Anna Livia　　　　　　　Photo: Pam Isherwood (Format)

Anna Livia was born in Dublin, and spent her childhood in Africa. She has been to university, studied to be a teacher, and had a variety of jobs cleaning, catering and servicing. She describes herself as lesbian, formerly Socialist, now radical feminist. She is currently working at Onlywomen Press, and is a member of two London women's housing associations, because of the shortage of lesbian accommodation. She has published a novel, *Relatively Norma* (Onlywomen Press, 1982) and short stories in *The Reach* (Onlywomen Press, 1984) and in *Everyday Matters 2* (Sheba Feminist Publishers, 1984).

She lives by herself 'in a basement flat in West London with the tenacity and insecurity that seem our only options.'

ANNA LIVIA

Accommodation Offered

The Women's Press

First published by The Women's Press Limited 1985
A member of the Namara Group
124 Shoreditch High Street London E1 6JE

British Library Cataloguing in Publication Data

Livia, Anna
  Accommodation offered.
  I. Title
  823'.914[F]   PR6068.I8/

  ISBN 0-7043-2857-7
  ISBN 0-7043-3951-X

Typeset by MC Typeset, Chatham, Kent
Printed and bound in Great Britain
by Nene Litho and Woolnough Bookbinding
both of Wellingborough, Northants

This book is also available on cassette, recorded by the author, for blind and
partially sighted women, from
  Feminist Audio Books,
  c/o A Woman's Place,
  Hungerford House,
  Victoria Embankment,
  London WC2.

For Irmgard, Waltraud, and Julian Brawn herself

Acknowledgments

I would like to thank Liz and Judith for reading the third draft, Caroline for the fourth, Dympna for parts of the fifth, Jen for her work on the sixth, Onlywomen Press for their lengthy, detailed and encouraging rejection letter, and especially Lilian, for her kindness and friendship.

Contents

 1 Liberty Boddesses   1
 2 Sheets of Oyster Satin   3
 3 Not Visitors   35
 4 Direct Intervention   43
 5 Forces of the Assumption   50
 6 Hiccups   67
 7 Penknives in the Park   83
 8 Problems of Scholarship   111
 9 Biodegradable   120
10 Mock Gothic   133
11 Axioms one, two and three   147
12 Three leopards (of which one is a tiger)   168

1
Liberty Boddesses

Hortus was a great botanical zoo of a place, a celestial Kew Gardens where Clianthus the Scarlet Desert Pea might shake stamens with the more matronly Lilac Buddleia; where the spikey, cabbage-like Hakea could greet old friends: Melaleuca, the melancholic paper bark; Quercus, the inflexible but not insensitive oak; friends whom, were it not for this bicentennial twig-wag, she would rarely get to see. There was to be a meeting of the Boddesses of Hortus to discuss a new water rate: a way of regulating rainfall without upsetting the Huwomen down below, for these are Liberty Boddesses, not like that uncouth crew on Olympus. All their varied Bodships of mountain, desert, and coastal plain were duly gathered together when one, Hakea's old friend Quercus, refused to continue.

'That woman is sinning,' she said.

'People are sinning all over the world,' said the others. 'It really doesn't do to be so sensitive.'

'There is a women in Stockwell sinning,' insisted Quercus. 'I can clearly see her. She is blocking out my sun.'

'Oh for Bodd's sake let's get on with the meeting!'

'Not while that woman's sinning.'

'All right, we'll send someone. Melaleuca, will you go?'

'Not me, sister, I've only just got comfy.'

'Hakea?'

'I've done my bit.'

'Clianthus, how about you?'

Finally Buddleia agreed. The problem was how to introduce her for she'd be quite out of place in Polly's garden.

'Does Polly have a female friend to whom she goes for some support?'

'She has a friend who has left her and another with troubles of her own.'

'A relation then or a workmate?'

1

'Her colleagues are all academics, her mother's hooked on the Highway Code.'

'Oh Bodd,' said the Boddesses, 'this could go on all decade. Isn't there anyone else? We have to work out the water rates. There were two cyclones and a hurricane last month – so irresponsible, so bad for the Huwomen's nerves.'

'There is . . .' said Buddleia haltingly.

'Yes?' thundered the other Boddesses.

'That is to say . . .'

'Well? Who does this woman have in whose guise you could prevent her from sinning?'

'She has a mother-in-law,' said Buddleia. 'An ex-mother-in-law, I should say, for the woman is separated from the son. But I'm not sure; they do say Huwomen hate their husbands' mothers. It's traditional I believe.'

'Bodd's teeth!' burst out Quercus, 'They should leave the legends to us if that's what they're going to do with them.'

'Maybe now the son's out the way . . .' ventured Melaleuca.

'Oh, I'll give it a whirl,' said Buddleia. 'What's her sin?'

'Despair,' said Quercus squeamishly. 'She has been ironing now for three hours, satin sheets of oyster cream. Puts me right off just watching her, don't know how she must feel. She has work to do in her study, the sun is shining outdoors, her friend left over a month ago and still she irons the sheets. Go to her as a mother-in-law; try to make her buck up. But move quickly for I think I hear the approach of visitors.'

'Not visitors,' said Melaleuca, 'she has scrubbed the whole of the house including the sides of the oven and the pale blue carpet on the stairs (such a stupid colour for a carpet), has scrubbed so hard in fact that it won't be dry before they come.'

'Not visitors, echoed Hakea, 'there are two empty rooms upstairs. She has advertised in a magazine for women to live in her house. Her friend left over a month ago and she grew tired of living alone.'

'The women will be there any moment eager to look around and Polly has cleaned the house for them but she doesn't think she can cope. Her friend left only a month ago and she would rather be on her own.'

'Go now, Buddleia,' said their Bodships. 'Find out why this woman sins. Tell us why her friend left while another has troubles of her own. Explain her desertion of her studies, her mother's faith in the Highway Code. Tell us why she irons the sheets and why the stair carpet is blue.'

'And for Bodd's sake make her buck up,' said Quercus, whose sun was totally eclipsed. 'I like direct sunlight and she has put me in the shade.'

2
Sheets of Oyster Satin

The radio blared out with painful jollity and Polly had ironed her way through two pairs of oyster-coloured satin sheets and pulled another from the airing cupboard before a full realisation of her actions fell upon her.

'Oh Bodd, oh Bodd what have I done?' And the answer rose up from the crisp sheets and the crumpled sheets, the warm ironing board and the steaming iron and from the aching muscles in her own right arm. She had been ironing for three hours. She looked down at the creamy satin and for a moment she could not bear it, slammed down the iron and turned away in revulsion. She, who in her heyday could wander round London entirely oblivious as to the state of the laundry, the holes in her stockings, the bareness of the larder, was now reduced to the ironing of sheets and the company of the radio. It seemed to her that she'd been standing for days at that ironing board, her back slightly bent, the board slightly wobbly, pressing away at the small creases (for satin can always benefit from a little more pressing, a little more smoothing out) and that the radio had played the same song a hundred times: a love song, and love lasts for ever.

'They're such pretty sheets,' Margot had said when she bought them. 'Look at them, Polly, laid out on the bed. You tuck in your side and we'll slip between as cool as water.'

'Laid out on the bed!' muttered Polly thinking of their oyster sheen, 'Like a winding sheet. Yes I'll lay them out and there they will stay, smooth and glacial with no one to crease or crumple them. And I'll creep in between, a long thin corpse in that wide matrimonial bed.'

Poignant though this image might be, she had not long to dwell on it for there came to her nostrils a thin acrid smell filling the air with the scent of funeral pyres. The iron, impatient with the straight lines it had been describing for the last three hours, had burned a hole downwards through the pile of satin sheets – this was easy for they resisted little; now it was doing its best to bore through the ironing board itself and though the asbestos covering was proving stubborn in its rebuffs yet with a little time and persistence the iron hoped one day to reach Australia . . . But, just as the outer coating was showing signs of submission, the power ebbed and the iron felt its very life-juices sapping out of its flex. Polly had flicked the switch. She stared at three hours' work: burned, hopelessly burned and the board itself ruined. Those incredibly expensive sheets no better than torn rags.

'Oh, I despair,' said Polly. 'Why not just burn the bloody house down?'

'Don't come the kamikaze with me,' said a voice behind a puff of smoke.

'Who are you?' asked Polly, seeing nothing.

'I'm Buddleia the Liberty Boddess, your mother-in-law,' said Buddleia. 'And you are a wicked sinner.'

'I am not,' said Polly.

'Yes you are; you despair. You said so yourself not a moment ago and if you don't buck up we can't start the meeting and then there'll be more tornados and hurricanes and I wouldn't be surprised if there wasn't an earthquake.'

'You mean you would be surprised if there was an earthquake.'

'No I wouldn't.'

'You said you wouldn't be if there wasn't,' explained Polly. 'That's a double negative.'

'You some kind of English teacher?'

'What's it to you?'

'Listen sweetie, you're in a state. Your lover's left you, you've burnt the ironing, the house is full of smoke and in another half hour you've two optimistic young home-makers coming to take up residence.'

'Don't rub it in. You even sound like my mother-in-law. On

4

and on and on.'

'Yes,' Buddleia agreed, 'but you never listened.'

It was all a bit much for poor Polly. Her arms ached, her back ached and her legs were stiff from standing. The smoke hurt her throat and made her eyes water. It was too bad of Margot to leave her; too bad of these women to want to come and look round. She could imagine them in the house now: two strangers, looking at her furniture with the eyes of strangers, seeing only what was immediately apparent, that the sofa was too big for the room and the corner cabinet didn't quite fit in the corner. No sense of history to tell them she had bounced on that sofa when she was five and her granny had promised she could have it. How was granny to know it would end up in a front room in Stockwell? As for the corner cabinet, it was such beautiful wood; couldn't they even see that? And she had scrubbed the whole house for them down to the sides of the oven and the pale blue carpet on the stairs (such a stupid colour for a carpet). But would they notice how clean it was? Oh no. Not they. They would take one look at the front room and decide the sofa was too big and the cabinet did not fit.

'Well, it's all Gerard's fault,' she said aloud, legs finally crumpling, body falling on to the overlarge sofa. The habit of blaming her husband was too ingrained for her to break merely because it was two years since she'd seen him. She had closed her eyes and sunk back, however, before she could develop the theme.

When at last she reopened them the fumes had vanished from the room, the windows were wide open and the ironing board had been put away. Even the smoke stains on the mantlepiece had been carefully wiped off.

'I've made you a nice cup of tea, love,' said her mother-in-law.

'How wonderful,' said Polly groggily, 'two sugars . . .'

'I remember, dear, I used to be married to your son.'

'You mean . . . Oh heck, why argue. Thanks Budd, you're a real sweetie.'

Polly drank as thirstily as that early morning cuppa, only the Teasmade never tasted like this.

'Feeling better now?'

'A little.'

'Good.' (Pause) 'Listen dear, a word of advice . . .'

5

'Just like old times.'

'I wouldn't mention the visitors to Gerard.'

'Why ever not?'

'Well, you know what he's like about money. He'd want to raise the rent. I had enough trouble persuading him to let you live here.'

'You persuaded him?'

'Yes, well, he listens to me.'

'He never did to me.'

'No, but then I gave up everything for him.'

'Whatever did you say to him? He was perfectly revolting when I left, and when I came back, two months later, he was as distant as a lofty peak and twice as icy but he agreed to my having the house in Stockwell practically without a murmur. I didn't know what to make of it.'

'Oh, I had a motherly chat with him.'

'About generosity to ex-wives? Losing with dignity?'

'Not exactly. I did some research into property values and it was clear that Stockwell was on the up. If he'd rented to anyone else he'd have had sitting tenants on his back just when he wanted to sell. He still has the place in Westminster, so can hardly claim Stockwell as his family home.'

'And when I met him in Dublin, he didn't have a bean!'

'Socialism's a great way for the blue-eyed boy to rise. Marx gives a firm grounding in high finance. It's that or be picked up by a football scout. Sign with United or bankroll your own communist weekly. Don't imagine there was ever anything pure about Gerard's politics, save his unadulterated thirst for liquid assets.'

'Oh, that overbearing, arrogant supercilious snob!'

'I always wondered why you married him.'

'I was all of eighteen when I met him, just started at Trinity, still living at home. And him, he wore green corduroy with leather patches on the elbows. Smoked a pipe and had pale blue eyes.'

'Like something out of *Look Back and Hanker*.'

'He said I was bourgeois.'

'He'd know.'

'I was angry because I thought that was vulgar. He was my first socialist, you see. I found communism more exciting than anything; much more fun than God or learning to drive. Only

6

apparently you couldn't call it communism until it arrived and you knew what form it would take.'

'Oh yes,' said Buddleia, 'like naming a baby.'

'I went to a meeting with my friend Suzette, sharing an umbrella and talking so earnestly we were in the upstairs room of a pub before I knew it. Me in a pub! Me in an upstairs room! But Suzette chatted on: the phonetic subtleties of the Irish language, how she would go to England and study Russian, until Gerard in his green jacket announced that the meeting would begin as the rain seemed to have deterred the great hordes expected. Of the speeches, I could afterwards remember nothing. The Two Nations* and the Belfast Dockers thundered over my head and I watched the blue veins in Gerard's wrists swell as he clutched his notes. I listened to that word 'socialism', so soft and comforting, it seemed to promise everything. To the Two Nations independence; to the dockers escape from tyranny; and to me an alternative to the clammy generosity of my father's house. A word to put between me and the alcoholics who lay out under the arches in all weather, the mad women who came to the door with stories you could not believe but dared not discount.

'My parents lived at Foxrock, you see. They were very rich: won the Davis Cup every year and avoided planning permission for their swimming pool by having it filled from the house with a hose. The garden was enormous, full of stone statues and green marble chips like a graveyard. The drive was crescent-shaped and the car tyres scrunched on the gravel outside my window as they pulled up at the house. It reminded me of eating fudge. My mother kept diabetic fruit pastilles under the dashboard for Romulus and Remus the Pekinese dogs. She wore an enormous number of clanking gold chains on her wrist and it would be true to say that in all her life she never once parked a car. "If God had meant us to park," she used to say, "he wouldn't make us do it backwards." She would simply stop in the middle of the street and hand the car keys over to that ubiquitous young man who seems forever willing to perform small favours for wealthy women. My mother tipped handsomely. The mornings she spent conducting a complicated gossip session on the telephone. She did not dare leave her post between calls but would shout

*Ulster and Eire

7

out orders for lunch from the red velvet phone-stool in the hall. When anyone looked to be talking too long she would signal to me and I would yell:

' "Mummy there's someone at the door. She says do you want any clothes pegs?" '

'Then she would simply have to dash, could replace the receiver and phone somebody else.'

'You two must be marvellous at bridge,' said Buddleia.

'We were,' sighed Polly, 'only, when my mother lost God she took up with the Highway Code.'

'Buddleia,' called a voice from Beyond, 'we haven't got all century.'

'She can't stop now,' protested Melaleuca, 'we sent her to answer certain questions; we must give her time to reply.'

'What about your father?' prompted Buddleia quickly.

'Oh, he worked in Dublin but spent most of his time at home in the studio painting wild scenes in thick oils. Every morning, Jimmy-the-Gardener drove him into town, left the car outside his office and took the bus back again. My father couldn't drive, you see, never learned, but there was a space out front for the Director and he wanted his car to be there. When he'd had enough business for one day he'd phone Jimmy up to come and fetch him.'

'Buddleia!'

'She only sounds a bit better but that's because I'm here. If I went now she might, you know, do it again behind my back: slough of despond, trough of ages, the whole bit.'

'Buddleia!'

'Don't be so heartless.'

'Buddleia, we call upon you and the Bodhead vested in you as a Liberty Boddess to . . .'

'Shut your stupid stamens and listen.'

'Quercus! You're out of order. Buddleia, it has been brought to our attention that in our haste to start the meeting and prevent another natural disaster (for the monsoons will soon be upon us) the Djugashvili Bonsais were unfortunately over-looked. You may therefore stay where you are until their arrival.'

8

'But remember to keep reporting back,' hissed Melaleuca.

Polly, hidden in history, was oblivious to interruption. 'That smile of Jimmy's as he walked up to catch the bus every day: too awful. Sometimes when the buses were running late he might only have been home an hour or two, be in the middle of training the roses, when the phone would ring and he'd have to go back out again. But he'd smile his little ingratiating smile and trot off to the bus stop. He always lowered his head when he spoke so that, though I was a foot shorter, he might still look up to me. A grown man lowering his head to a girl. Socialism was going to change all that.'

Polly paused a while.

'Gerard used to get at me for having no Irish, though they did say his own was like English spoken backwards. My parents found him beautiful, and he was in a way. In that way young men have of being beautiful as, moving from youth to manhood, they realise they need no longer be kind. But my father's firm was doing badly and I think they had other worries.'

Polly grew silent.

'And we, his parents,' prompted Buddleia, 'we were Catholic . . .'

'Yes,' laughed Polly, 'but embarrassingly wealthy for a freedom fighter. At meetings he'd say his father was a baker.'

'No doubt neglecting to add it was my husband *owned* the bakery.'

'Two years after I met him I married him and we moved to London. I'd only just finished my degree and didn't have any better suggestions. He became economic adviser to his firm and he used to say no one could be a better trouble-shooter for capitalism than himself who had plotted for its downfall. He had nothing but admiration for a successful capitalist, the only trouble was that the system didn't work and he wanted to be on the winning side.'

'How clever,' commented Buddleia. 'I wonder did he think that up himself?'

'I thought he was wonderful, doing all that high-powered thinking, and if I noticed any of his little contradictions he'd say, "Well done, that's what the world is based on. Change only comes from the cracks in between." After staying with you in

9

Cork, we'd be stopped and searched at Fishguard. Gerard would feel proud because the British knew what a threat he was to their national security. I used to dust the complete works of Marx and Lenin and despair . . .'

'Not again!' writhed Quercus.

'. . . they filled a whole bookcase by themselves. But Gerard said if I just read the papers I'd catch up. We bought a dear little house in Westminster and I used to think if I had a child I'd call her Pimlico. Only it never seemed worth the effort really, just for that. I was happy. At least, I can't remember not being. I went for walks in all the parks in London though it used to worry me the way they went yellow at the end of the summer. Then I'd come home and play Beethoven's *Hymn to Joy*. You know, Side Two where it starts on the crashing and banging. Gerard said did I only put it on to block out conversation seeing as I never listened right through.

'Ten years and no children later I started my PhD; Suzette was teaching at SEES; I was still happy.'

'What an achievement.'

'Ah, but it couldn't last. It was his fault you know. His bloody fault. I never got depressed or lonely. Do you know I was thirty before I learned to be bored? Oh, he was an education all right. What a splendidly autonomous creature I was. And look at me now! Scrub the whole house from top to bottom for two people I don't even know. Oh, Margot!' And Polly began to cry.

'There, there,' soothed Buddleia. 'Would you like another cup of tea now? A clean carpet is not a bad thing in itself.'

'You noticed?' said Polly, looking up behind brimming tears.

'Well, it's still a little wet . . .'

'Ye Bodds,' yelped Polly. 'Those two will be arriving any minute and here I sit yapping.'

'Polly!' scolded Buddleia. 'It's not like you to be discourteous dear. We don't very often see each other, why begrudge our little chat?'

'Oh, I'm sorry. I wasn't trying to hurt your feelings.'

'For someone who wasn't trying you succeeded very well.' Sniff.

'Dear Buddleia, I'm terribly pleased to see you, really am. You taught me how to bake soda-bread: I haven't forgotten.

And now here you are and you've cleaned up the ironing and everything.'

'And I wiped the smoke stains off the mantelpiece.'

'You did, you did. You're very good.'

'So,' said Buddleia, 'will you go on with the story now?'

'All right sweetie, if that's what you want. But where was I?'

'Beethoven was crashing and banging and you were still happy.'

'Well, every evening Gerard would come home . . .'

'Poor Polly . . .'

'. . . and ask me what I'd been doing. "Another boring day by yourself?" he'd say, because I was struggling with my thesis. I'm sure he saw a PhD as a kind of academic finishing school.'

'Instead of teaching you how to marry the man in charge, it tells you how to study him, how to record his achievements. It certainly doesn't suggest how you might take charge yourself.' Buddleia announced emphatically.

'Your disapproval's quite wasted you know, Buddleia. I went through all that with Margot. I started my MA at Birkbeck because Suzette was round the corner at SEES. I only put down for English because that was Thursdays and she played squash till eight o'clock. I'd been giving dinner parties for ten years and Suzette was still my only friend.'

'I thought you started your thesis because you fell suddenly and passionately in love with your great auntie.'

'With who?'

'Dorica Maud.'

'No, that was afterwards. My life is full of retrospective explanation. I'd registered for an MA before I knew what I was going to do it on, and I only read Maud because she was a family connection. Didn't realise how closely connected till I was half way through her third novel.'

'And what had Gerard to say about it?'

'At first he felt a certain cachet in putting his wife through her doctorate but the more involved I became, the more resentful he was. He'd bring me back things from the office to type, though his secretary did a much better job; or he'd need the dining-room table to lay out his graphs. Transparent as a two-year-old. Sometimes when I was really engrossed he would pour me a glass of sherry and recommend exhibitions and daytime lectures, commiserate with me for the dullness of my days. I would sit, frozen to the chair, panicking quietly, thinking I would never, never do what I wanted, Gerard would never stop talking, the clock would not stop ticking nor the dust falling. I would stare at the beautiful mahogany table that had always to be polished and protected, the black chairs inlaid with mother-of-pearl too small to sit on, the double glazing that muffled the street, and I would wonder what they were and how I came to live amongst them. Gerard would talk and the clock would tick and the dust would fall and I would think: this is my life I'm living, now, at this moment, my life. Of all the incredible beauty and diversity I have chosen this. On the middle of the table was a bowl of fruit: apples, pears, grapes: that blue, satiny shine on the plums, that feathery down on the peaches, a perfect likeness but made of stone. We had them at Rathmine and Mummy let me take them with me. I reached out and took one, a hard green apple, opened my mouth to bite it when Gerard, still talking, picked it out of my hands. I wanted to bite him; sink my teeth into those bulging veins that stood out on his wrist; break my teeth on the stone apple in his hand; spit blood and tooth over the still-life scenes on the dinner mats the French more fittingly call "dead nature".

' "Been to see the ducks?" he'd ask with an offhand interest in my affairs, throwing the apple in the air and catching it before popping it back in the basket.

'And I'd remember the old woman with the bag of Slimcea sitting on a bench in the park, chewing the bread herself first before offering it to the mallards. To my embarrassment she caught me watching but she pointed at a sign near the water's edge: "Please do not feed the birds; large pieces of bread stick in their throats."

'She passed the bag over to me. "It's all right," she said, "it's completely tasteless." There is an art to chewing bread for birds and I think I may have acquired it during that quiet afternoon. We talked of all sorts of things: of planets lining up and the new ice age.'

'Planets lining up?' repeated Melaleuca. 'That rings a bell.'

Hakea grinned, 'One likes to drop in occasionally. Clianthus said as long as I refrained from meddling she could see no possible harm.'

12

'Around the bench were paths in all directions. Because I could have gone at any time, I didn't want to.

'Gerard would have friends round, men from the Party. I would stock up on sherry and hope they'd deal a round of cards so I could slip off.

' "Well, have you?" Gerard would repeat.

' "Her . . . Howmuch?" I'd stutter, squeezing out the fairy liquid, having quite forgotten the question.

' "Been to feed the ducks today? Don't know how those poor birds would survive the winter if it wasn't for my wife's tender mercies."

' "Oh, there's an old woman who's always there," I would start. Sometimes. Sometimes I wouldn't bother; only when a woman is first married she does have some expectation of talking to her husband. Though it wears off.

' "So that's what becomes of our taxes," laughed one of the men. "We carry the Welfare State so the lumpen proletariat can throw our money to the birds."

' "She was so interesting," I said, "I enjoyed talking to her – about the solar system and the elements, how Saturn was coming nearer . . ."

' "Course she'd know," sniggered Gerard.

' "She told me about the plants in the park; far-fetched I suppose, but convention didn't seem to reach her. She was ..." I stumbled for the right word, "... she was a liberated woman."

' "Oh liberation!" Gerard whooped. "Women's Liberation."

'And then he sang, slowly he sang so the others could join in: men who'd enquired after my thesis, men who'd offered to wash up, "Liberate the women, lads; give every man his fuck."

'They found it a little risqué that he should talk like that before his wife but he'd slip back into his Irish accent as if that made him untouchable.

'So there I was,' said Polly, summing up . . .

'And then?' Melaleuca whispered to Buddleia. 'Did she walk out on him then and there? Wipe the dust from her feet saying he was devoid of both charm and politics?'

'I doubt it,' said Hakea. 'Where could she go? Back to Mummy and the twin Pekinese?'

'If I'd been her,' said Quercus, 'which Bodd forbid! I would have gone out and got a job. Let me see, something with a

13

social conscience: a home for retired worker bees, a crossings'
lady for hedgehogs.'

'Don't be facetious.'

'There is no action so vile, so wicked nor so ludicrous but
someone somewhere is the national co-ordinator. I can see it
all. She has a chat to the Careers' Guidance Officer; he suggests
she train to be a teacher as she's too refined for an air hostess
and doesn't want to be a nurse. She tells him she is chaotic and
innately unjust. He asks has she thought of working in a bank.
She tells him she is a socialist and does not approve of banking.
"Well what do you enjoy?" he asks. "Let's start from there."
She smiles vaguely, "Oh I used to like wandering around
looking at things," she says. "I used to think a lot, but it
annoyed my husband."'

'Polly's not nearly as fey as that,' Melaleuca objected.

'And I like the way *she* tells it better,' said Hakea.

'What did you do then?' asked Buddleia.

'Oh,' said Polly, 'I thought about getting a job.'

'Huh!' Quercus snorted. 'Was I right or was I right?
Huwomen are so predictable.'

'But that's just what Gerard would have wanted and I didn't
want to give up my thesis.'

'Suck dewbells Quercus,' said Melaleuca. 'Polly's one step
ahead of you.'

'Things had gone badly with Gerard for some time,' Polly
continued, 'particularly in bed.'

'Oh good,' piped up Quercus, the irrepressible, 'I was afraid
there wouldn't be any sex in this story. Adds bodily interest,
don't you find?'

'Quercus, you are a pestilence,' said Melaleuca, 'a blight
upon the face of the earth.'

'Quercus,' chimed in Hakea, 'you are the yellow spores in the
mildew; the furry growth in the mould; an entire crop of
loganberries lacerated by greenfly.'

'Quercus,' Melaleuca concluded, 'you make my leaves curl.'

14

Polly contined, blithely unaware of celestial interruption. 'I faked as often as I came, then gave up coming altogether as too heavy on the diaphragm and anyway it made my thighs ache. Gerard was pleased because I seemed to be concentrating more on him. Perhaps his pleasure would excite me, that'd make sense, psychosexually speaking. I wanted to throw my fake orgasms in his face but I was afraid he wouldn't mind enough. "If you do too much for a woman, she gets greedy." I was greedy. He must have done too much for me. He said the way I rubbed myself against him he might as well be a vibrator. I went out and bought one.'

'Where on earth from?' asked Buddleia.

'Funny little shop off the Charing Cross Road; I used to pass it on my walks. It sold all sorts of things: spare limbs, surgical shoes and then this white plastic gizmo like a torch which had a picture of a woman with a stiff neck and a warning note: "Do Not Use On Unexplained Calf Pain." '

'Did it work?'

'Admirably for post-coital triste but it wasn't much cop as a lover and as it was made in Taiwan I thought it probably wasn't socialist.'

'Coming now quite happily on her own,' commented Quercus, 'she told Gerard of her joyous discovery.'

'He was furious,' continued Melaleuca, 'then, caught by her spirit of adventure, suggested they try something new.'

'There was an ad in Forum for a bi-girl,' said Hakea. 'He made her answer it. It was a man wanting a partner for his wife.'

'There was an ad in Forum for a bi-girl,' said Quercus. 'He made her answer it. It was a young woman seeking friendship; she had a passion for David Bowie.'

'There was an ad in Forum for a bi-girl,' said Polly. 'Gerard used to buy it but he never dreamed I'd reply. Sounds terribly sordid doesn't it? I answered because I couldn't bear being lonely any more. They did a survey: it said for every lonely heart there were at least fifty replies. It seems odd now to equate loneliness with sex, but I thought that's how one made friends. I only answered the bi-sexuals, sounded so much safer than lesbians; of course one ran the risk of having to deal with her boyfriend but that simply didn't occur to me. The woman rang. I was so alarmed I put the phone down. She rang again. Said she was sorry she'd alarmed me, she really did want to meet me: out of fifty replies I was the only one who hadn't sent a photograph. She would never have the courage to advertise again. Said her name was Margot.'

Melaleuca and Hakea exchanged significant glances.

'I met her at the V&A. She was nice. It was all so fearfully embarrassing and neither of us had any idea what we wanted so we actually had quite a good time together. Only I didn't fancy her at all, though I tried and tried. We even went to bed and her skin smelt so silky I thought it might be all right. But it wasn't. It was awful and I panicked. Decided I was one of Bodd's holy celibates and would never do it again with anyone be she fish, flesh, fowl or good red herring.'

'So what went wrong?' asked Buddleia.

'We took our trousers off,' said Polly.

'Always a difficult moment.'

'She'd done it before with a woman and I hadn't. She undressed and I just sat on that bed thinking it wasn't right to look at women's bodies because it embarrassed them. You know, like changing on the beach and a bit of breast flashes out and you have to pretend you haven't seen it. I was curious though. I wanted to see how she went and if it was different from me. Margot pulled the covers back and said: "Listen, Polly, I'll put a line of shoes down the bed so you don't have to touch me, but don't just sit there shivering. You make me feel like a wicked seductress."

'She made me feel like an adolescent.

' "It felt so easy when we had all our clothes on and were just kissing."

' "Just kissing!" said Margot. "Polly, what grey horrors are to follow?"

' "Oh," I said. "Couldn't we sort of lie here and pretend we weren't doing anything?"

' "I don't think so."

'So I felt bad, but it was as though, because of the ad, I did have to go through with it even though I wasn't sure quite what it was.

'I got into bed and lay alongside her. Then I had an attack of

16

the tickles, felt if she so much as stroked me I'd shriek. I started touching her instead. Oh those heady days of sexual discovery, but I was thirty-five years old. I put my hand on her breast, her stomach and whatnot but all I could think was "goodness me, so that's what that feels like from the outside". I didn't feel anything inside, just sort of interested. I mean, I didn't think at last I'd come home or anything. When I stroked her breasts it was lovely: her skin was as smooth as water; and when I sucked her nipples I could feel it inside me. A bit like someone else sucking mine, and I began to think maybe it'd be all right after all.

'It wasn't till I moved my hand down to her pubic hair that I began to think, "This is disgusting, I am using this woman as a guinea pig." Before that it just felt like we were both experimenting, with some affection thrown in. I liked the way she frowned: an innocent, curious frown as though she was thinking something deep but when it came out it would be funny. With my hand on her pubic hair, well, I stroked it because it was hair but with no idea how that might feel to her. And when I reached further I couldn't recognise any part of her as similar in any way to me. It all felt most peculiar. It seemed very wet but I could find nothing save hair and I was afraid that unless I went down and looked to sort things out I wouldn't find a way in without hurting her. I was scared: of playing Gerard, of not being guided by an uncontrollable passion which would tell me what she wanted. Mind you, Gerard's passion never seemed to work like that.

'As I stroked, Margot got wetter and wetter and suddenly I found myself inside her, and that felt absolutely incredible. I can't describe it. For a while I just stroked and explored a bit with my fingers. It was so exciting. I hoped she was enjoying it too, but I thought she must be or she'd get me to stop. Only then . . .'

'Only then you started wondering where her clitoris was: would it be in the same place as yours; did she want you to touch it directly, hard against the bone or just flow over it . . .'

'Only then I started to worry about how you said that word "clitoris". Did it rhyme with "liquorice" or "walrus"? Gerard and I didn't mention such things and I wondered would it sound too formal and did other lesbians use less medical terms for things.

'I got as far as telling Margot about not being quite sure what she wanted when she took hold of my hand and said, "You only have to ask," and that rather put paid to discussion.'

'And after that,' said Buddleia, 'everyone was gasping for breath and moaning with pleasure and the biggest problem was whether to groan softly so as not to disturb the neighbours, or loudly to encourage others.'

'Not quite,' said Polly. 'I kept on thinking she was going to come, so I kept on stroking but then she let herself flop on to the bed and stopped moving. Was that an orgasm or a complaint? I felt awful, and she felt awful. My brain was tired from all that thinking so we went to sleep.

'She rolled so far away from me she might as well have put those shoes down the middle of the bed.

'On the slow ride home on the bus next day I remember thinking: Well I've done it now. I've done it with a woman and I didn't like it. I must be normal. Normal. What a relief. I still hoped we could be friends and maybe laugh later on at the thought of being lovers. So I phoned her.

'We went to a play by Gay Sweatshop. It was at the ICA: *Any Woman Can*. I'd never heard of it; I don't think either of us knew quite what to expect. I'd been too nervous to eat beforehand and then, right in the middle of the play, I got so hungry my stomach started rumbling. All through the quiet, intense bits. I was sure everyone could hear. All there was to eat was a grapefruit Margot had for her diet. I always wonder when I get hunger pangs is it for food or for sex. This time I thought it'd be safer to eat. I kept thinking: Margot is sitting beside me. Margot! And wondering if anyone could tell; . . . quite what there was to tell . . . There'd been such a strong smell on my fingers afterwards.

'There I was watching this play, sitting next to this woman, opening this grapefruit and all of a sudden my fingers were inside it. It felt so wet . . . I was so surprised I dropped it. Margot stared at me wondering what was going on. I picked up the grapefruit, put it into her hands, made her put her fingers inside it just as I had. First she looked completely blank, then she started to giggle. I felt like leaving the theatre and trying again right then.'

'And did you?'

'Oh, we'd paid for our tickets and the show was very good.

18

The next time was much easier though. I mean there actually was a next time. I'd sort of decided that if kissing was so nice maybe the rest could be too. Also I'd brought my vibrator. I thought if I daren't say I wanted to use it I didn't trust her enough to have sex with.'

'Bodd in Hortus!' exclaimed Quercus. 'The tests Huwomen set themselves and fail every day.'

'But couldn't you masturbate or say you wanted something different?' asked Buddleia.
'Dear Forum, Is the first date too soon to masturbate?' said Polly. 'Buddleia, you make me feel like I'm being eaten. Why do I have to answer all the questions?'
'Because it's your story, Polly.'
'Well, I was used to Gerard being faintly nauseated by whatever it was I wanted and why should Margot feel any different? I mean, we weren't old friends or anything.
'We went to a bar after the play, a place off the King's Road that Margot knew about. All women. I had Tia Maria and milk. I was surprised how expensive it was. I wondered did it go any further if you asked for ice or did that just dilute it. I wanted to be drunk. It was the first cocktail I had to pay for myself. Things happen when you're thirty-five. Margot drank orange juice, but then she was a doctor and believed in livers.
'It was too noisy to talk and too crowded to sit down. I didn't really mind. We stood at the bar and looked at the other women. I felt all these words rushing through my brain:
' "It began as a blind date . . ."
' "An ad in a sex mag . . ."
' "Don't look like perverts."
' "Discreet deviants, worst kind."
Margot was fiddling with her cardigan, trying to knot a dropped stitch on her button hole.
' "Give me," I yelled against the music. "I've longer nails." I pulled through one strand and succeeded in tying it.
' "See, really you should sew it in," I shouted.
' "What?" she mouthed.
' "Sew it up," I repeated.
' "There you are," said the voices in my head while the other women in the room were busy laughing and dancing, "knitting

19

patterns. Normal."

' "If I sew it up I won't be able to button my cardigan," shouted Margot.

' "Howmuch?" I yelled back.

'She came right up to me, cupped her hand to my ear, and yelled into it. My ear buzzed and crackled sending highly ambiguous messages to the base of my spine.

' "What was that then?" said the voices.

' "Not what you imagine . . ."

' "In a grey flannel suit . . ."

' "The music's really very loud . . ."

' "Can't hear yourself think . . ."

'Lucky that, I thought, as Margot whispered something else.

'It was late when we left. Neither of us relished going home. We walked back to Margot's flat in Fulham. I rang Gerard, told him I'd missed the last tube. Knowing he'd offer to drive me, knowing he'd rather not. Margot and I lay on her bed together. I was drunk and she wasn't. You don't get very drunk on orange juice. We took off our clothes and got into bed. Business-like this time. I felt very close to her. She was rather tall and upright; wore a lot of cream and beige but there was always something to throw you: green dolphin buttons, lilac rims to her glasses.'

'We were in bed with no clothes on, kissing. I was beginning to feel like urgent intensification when Margot drew apart from me, leaned up on her elbow and began saying how good the play was. She was right. It was a very good play: funny but with a serious message and nice positive images of lesbians but Jesusbodd! A time and a place. All I wanted was for her to put her soft tongue to my clitoris, however you pronouce the bodding word, and lick it gently till I came. Oh. Er . . . I mean. Well, yes, that is exactly what I wanted actually. But if something was wrong I wished we could talk about that instead of the play. Pander to my sense of logic.

' "No, Polly, nothing's wrong," Margot said coldly. "You're not upset are you? So how could anything be wrong? I just think I'd rather sleep on my own."

'It was the middle of the night. I didn't want to have to go when things were feeling warm and tender. I wondered what it was Margot wanted to do. Fart or pick her nose so I could assure her I didn't mind and we could still sleep together.

20

' "We hardly know each other, Polly," she said, "yet we always end up in bed."

' "Always? This is only the second time we've been out together. Besides, sex is a good way to get to know someone."

' "Is it?"

' "I don't know. But it might be." '

'Well, I spose it might,' conceded Buddleia, 'but not the way you two were going about it.'

'What do you mean?' snapped Polly.

'Something's missing, Polly; a large, integral piece has somehow been mislaid, removed perhaps, I'd be prepared to believe that, from the very centre of the story. The point, Polly; your story has no point to it. It is a well-thumbed page from a sex manual of the Seventies. Two bored and boring women seek solace in sex, after initial fumblings and much mutual embarrassment, they manage to get the hang of it. What happens next? Does Gerard make it a happy threesome?'

'No!'

'Sounds like the more organs the merrier.'

'How dare you!'

'What do you think went wrong when you were in bed with Margot? When she started off about the play, maybe she just wanted to talk to you. That ever cross your mind?'

Polly jerked her head away. She had a sudden strong vision of herself, a small grey figure, smart enough to pass unnoticed, treading silently down the vaulted concourse of her college, marble busts and bland seascapes looking discreetly away. She was a grey chameleon perched upon a stone, hoping only that no one would tread on her before she turned into a wall. How could she show that to Margot?

'I wanted to get to know her,' said Polly softly. 'She started off as my guilty secret, someone I washed my knickers for, then London began to open up as a place two people could walk in: once or twice I even left my book behind. I began to remember how long conversations take, how you can sit across a teapot all day and not notice you haven't been out. It's funny, I was much closer to Margot in her kitchen than her bedroom.'

'Extraordinary,' said Buddleia.

'For the next few weeks I didn't see her. I didn't go into college much those days either: post-grads only attended research seminars and they went right through me like a tomato skin through the body. I stayed home filling the hours with small, undemanding activities, nothing that required planning. I would empty all the ashtrays, wash them, dry them, and put them back; I would wipe the ring underneath the ashtrays with a damp cloth, then rinse the cloth; I would empty all the waste-paper baskets, throw out the old paper, reline them and put them back; I would roll the rest of the paper up and put it in the drawer; I would empty the pedal bin into the dustbin, sluice it out with disinfectant and leave it upended in the area. I might pop out to Safeways for loo paper, and again later if I'd forgotten toothpaste. I might find a ball of string it would take me hours to unravel. I would read the paper from beginning to end; try and keep it going till at least ten o'clock.

'One morning I searched all over: Gerard had taken it to work, leaving me with the *Morning Star*. It was only a quarter to nine. The Women's Page had a feature on overcrowding in men's prisons. I dreamed of going to jail because at least you'd have the company. I thought about going for a check-up so someone would be concerned about my body. I considered waiting at a bus stop: we could discuss the likelihood of a bus. And finally I went out, put on my grey coat and went out, walked down the street a little way but the tears kept welling up in my eyes and my throat hurt so much I couldn't talk. I felt I was staring, all the time staring, that my forehead must be marked with an enormous L: "Warning, this women is lonely, approach with extreme caution. Do not look at her too long; do not show by any sign that you have seen her; do not speak, as you value your sanity do not speak to her." It is a terrible thing to walk down a street alone. On the other side of the road was Nora from the Party, looking in a shop window, and I suddenly thought she might see me and if I opened my mouth I would cry and Gerard would know how lonely I was so I turned round hastily and bolted back home.

'In the evening when Ger came in he poured us both a drink and looked at me. I wondered was I giving myself away, had I put my shoes on the wrong feet, was I still wearing my slippers? He said, "Aren't you lonely, Polly? Here by yourself all day?"

'The first time in fifteen years. I wanted to open up to him, confess I'd slept with a woman, hear him say consolingly, as he used to when we addressed meetings together that scarcely anyone attended: "Never mind, you're better off embarrassed than dead." Only I couldn't bear to go into details that I knew he'd not believe me without.

' "No," he answered his own question. "You never get lonely. Lord sakes, I should know that by now."

'And I went to the cupboard for the ground glass I keep there for special occasions and I poured him out some more whiskey and after he drank he fell down dead before me, writhing in terrible agony; and I went to the cupboard for the paraquat I keep there for special occasions and I poured it into the vichyssoise and when he asked what the smell was I said it was the turpentine I had used on the stain on his trouser leg and after he drank he fell down dead before me, writhing in terrible agony; and I went to the cupboard for the coil I keep there for special occasions, made in the fashion of Resistance prostitutes for use against the German Occupation, an aluminium cylinder with a razor-blade down the centre and after he put his prick inside me it split open like a runner bean under a thumb nail and he fell down dead before me writhing in terrible agony.'

'How foul!' exclaimed Buddleia. 'To be so involved in his physical presence.'

'Ah,' said Polly, 'but he anticipated me. He offered me another sherry and I dropped my glass on the grey slate floor of the kitchen and he went to the cupboard for the dustpan I keep there for all occasions and swept up the mess most carefully, wrapping the tiny shards in newspaper so the dustmen would not cut their fingers.

'Next day I phoned Margot, suggested a safe date for lunch with an option on looking at Art. We sat in the National Theatre which was suitably spacious and gloomy. I was drinking filter coffee, she was drinking milk. We'd been listening to a steel band in Jubilee Gardens, followed by the local brass; they clashed rather but you were free to come and go.

' "I think sex is difficult for both of us," I ventured, staring at the unplastered concrete. "I hope you don't feel it's all to do with you . . ."

' "It has nothing to do with me at all as far as I can see," retorted Margot and for a moment I gave way to the most awful paranoia. Gerard used to say that, and I'd been so pleased to feel sexual with Margot, as though my arousal was a bloody gift. I glared round at the other customers in their dun coats and their pinstripes. They knew what women wanted, no one had to

23

tell them.

'I just wanted Margot to be my friend, go on meeting me for coffee, go on talking. But what was I to say? "I so enjoyed going to the V&A with you; I liked your fascination with waistcoats; the way you bought all those postcards to send to your 43 best friends?"

'I waited for the indeterminate person in the astrakhan to finish noting down concession prices: student, pensioner, unemployed, she could not have been all three. Margot was silent, then she picked up her coat and started off down the stairs. What could I say? That I admired her taste in clothes? It was similar to mine. That she was brave to put the ad in? I was brave too for answering. I ran down the mauve-carpeted staircase and all the static electricity in the building welled up in the stair-rail and sputtered at my fingers as I clenched it. She was waiting for me at the bottom.

' "Who am I, Polly?" she demanded, "how long have I lived in London? Do I know how to roller skate? What do I think of abortion, speaking as a doctor?"

'I stared at her then shouted: "And me, Margot? what part of Dublin am I from? Do I have any sisters or brothers?"

' "What a coincidence we're both Irish," she said.

' "What a coincidence we're both women," ' I said.

' "Polly," she said, "I really enjoyed the V&A. I liked you looking inconspicuous in your little grey coat, your total and professed ignorance on the finer points of embroidery, how cross you were with the stone fruit because they meant your mother's weren't unique." '

' "Oh no," I said, "that wasn't it at all." And I began to tell her, wondering if I ought, but it didn't seem to put her off me. We went back across the gardens, over Hungerford Bridge and down the Embankment to Westminster. Sometimes she told me about the hospital, pathological definitions of homosexuals; her ex-lover who was a medic and had volunteered for aversion therapy. Sometimes I talked about my parents, Gerard, the Party. Sometimes we both talked together.'

Polly had fallen silent. She sighed.

'Do you know by now in a hundred different ways half of me is Margot? At first her expressions amused me, then I imitated them and now they're mine. I frown her frown: that innocent, curious look, precursor of a funny remark that so intrigued me

24

when I first met her. When I'm hurt or scared, my eyes go cold stone like hers. Like the fine layer of skin you lose every day and which reappears under the bed as dust, I lost some of the mannerisms I absorbed from Gerard and grew into new ones. And somewhere back in Dublin at this moment is a woman saying "howmuch?", and she says it because I say it and that woman is Margot. My Bodd! When I talk about her I feel as ludicrous as my mother telling Romulus to "come to mummy". One month, only four miserable weeks ago, she left me and who was I to turn to? Aunty Ag's Problem Page?' And Polly cried for Margot, for the satin sheets, for the untouched work upstairs. She cried because the house was Gerard's and the furniture too big.

'Your husband leaves you, it's the end of the world, everybody sympathises. Margot moves out – it's a shameful little interlude best forgotten. If Suzette were here she'd rally round, but she's busy at the moment and she never did like Margot much. But it's just no good, is it? I mean. If Margot was a man I could have a long chat about her to the dry-cleaning lady; I could even tell the bus conductor. They do you know, I've heard them, other women.

'It's because we're lesbians. No, I know that sounds a bit naive. I mean, of course it's because we're lesbians. But it's cyclical, isn't it, feeling hard done by, and every now and then it hits you a little bit harder, biteš a little bit deeper just how thoroughly vile and wicked the world is. If you hadn't dropped in like that, I don't know what I would have done. But one can't rely on one's mother-in-law stopping by for tea at the right moment. Would you stay a little while now you're here? I'd love it if you did.'

'I will, petal,' said Buddleia. 'I've unfinished business of my own. A little fresh air and sunshine and I'll be perfectly happy.'

'Can't really guarantee the sunshine,' said Polly.

'I know,' said Buddleia, 'I know. Still, when in Rome. But you were saying: about you and Margot being lesbians.'

'Well, I looked us up in the public library, you know, in one of those books that falls open on "Oral sex can be satisfying for either partner", and under "Lesbians" it said, "Mutual Masturbation". Well, we didn't do that. I mean, it's a bit difficult being mutual, you have to concentrate. Everywhere I looked those days I saw that word: "Lesbian" and thought, "they mean me". Sometimes I looked again and it really said "Lebanese" or "Lesion", but my heart beat just the same. For a while I wouldn't sit next to women on tubes or look them in the eye in shops, in case they knew I was one.

'I didn't want a sex manual that would tell us where to put what, we'd worked that one out on our own, but something that would say we weren't the first, that other women did it too. I met Margot for lunch one day at her hospital. We were going to say I was her sister up from Taunton. She showed me this book they had in the nurses' library, a yellow hardback with *HOMOSEXUALITY** in square letters down the spine. We flicked through it.

' "Women seem more liable than men to form emotional attachments to members of their own sex. They stop short of going to bed together but their feelings often exceed in intensity . . ." '

'Stop short of going to bed together?' repeated Buddleia. 'Why? Passion overtake them on the parquet?'

'Oh Buddleia, we could have done with you then. We looked round the library and put two weighty tomes on the table to hide what we were reading.'

' ". . . promiscuous lesbians . . . comparatively rare birds . . . particularly dangerous . . . dominant, forceful personalities . . . weaker, more pliant women . . ." Far worse than "Mutual masturbation". "The butch or 'dyke' type, swagger along in men's trousers and parody the normal male . . . exhibitionistic minority . . . more discreet deviants . . ."

' "Wotcha, Clit, lend us a fiver . . ."

' "Ssh, Jock, not so loud . . ."

'Margot started to laugh. I was outraged; I took it all very seriously, didn't want nurses reading that about me. And I didn't quite trust Margot's heartiness as she stood beside me in her white doctor's coat. Who ever heard of a lesbian gynaecologist?

' "Go on, pokerface," she said, "have a little giggle: it's on us."

' " We can't leave this stuff lying around," I said, "someone might see it."

' "What do you want to do, then? Confiscate the wanton

*by D J West

26

tome? Lob it out the window? March up to the desk and demand this sort of obscenity be removed at once from the shelves?"

' "We could just pick it up and walk out."

' "Finish it in bed tonight, eh? No, they've metal strips down the spine so a buzzer goes off."

' "Then let's hide it."

' "You want to hide a book in a library?"

'In the end we decided to change the classification and put it back in the wrong place, thus *HOMOSEXUALITY* became *Hiccups in the Cardiovascular System.* We only hoped . . .'

'Oh Polly,' Buddleia interrupted, 'there's a couple of very good . . .'

'I know,' said Polly. 'I've read them. You remind me of Suzette. She could always lend me the latest proud statement, though I don't know why she needed them. She had it easy. Met her Jane in Leàmington with the full support of her varsity colleagues.'

'I doubt it,' said Buddleia.

'I read Suzette's books, only the more I read, the angrier I got. First with her and Jane: sure they never cried because it was all too true too late. Then with Gerard and my parents and all the people who write library books because they don't have to search out any short article in a mine of scholarship, any chapter in a volume on perversion, any sentence in a paragraph, any bracket, any kind adjective. Oh no. They just go down the public library to discover that oral sex can be satisfying for either partner.

'We grew tired of clandestine meetings, thought we should regularise the situation, and I introduced Margot to Gerard. Polly the eternal adventuress! But what Margot really adored was bad taste and social climbers so there was just a chance they'd hit it off. So much better than all that exhausting bitterness. She was very funny in a subtle, subversive way because one was always on the point of believing her serious. At least I was. She'd do her solemn little frown, I'd put my compassionate face on and she'd crack it up into little laughing wrinkles. I'm sure I was the most grateful fall guy ever made. Gerard had a brother named Stephen.'

'Oh yes,' said Buddleia, 'I remember Stephen. Dear little boy. Used to take off his nappy and rub shit in his hair.'

'Yes, well, Stephen's wedding was approaching and it seemed like a good time to produce Margot. Everyone on their best behaviour, clothes too tight to brawl in. Though I was torn between keeping things smooth for Gerard and feeding Margot titbits to make fun of. Honestly. Made me feel like a blotchy chameleon.'

'Mmm, sounds like a recipe for disaster,' commented Buddleia. 'Was that what you wanted?'

'Margot and I had a terrible coolness over it. She said she'd not go anywhere near him. I said, "Margot, that's not fair; I always see you at your house. I know all your friends, your sister, everyone. Who've you met of mine but Suzette?"

' "And she doesn't like me."

' "She hardly knows you."

' "Well why don't you leave your beastly husband and move in with me?"

'Margot was always saying this.

' "Don't be silly. Your flat's too small," I said. "Where would I put all my books? No. If I leave Gerard I lose everything."

'Margot and I arrived at the church together. Gerard was best man of course and had gone round to Stephen's to practise his speech. Margot was being very good, didn't limp or make us late but I could see it was a strain for her. She went on being good right up till the bride and groom went to sign the register. The bride's brother had composed a wedding march; while we were waiting to sing the last hymn and start getting sloshed at the reception, he came and sat with his cello on the altar steps. I think it was supposed to look casual. It was too much for Margot to miss. She felt she owed herself one after all the handshakes and "friends of the bride or the groom?"

'She listened for a few rapt moments, sighed then turned to me sobbing with feeling and whispered loudly: "It's too much. All this and a cello too. I shall have to kneel."

'So she knelt. The only one in the whole bodding church. And we were practically in the front row so she was very conspicuous. Of course everyone turned and started whispering, and them in their garden party hats. The cellist looked up from his score but couldn't see anything untoward, missed a beat in his adagio and the march turned into a mazurka.

'That might have got it out of her system, only at the reception Gerard made this drivelling speech about his

28

brother's sobriety, cleanliness and devotion and if anyone knew any different they should all meet down the pub afterwards. Oh, you know wedding speeches.'

'Yes dear,' said Buddleia. 'As the groom's mother I did have to put in an appearance.'

'Of course, I was forgetting. Well, at the mention of devotion Margot muttered a passionate: "Well said! Oh well said! There's so many as forget these days." So no one was allowed to laugh. Then there was a queue for food. Gerard was at the front so it seemed like a useful time to effect an introduction. Somehow with the formal commotion of the church we hadn't met up before the ceremony.

' "Gerard darling," I said, "this is my girlfriend Margot, I don't believe you've met."

'Margot gave him a nonchalant grin and gazed past at the food. Gerard smiled back, still a little deflated about his speech. Margot patted his arm with her beige gloves and pointed.

' "Tell me now, what would those little chimneys be?"

' "I believe they're called vol-au-vents," said Gerard. "A sort of pastry Gone with the Wind."

' "Howmuch?" said Margot.

' "Vol-au-vents. French. You know, gourmet."

' "Oh," said Margot, "French is it? How very rude of me."

' "Shouldn't worry, my dear, acquired taste."

' "I wonder now, would any of them have prawns in?" Gerard passed her some over. These little pretty pastry cases full of savoury cream and a small pink prawn somewhere in the middle of each. Margot removed her gloves and very carefully hoiked the prawns out with her little finger, licking the cream daintily off afterwards. So neat you'd think she'd been practising. Then she handed the plundered pastries back to Gerard, smiled sweetly and said:

' "Waste not, want not. Would you be so kind as to replace these for me?" I was furious.'

'Should think so too,' said Buddleia, 'all that work. Puff pastry. Do you know you have to wash the butter first?'

'Gerard was fascinated. I could see him thinking her a real eccentric, deciding to draw her out. I was a bit nervous but so sure she'd prove more than a match for him that I hesitated to intervene. I longed for her to grind her heel upon his neck. She was being the simple Irish woman who thinks a lot but is easily abashed. Gerard was delighted, said he just loved her accent so she pronounced a few more haitches and he started to mimic her. Made me feel blotchier than ever. Gerard's father spoke like that; my mother too, though not as pure. But Margot's an Ascendancy thoroughbred. She had Gerard eating out of her hand; got him on to Russia and I wondered was she trying to show me he was a hypocrite. He'd done that himself quite successfully.

' "How do you like it here in Sassena, fine Irish Colleen like yourself?"

' "I like it fine," she said, looking like given half a chance she'd drop a curtsey and call him sir. "But I've always wanted to travel."

' "Have you now? And where is it your heart's set on going?"

' "Oh, the Soviet Union, sir," she replied with all the red-headed fervour of her Celtic soul.

'I knew there was a "sir" in there somewhere.

' "Hmph, Russia," he grunted dropping the accent. It's not all pine forests, you know."

' "No indeed," said Margot earnestly. "They have that planned economy as well."

'Now it sounded like me she was mimicking.

' "Planned economy!" harumphed Gerard. "If it takes four men to move eight crates of oranges the Russians would deliver them rotten. You wouldn't want to go there."

' "Ah," said Margot simply, "I feel they ought to know something of the lives of ordinary homosexuals over here. Would you not agree that's most important?"

' "What are you insinuating?" Gerard snapped. "You're treading a very thin line, young lady, very thin."

'He was boozy with champagne and looked outraged. When she thought he wasn't looking Margot winked and blew a kiss across at me. She didn't need to be drunk to go over the top. Gerard turned and certainly intercepted something. He was all red and puffy. I thought he was going to hit one of us. Then he laughed.

' "All right," he said. "You got me. I'll give you two out of three. Now that's not bad. If I had those odds in my job I'd be laughing. I am Irish, born in Cork City and proud of it, so the accent was right. One point. In my youth I was quite a tearaway, ask Polly, that's how she met me. I was even, don't laugh, a Communist and I thought Moscow had all the answers. Two points. But," (and here he chuckled) " 'the lives of ordinary homosexuals'; good try, Margot, good try. You very nearly scored three in a row. Unfortunately, and again it's your friend who's my witness, I'm a happily married man."

'He drew me towards him and we stood, side by side, a picture of marital harmony. I could feel his heart pounding in his ribs. He looked terribly pleased with himself.

'Stephen came up to us then. He and Gerard had a bit of a crack about honeymoons and first nights and soon they got on to dirty jokes, their major channel of communication. Margot was filling herself with red caviar, explaining that she never touched black. I was beginning to breathe again whan Gerard remembered a really good one. He began to laugh uproariously before he could even get the words out.

' "Did you hear the one about the . . . hey Margot, honey, this'd be one for you . . . 'the lives of ordinary homosexuals', don't worry I've not forgotten." He took hold of her arm. "You see there were two lesbians in the bath. One says 'Where's the soap?' And her little mate replies 'Yes it does, doesn't it.' D'you geddit? Eh? Do you? 'Wears the soap.' Oh forget it. Slow isn't she?"

'Then he put his arm round Stephen. Took another swig and spluttered: "Two lesbians in bed together. One says 'Let me be frank', so the other one says . . ." and here he had to stop for a moment he was laughing so much. He coughed and coughed and did the nose trick, had liquid coming out of every hole in his face. " 'You were Frank last time, it's my turn.' Come on Margot, spill the beans, my joyful little songbird, which one of you is Frank?"

'He leered at her, forcing her back against the tables.

' "Who's going to be Frank tonight eh? Who's going to be Gerard?" He grabbed hold of her left hand and started playing with her fingers. "Which one do you use? This one, is it? Or this one? No, of course it'd be the ring finger, more sacrilegious." He held her hand in his. "You're very sexy, you know. You're wasted on my wife; anyway she doesn't need you, doesn't need anyone. She's got a plastic one, a plastic dick with batteries that goes throb, throb, throb." For one awful moment I thought he was going to take out my vibrator and put it on the table; let everyone watch it rocking and imagine me and Margot using it.

Just like him to embarrass himself as long as it hurts me.

'He started coughing again and choking. Had to sit down. I don't know who drove him home, me and Margot had already left. We went to her place, both shaking.

' "I'm sorry, Margot, I'm so sorry."

' "Yuk, men. I'd forgotten how vile they are, the size of them and the smell of them and the little crack in their voices that says, really I'm terrified, really you must protect me."

' "I know, I know; I'm sorry."

' "What'll you do? We could collect your things while he's at work and bring them back here."

' "To your luxury penthouse? It's sweet of you and your double bed's very comfy, but I'm going to want to get out of it occasionally."

' "Well it's an offer."

' "I know and I'm grateful but I can't go straight from his life to yours. I'm sorry."

' "Stop saying that; you'll apologise yourself into the pavement."

' "But I am. I'm an enormous, quivering mass of cosmic, transcendental sorry. I just never dreamed that Gerard could be that sick."

' "Come off it, Polly. It was obvious that was coming. I knew as soon as I started talking to him."

' "What do you mean you knew? What did you know? Margot! You did it on purpose."

' "Oh, don't take it like that. Why did you invite me?"

' "You wanted me to see what an evil little wimp I'd married so I'd come and live with you. Can't I fight my own battles? Don't I make my own decisions?"

'I was so angry with Margot I went to stay at Suzette's. All the way up in the train I stared out of the window, at sheep slumped morosely in fields till night fell and they were merely lighter puddles against the dark and I found myself gazing at my own reflection with telegraph poles looming near and leaping past. "It was obvious that was coming." I sat there and gazed and it was all tremendously obvious. It didn't really matter which little wimp I married. My childhood, I think, was the usual round of rage and resignation and at eighteen I had woken up briefly but long enough to recognise my father's wealth and marry Gerard. Then I had fallen asleep again – a sleep from which both Gerard's arrogance and my flirtation with scholarship failed to rouse me – until I found myself to be thirty-five, friendless and living in London, entirely dependent on my husband. It was while we were having sex that I first stirred; it is somehow more difficult to disappear when a man's body lies smeared across you, sucking your mouth, denting your chest so that every breath comes courtesy to him. I think perhaps I coughed. And perhaps that is why sex was so important with Margot: I was in mortal fear of drowsing off again. But even then, despite the books in the library, the difficulty of seeing each other at all, the shouts after us in the street: "Are you married? Which one's the man?" Which we never mentioned even to each other for fear one of us would decide it was all a hideous mistake; the code we had for phone calls if Margot was at work: "Hello, Mum, it's me. How's the arthritis?" If Gerard was around: "I can let you have the rough draft by Thursday"; I still felt my father's wealth protecting me like the stale cotton-wool smell of an air-conditioned room.

'As I walked through the swaying corridor to the buffet for a little bottle of Benedictine I wondered that Margot's patience had lasted so long. As the sweet syrup rolled on my tongue I realised I was half way between Euston and Warwick with no clean knickers and only a joint bank card to my name; that the college had accepted me because my husband paid my fees; that my share in the world was the other half of Margot's bed or the seat by the window with my lime cardigan draped over the back.

'You know, Forum was not the first advert I answered. On the corner of our road was a small job agency; they were delighted with my accent but dubious of my Dublin degree. I could offer no work experience though I was expert at not minding and pressing on regardless. They sent me to a place in Victoria where I would check one list of figures against another, would start at eight and finish at six, see no daylight in the winter months, have no knowledge of the weather save the absence or presence of umbrellas on the arms of the lower management.'

'But you made it up with Margot?' said Buddleia. 'She went to see you at Suzette's?'

'Oh yes. And Gerard and I settled things diplomatically, mostly due to your good services.'

'Well he was playing at being indifferent so he couldn't very well make a scene. Though . . .'

But at that moment there came a knock at the door.

'Oh no!' cried Melaleuca. 'You can't stop now. Polly's only just left Gerard. Took her time about it too. Margot hasn't moved in yet and you were to find out why she went.'

'But Polly has to answer the door,' said Buddleia.

'And we,' boomed another voice, 'have the water rates to attend to. Have you not done prevaricating?'

'The Djugashvili Bonsais have arrived . . .'

'The women have come to look around . . .'

'Polly must answer the door . . .'

'And Buddleia return from whence she came.'

'. . . Though . . . what?' asked Polly. 'Buddleia, don't sound so ominous.'

'Well, he's letting you live in his house but don't think he's doing you a favour.'

'I know, he just doesn't fancy the stain of his wife in a YWCA.'

'You mean he doesn't want the squatters in.'

'The rent's very reasonable, and he still pays the rates.'

'Just in case he wants the house back.'

'But Margot and I did all the work on it: she picked the colours, I did the papering and we took turns waiting for the gasboard.'

'How satisfactory,' said Buddleia. 'So what made her leave?'

'I asked her to,' said Polly, adding cryptically, 'Political Differences.'

'I doubt it,' countered Buddleia.

Polly gave one last look round her home. Whoever came to move in, it would not be the same again.

Buddleia hovered between going and staying. She had been sent to answer certain questions and now had the answers to some of them; but too brief, too sketchy. Polly had asked her to stay; for how long was she to be responsible? In the absence of a clear collective voice she followed her own wishes in the matter and planted herself in the back garden there to await further events.

34

3
Not Visitors

Accom Offered
Two lesbians wanted for nice little house by
the tube, SW9, £13pw. Ring Polly 273 6347.

Polly looked again at her ad. What vital detail was missing? Too late now for that.

As soon as the new *Spare Rib* was pushed through the letter-box, Kim rushed upstairs to read it. She made a note of Polly's number on a separate piece of paper.

'Wouldn't do for the others to find out,' she muttered. 'Not till I'm safely out of here.'

Bev had woken Sadie and shoved the ad under her nose.

'Oh Bev,' said Sadie. 'Why did you wake me? I was having such a lovely dream.'

'Look, Sadie, at least try it,' said Bev. 'You can't stay here for ever.'

'All right, I'll call her. But you've got to stand by the phone.'

While Polly was talking to Buddleia, Kim was still calmly drinking her tea though she was sure to be offered one as soon as she got to Polly's. Then she stood up and rinsed her cup in the sink, studiously ignoring the pile of knives and plates which had already collected, product of a day's worth of toast and sandwiches. She cleared a space for her cup on the drying rack.

'Just popping out,' she called, scrawling her name in the 'save' column of the dinner rota.

Riza looked up briefly but Quinton and Lee were discussing whose turn it was to wash up and Kim snuck out by the French windows. If Polly's proved impossible she'd be back in a few hours and no one any the wiser. One or other of them was always threatening to move out: a kind of housing suicide unless

35

things improved. Kim looked the new place up on the A–Z. If she moved in she'd still be living on page 78.

Polly ran her fingers along the stair carpet. It was still a little damp. Maybe she should have used the dry shampoo only how was one to tell? If she asked at the shop the assistant would think she ought to know already. A woman of her age.

'Sadie, couldn't you at least put on clean shorts?' said Bev, feeling increasingly exasperated.

'What clean shorts?'

'Well, borrow something of mine then. And your feet are filthy.'

'Shit, Bev, it's only surface dirt. That's easy to clean.'

'So why don't you? You could scrub your mouth out while you're at it. Honestly. The language Claire's coming out with at nursery the other mothers will stop their kids playing with her. Are you listening? Don't give a monkey's do you? Some of us have to live in this world you know.'

'Stunning. You sleep with me cos I'm easy and as soon as it gets a bit difficult I'm out on my fucking ear.'

'Shh. Sadie! Claire'll hear you. Look love, I took you in, didn't I? Gave you a place to stay but I said it couldn't be permanent. I mean, I made that clear from the start.'

'Spose you did, Bev. Spose you did. Only, well, I thought you liked me being here.'

'Sometimes. Look sweetheart, you should get out and make your own friends.'

The place was easy to find, only across the main road and into the back streets a little way. The houses were small. Kim peered through the transparently clean front window. 'Tasteful', she thought. Hefty furniture. Perhaps the owner had come down in the world. For a moment Kim turned back to the street. Polly seemed a long time answering. At the corner of the road stood two women talking. Were they both coming to see the house? Oh no. One was walking back the way she'd come.

'Dear Bodd,' said Kim earnestly, 'let it all be all right. Don't make me go back there. I'll never feel angry enough again.'

Always when her period started she felt a rush of energy which it didn't do to ignore. It might make her fidgety and

36

uncomfortable but this was the time when, her toleration level low, she was forced into making changes.

As Polly walked towards the door she felt overcome by fatigue. She really could not go through all this again. Suzette, without tenure in her department, had been offered a transfer to King's and knowing Polly had spare rooms had suggested she and Jane move in. Dubious when the plan was first mooted, Polly now warmed to the idea. She could readily picture Jane sorting out the garden; Suzette borrowing books from her room, staying to chat a while. Why feel cowardly? Everyone picked the safe option.

'I'll go as far as the corner with you, but the rest you must do on your own,' said Beverly firmly.

'Thanks Bev,' said Sadie. 'I'm not very good at gratitude but if you hadn't seen that ad . . .'

'You'd still be asleep in my bed! Oh climb down, Sadie, it was only a joke. Good luck love.'

'I'm all right, aren't I? I mean, I'm not always like this.'

'Sadie stop it. You want somewhere to live, she wants someone to live with. She's even looking for a dyke.'

'Not this dyke she's not.'

Beverly turned and walked away. Sadie moved her feet slowly along the street. She'd been a millstone far too long. It wasn't fair. She'd gone to Bev in an emergency but the emergency'd run out of steam.

'Hello, both of you together? Do you know each other then?' Polly felt the gloom settle firmly on her shoulders. These two were far too young and hopeful. It was going to have to be Suzette and Jane.

Kim felt surprised. How old was that woman, Polly presumably, with the grey hair? Was it earned or dyed? Her trousers were grey flannel with darts and certainly lined. Her blouse, for it was a blouse not a shirt, had a little rounded collar. She smelt crisp, like a hot iron. Did she own the house?

'Well, you've come to the right place so you'd better step on in.'

She kept a tight rein, obviously not one to be invaded. Perhaps she had just left her husband. She was far too posh for

Stockwell. Kim imagined a romantic story based on coffee mornings: two women's hands reaching for the milk jug; the husband finding out, being saddened not angry; the children fortunately too old for a custody case; the final decision to live apart.

Kim looked at Sadie standing gawkily beside her, so tall and awkward, big, with the shoulders of a swimmer. Kim could imagine her: here one day, gone the next to chase up a story, make a film, hitch with her lover to Tibet. Loose khaki shorts, hands in pockets; Kim expected she played the saxophone, took a lot of nice drugs and spent the summer in Crete.

Sadie wondered how long she would be able to put off that awful moment when she would have to look at the other two, aware of the bulk that their bodies made in the air next to her. Soon she would leave behind the street, the low walls and cracked paving stones where one might find a penny or a halfpenny. Already Polly's voice was there between them, surrounding them, drawing them into the house. Sadie plunged her hands into the pockets of her shorts, her skin was warm, her muscles tightened as she moved.

'I expect you'd like to see round first,' said Polly. Was that right? Or did one offer a cup of tea? 'Um, I'll just run and put the kettle on and it'll be boiling by the time we're through. We'll start upstairs and work down.'

The stair carpet was light blue and must need scrubbing once a week. Had Polly a collection of her husband's old shirts specially kept for the cleaning? No one would dream of sweeping the stairs at home, with seven of them rushing up and down they'd only get dirty again. Though Kim would have liked a clean house. She watched as Sadie followed Polly upstairs, bending slightly as though experience had taught her ceilings were always too low. 'So tall', thought Kim. She felt irritated. It seemed an arrogant gesture for all its apparent submissiveness.

The stair carpet was light blue. It had little specks of white and a beautiful soft grain like a shetland jumper. Sadie would have liked to crouch down and roll in it, stroking it against her cheek. The bannisters were a smooth, glossy white with here and there a drop of paint suspended in motion, cut short on its slow journey to the bottom. Sadie bent and followed one of the little paths with her finger but dared not linger long.

'This is my room,' said Polly opening a door at the end of the corridor, standing back to let them pass. Perhaps it was wrong to start with your own room, perhaps you only took them to see the spare rooms, the ones they might move into. It must be different from showing friends round.

Blue and pale gold striped wallpaper, tradescantia by the window, a pine bedstead with a patchwork quilt in Laura Ashley hexagons and a rainbow of neatly folded sweaters. Somebody had to say something, break the respectful silence.

'What's in there?' asked Kim, pointing to a door next to the wardrobe.

'My study,' said Polly reluctantly. She didn't want them going in there; her academic defeat was her own business.

'Let's see,' said Kim.

A tiny room lined with bookshelves, a desk covered with paper and pens, total disorder.

'What is it you do in here?' asked Kim.

The question Polly was dreading.

'Fart,' said Sadie, the first word she'd spoken.

Polly's hand played with the round collar of her blouse.

'Well, er . . .' she faltered. It was just the sort of thing Margot might have come up with, though Margot would have been trying it on.

Sadie turned towards Polly and smiled. First she gazed, then the corners of her eyes tightened, the thin lines of her mouth and eyebrows became curves, her cheeks rounded. She put her head on one side and grinned down wholly, directly, at Polly.

'It's a nice house,' she said solemnly.

The last slice of a two-year-old's imaginary cake saved especially for you.

'How sweet of you, dear,' said Polly.

The smile filled her with the most incredible wave of optimism. Everything was going to be all right; Sadie and Kim would move in and they would all be incredibly happy together; everyone was terribly beautiful and it was all just perfect. There was a golden glow like a halo over the house in Stockwell. Polly looked again at Sadie. The smile, though still flickering in the corners, had all but gone. It left a rosy aftertaste. Maybe this time things would work out. Polly recollected herself. Kim had gone off to explore.

'Would you like to see the middle room?' Polly asked Sadie, hoping something in it would please her because then she might smile again. Sadie gazed along the corridor in assent. The other room was small, an odd pentagonal shape so that the furniture was forced away from the walls.

'The epicentre,' said Sadie.

This time Polly smiled. (Rather a boring society smile after that great beam of joy she sent me.) She worried lest Sadie feel short-changed.

Back downstairs.

Polly looked at Kim from behind the coffee pot. They said they wanted coffee. She herself was drinking hot water, far too much tannin for one day. She supposed she ought to ask questions but Kim looked up and said abruptly:

'I live in a mixed house.'

There was no point beating about the bush, they'd better know that from the start.

There was a silence. Kim wondered were they both thinking what on earth is she doing here then?

'Mixed?' repeated Polly. 'You mean . . .?'

'Men,' Kim supplied gloomily.

'That,' said Sadie.

'It's a squat actually.'

So now it was out. Polly would despise her for not paying rent. She was beneath Sadie's contempt because she associated with the enemy. Well, they weren't going to put her down without a word.

'We share cooking and cleaning, do the shopping together and have a house account for the big things. Lee, that's one of the blokes, does a wholefood run once a month because he's the one with access to a van.'

'It sounds nice,' Polly said.

'Yes,' said Kim, surprised but pleased. 'It is nice, but it's difficult.' Quite how difficult suddenly hit her. In an hour at most she would be back there having dinner with the others.

'You see,' she said, 'it's just me and three heterosexual couples.'

'Fucking Hell,' said Sadie astutely.

Kim wondered why she was telling them all this.

'But it's not like that,' she protested. 'In a way it makes the house very stable.'

It was true. Chris and Riza cared about her in a way she could not expect from the nebulous lesbian community.

40

'It's only that after dinner they all go off to each other's rooms. Except Riza and Lee and they'll be having an argument. Riza will tell me all about it while I wash up. I don't always do the dishes, don't get that impression. I think I just mind more. Lower threshold of dirt. After I've gone to bed there'll be a knock and Lee will want to know what we've been talking about.'

'What happens if you have company?' asked Polly.

'I don't,' said Kim. 'I mean. Well. We wouldn't go to my place.'

'Selfish pricks,' said Sadie. 'Invite the heaviest dykes in the neighbourhood round.'

'I don't think they'd be seen dead in my house,' said Kim, wondering wasn't anyone else going to say anything.

'I got evicted,' said Sadie casually. 'My flat was declared unfit for human habitation.'

'And my lover's just moved out,' said Polly. 'Don't we just sound like a bunch of wet rags.'

A little more conversation. Comments on the house. How long had Polly lived there? Where was the loo? A little more coffee. A quick look at the garden; amid a patch of yellow lawn blossomed a precocious lilac buddleia.

'My mother-in-law,' explained Polly vaguely. The others nodded.

'Are you from round here?' Kim asked Polly conversationally, 'Your accent sounds . . .'

'I'm Irish,' Polly answered, too quickly. Suddenly remembering that when she first came over with Gerard, and they'd been looking for rooms, every single place seemed to have an orange geranium on the sill and a large cardboard sign in the window: 'No Irish, No Hawkers, No Canvassers.'

'I was born in New Zealand,' Sadie intoned laconically, 'on holiday from London; moved to Africa when I was four, then moved back again when I was fifteen. The last two years I've spent in France.' She picked a blade of grass and chewed it, her expression almost – brazen, Polly thought.

'Well,' said Kim, 'I grew up in Streatham. Got born in the South London Women's Hospital, opposite Clapham South tube.'

Inside again. Sadie balanced the coffee cup on her bare knee, dabbling in the condensation until it got too hot and she changed legs. Whatever was she thinking about, Polly wondered.

Sadie gazed at the biscuit tin. It formed a comforting cylindrical presence in front of her. Were any of the knights on the lid women? How could you tell? Perhaps that helmet was really a wimple.

Kim gazed at the biscuit tin, wondering whether to have another biscuit. She'd eaten two already, but as she dipped one in her coffee it melted and flopped to the bottom of her cup.

'Plop,' said Sadie pleasantly.

Kim stared at her. Did she find the habit disgusting? Sadie looked away. Too big, too silent, too abrupt.

'I was away when they did moderation,' she said.

Kim smiled. 'Where are you staying at the moment?' she asked kindly.

'With an old friend who regrets her generosity.'

'The woman you were talking to in the street?'

'It's not her fault. She has a two-room flat and a four-year-old.'

'Well,' said Polly summarily, 'I think we should pat ourselves on the back for surviving.'

And as suddenly it was over. Kim and Sadie had gone. Their empty cups sat on the armrests where they'd left them. One had biscuit mush at the bottom; Polly guessed it was Kim's. She had trotted off home for her dinner. Polly hoped the others remembered to save some. Sadie had stood a moment gangling against the door frame.

'I'd best be off,' she said.

Whether she had decided to try again with the regretfully generous friend, or pick up her rucksack and move on, Polly had no way of knowing.

4
Direct Intervention

The Bonsais had arrived in Hortus; the water rates had begun. Discussion had so far limited itself to a definition of what was not to be included.

'I think we should leave out earthquakes,' ventured Hakea. 'They are a natural disaster but . . .'

'They're not really caused by water, no dear,' said the Bonsais condescendingly. 'I think we can safely consign earthquakes and other subterranean convulsions to a quiet footnote at the bottom of the era.'

'Nor volcanoes;' said Melaleuca, 'a little disruptive at the time but such marvellous top soil.'

Quercus snorted.

'Nor the planets lining up,' said Hakea. 'Though they are the cause of many break ups and much instability . . .'

'Hell's Bodds,' said the Djugashvili Bonsais with one voice – they were small but they stuck together – 'Haven't you worked out a frame of reference? What in Hortus have you been doing while we've been stunting our trunks to get here?'

'Frame of reference?' echoed Quercus: 'Bleedin' snobs, we all know what water is.'

'Perhaps we'd better take a break,' said the others, 'while we read over the minutes of the previous meeetings. This is surely not the first time it's come up. Besides, Buddleia hasn't reported back yet.'

'Where is she?' demanded the Bonsais, who didn't like to feel anything had slipped past them.

Clianthus began to explain while the other Boddesses leafed through the minute book.

'Phew,' breathed Melaleuca as she and Hakea drifted off, 'thought we'd never get out of there.'

'I was sure the Bonsais would move straight to a vote.'

'Then we would have had to pay attention and we'd never know what happened in Polly's house.'

'She was so anxious answering the door . . .'

'But it wasn't as bad as she thought.'

'Kim seemed nice. Nervous but nice.'

'Odds Boddkins they were all nervous.'

'I could see Polly and Sadie getting on.'

'Well I couldn't,' said Quercus, coming up behind them. 'She looked like she was about to crack up.'

'Just ignore her,' whispered Melaleuca to Hakea.

'Oh, come on you two,' said Quercus. 'You wouldn't know anything about it if I hadn't sent Buddleia to talk to Polly.'

'Go plant a little acorn, Quercus.'

'And I got you out of that bodding meeting.'

'You got us out?'

'If it'd been left to you two we'd still be in there wondering whether to include ornamental fountains and dripping taps.'

' "We all know what water is", salt-of-the-earth Quercus. Of course we know what water is but we didn't want to stay there and discuss it.'

'All right, all right,' conceded Quercus. 'But that Sadie, I mean, she's not all there.'

'Polly liked her,' said Melaleuca. 'Reminded her of her long lost Margot.'

'No,' said Hakea, 'Quercus is right. Sadie could hardly walk down the street without Beverly.'

'So what are we going to do? Set Buddleia on to her?'

'Buddleia is now firmly entrenched in Polly's garden,' Hakea observed. 'A bit abundant but perfectly happy. Pity to uproot her.'

'I should think so,' said Buddleia whose anthers must have been twitching. 'I'm staying put.'

'Well what do you reckon . . . ?'

'Ssh,' Buddleia commanded, 'Polly's thinking.'

Sharing with Suzette and Jane might not be so bad. As Kim had said, there was a lot of security in a couple. They would live their lives along their own pre-established pattern and she would have company if she wanted it. Of course it'd be difficult at first what with Suzette's transfer and Jane at a loose end but Suzette was a very old friend . . .

'Over my dead Bodd!' squealed Buddleia. 'She's going to let

44

Jane move in and do you know what that woman does to plants? Why she pares them and prunes them and cuts them back till they look for all the world like a French shrubbery.' Buddleia spat. 'She even ties up daffodil stalks.'

. . . They could share the cost of a freezer, buy food in bulk like Kim's house . . .

'No!' said Buddleia. 'No, no, no.'

. . . Well perhaps not, thought Polly. Suzette and Jane would extend their enveloping 'we' to include her, her house would be their house and they would inform her loudly but tacitly when her independence got out of hand.

One weekend at Leamington she had waited till Jane went to bed and, in a fit of confidence, told Suzette about Margot. In the morning Jane had put her arms round her, 'Never mind, poor Polly, it's so difficult buying food for one again.' She meant to speak worlds of understanding but Polly could just see Suzette snuggling in beside her and relating their whole conversation. It was like the letters which Suzette inevitably signed for both of them. Couples were all very well, but would you want one in the house? Better to live with Kim and Sadie . . .

'Much better,' muttered Buddleia. 'Oh much, much better.'

. . . They seemed to operate in quite different realms from herself whereas she and Suzette had always been rather competitive. She thought about Sadie for a while. her height, her monosyllables, her dirty knees, and she warmed to her. Sadie was as out of place as the living-room sofa. Then Polly remembered her smile: total and immediate as if it was too much effort to lie. And Kim? A bit ordinary, but why not? She was open, sensitive and tidy. Qualities that Polly could admire even as she declined to emulate.

But oh dear, what to tell Gerard? It was still his house and she had no idea what his plans were. And was she really in a fit state to handle the problems of newcomers? Wasn't she in need of a bit of coddling herself? She stretched her legs out on the sofa and lay back. Suzette and Jane? Kim and Sadie? Heads it's

Suzette, tails it's Sadie. Might as well toss for it, yes I will, I'll toss.

As Polly rummaged in her purse for a coin the Boddesses were pushing and shoving, anxious to see which way it would land, and none more anxious than Buddleia, fearful lest it fall on Jane who would certainly cut her down to size.

Polly threw a twenty pence coin in the air. Hope it's heads, she thought nervously. However would I cope with those two young ones?

Buddleia peered at the coin as it spun. Heads. Unless prompt action were taken Polly was going to get her wish. Quick as a flash, Quercus reached out and turned the coin round.

'Odds Boddesses!' exclaimed an awed Melaleuca. '*You're* gonna catch it.'

'That was Direct Intervention,' said Hakea, shocked at this tremendous audacity. 'Only the assembled Boddesses of the Angelica Archangelica are allowed to do that, and even then it has to pass three hearings and a veto.'

'Don't make me quake,' scoffed Quercus.

The coin fell back on to the cushion. Polly's hand was over it before she could see which way up it was. That's how it works, she thought. When it's actually spinning down toward you, you know how you want it to end up. So you choose for yourself anyway. I'll ring Suzette directly.

She raised her hand to look at the coin. Tails, it said: Sadie. Too bad, thought Polly. I'm not letting chance dictate my life.

'Did you see that?' wailed Quercus. 'Huwomen! They don't deserve to have us.'

'Oh Quercus,' said Hakea, 'your Heraic gesture. You risked the Archangelica all for nothing.'

Polly picked up the phone and dialled.

'Hello, Suzette? It's Polly.'

'Polly! What a coincidence, I was going to call you. We've been talking about it, you know, King's College and the move to London and Jane's absolutely heartbroken. Doesn't want to leave the garden. Makes me feel terribly callous, didn't realise how much it meant to her. I've decided to stay on at Warwick as a part-timer. Of course it's a drop in salary but we all have to compromise. Jane's delighted, skipped out to clip the hedge.'

'I bet she did,' murmured Buddleia.

'Anyway, how are you? Sorry to leave you in the lurch.'
'No, no, I . . .'
'Has someone been to look round? Do tell. What do they do?'
'Well, I think Sadie travels and Kim seems to um . . . I don't rightly know.'
'Oh Polly, not two more lost causes.'
'Suzette, I don't know. Do you really think it wouldn't work?'
'But I don't know anything about them. Neither do you, come to that. I expect they're fearfully interesting and rather sad.' If Suzette so much as mentioned Margot, Polly resolved to hang up.
'No,' said Polly, 'but the gas wants paying and actually I rather liked them.'
'I'd pay your bills for you, dearheart, sooner than see you involved in any more walking tragedies.'
Polly hung up. She knew Suzette would try to ring back and apologise so she kept the receiver in her hand and dialled Sadie's number.

'Best hot root it back to Hortus,' said Hakea, 'before our absence offends.'

'OK, OK,' said the Djugashvili Bonsais when the minutes of the previous five hundred and forty-two meetings, and the minutes of the minutes of the previous two hundred and thirty-three, had duly been cross-questioned, anatomised and vivisected. 'So let's keep this discussion strictly hydrological. And please, no earthquakes, no volcanoes and definitely no planets, lining up, lying down or falling out.'
This last was directed with unutterable scorn at the place which Hakea had vacated. As all eyes turned to the spot, some with sympathy, others with malice but most bearing idle curiosity, the empty seat proclaimed the unfortunate Boddess to be out of reach of any of them. No one likes their malice to

be wasted, let alone their sympathy or scorn: their assembled Bodships were disconcerted, the Djugashvili Bonsais outraged.

'One of our number is missing,' they hissed.

'We are not quorate,' they croaked.

'Our decrees are numb and avoidable, we must have a roll call at once.'

There was surely no justice in Hortus if everyone had to plough through seven hundred and seventy-five minutes while Hakea could just skip off. And the cry went up:

'Roll call, roll call, roll call, ' in two urgent, unvarying beats. And so the list was read, a powerful incantation in itself.

'Acer, Acacia and Casuarina.

'Brassica, Lobelia, Plumbago and Phlox.

'Quamoclit, Quisqualis, Schizocentron stop jiggling about.

'Fatsia Japonica, Ficus Elastica, Oxalis Europaea, Digitalis Purpurea.

'Rhododendron, Philodendron.

'Ilex and Ulex, Salix and Rumex.'

And so on until every Boddess in the place, hard stemmed or soft, bulb or seed grown, mono or dicotyledonous had had her name pronounced and recognised. Only three of that mighty throng remained unanswered; as if to add living proof to the already damning testimony of the roll call, the absentees chose that moment to grow back into their places.

'Where have you been?' the question boomed. Could any reply justify an absence so flagrant in its delict? Malaleuca was silent. It was obvious the roll had been called. Still, if no one pushed it they might get away with taking minutes.

'Sister Boddesses we are wasting time,' said Clianthus. 'I suggest the Minute Book be passed to the three absentees so they can catch up with progress to date.'

Stout Bodd, Clianthus, thought Melaleuca, but she reckoned without Quercus.

'Take the Minutes!' burst out that turbulent Boddess. 'While Huwomen take their own lives we sit here wittering about water. Does it not occur to you that women are more likely to die crossing the road than blown away by a hurricane, washed up by a tornado or deluged by monsoon? Why, if it wasn't for me, Sadie might have thrown herself under a bus.'

'If it wasn't for you doing what, Quercus?' said Clianthus. Malaleuca, fearing another outburst, looked at Clianthus and said, 'I think you should see for yourselves what happened and how Quercus came to intervene.' Intervene. The word was out and it was Melaleuca who had spoken it.

'You know what you are proposing, Melaleuca?' asked Clianthus. Melaleuca knew.

'We must put it to the Archangelica,' said Clianthus. 'First we will see the events, then we will listen to your motives, finally we must judge of the outcome. We will know your actions as you yourselves know them. Do you agree to this?'

'Oh, why not just banish us now and have done?' said Quercus. Banishment. Another word out. Banishment followed intervention as flooding follows monsoons.

Every Boddess whose name had been called on the roll sat with roots entwined round every other Boddess and together they grew backwards until Quercus, Hakea and Melaleuca had skipped off, and Kim and Sadie walked towards Polly's door. They watched as the three women trooped upstairs and came down again for coffee. No detail was spared examination: not the tiny drop of dry paint whose slow roll down the bannisters Sadie had paused to examine, not Polly's dietetic switch from tannin to hot water, nor Kim's wet munching of a soggy biscuit. At the end their corollas were grave.

Quercus waited impatiently till it was her turn to speak. 'I don't care if you send me away,' she said, 'but I must tell you what else we saw.'

'We've seen it through your eyes already,' said Clianthus patiently.

'Only what *we* did and thought,' protested Quercus. 'This is someone else . . .'

'You must speak from your own experience.'

'But Sadie's experience is ours because we know about it.'

The Archangelica considered. 'We will hear you out,' they agreed, 'but it is no more than hearsay.'

'What else is there?' said Quercus. 'Now, I'm not going to begin till it's so quiet I can hear the wind drop. Show a little respect for the damned.'

5
Forces of the Assumption

The 73 bus stopped in Stoke Newington Church Street and refused to go any further. It was only on exceptional journeys, the conductor was quick to point out, that they went all the way to Tottenham.

'You were lucky,' she added, 'that we weren't turned further back at Newington Green or even Angel, what with the Friday-night traffic.'

Sadie did not mind walking, it would give her more time to think, take possession of the streets again, let them welcome her back. She was the last to get off the bus. The weight of her rucksack slowed her down. In front of her an old woman struggled with a shopping trolley.

'Would you like me to hand it down to you?' asked Sadie, aware of speaking English, wondering what mistakes she had made.

'Thanks a lot darlin',' said the woman as she trudged off, 'that was a real help.'

Sadie stopped on the kerb and bent slightly, tugging the straps over her shoulders. She was sure there was a hardback digging into her spine. Bougainvillea, Fenland, West Bank, home. The street names skipped off her memory. Four corners. She always promised herself there would be only four corners to turn. Like the last hill before the sea. And the corners were on the right side of the road now after Paris.

The right side. The Assumption. According to the Assumption everyone was white, middle class and heterosexual, aged about forty. They were also male. Of course the Assumption knew that some people were working class, black or homosexual. They were also female. But if a person was walking down the street his skin was 'flesh' coloured, his suit expensive, he had half an eye out for pretty girls and probably voted C of E. People were men.

Sadie was walking down the street. She was a tall, foreign

lesbian who still thought in terms of the Assumption, a widespread, powerful organisation which must despise her for her itinerant idleness if not her height or nationality. She had just come back from France, her feet hurt and there was a hardback digging into her spine. It was the hardback not her deviance which caused her the most present anguish. She thought it was the left-hand corner of the Petit Robert and wondered when the little trianglar indentation in the small of her back would turn into a permanent scar. She decided not to stop and shift things around, it was more important to get on.

Through all the stopping and starting of the previous days, bus to the metro, metro to the Gare du Nord, lumbering down from the train at Dunkirk, waiting all night with the other strike-bound passengers, curling up in her sleeping bag to avoid the Dunkirk spirit, the coach to Calais, the crossing, the wait at Dover for the British train and two more buses; through it all that hardback had been digging into her spine. She would not stop now, now there were only three more corners.

The streets formed the right pattern before her: little girls in white knee socks, their hair in bunches held by red plastic bobbles, who executed complicated patterns with a piece of elastic. As they picked the band up with their feet Sadie reflected that though the little girls were not the same ones she had left, the elastic, grey and knotted as it was, might very well be the same piece.

She turned from Hilldrop into West Bank. It was still light but already there were cars kerb-crawling, their windows open, men with one arm on the steering wheel leaning across and yelling:

'Got the time, love?'

Once Lorraine had left a party to make a phone call, her half-full glass in her hand. A car had stopped beside her, as usual on West Bank, and one of the passengers called out:

'Gonna show us a good time?'

'No I am not. Piss off.'

'What did you say?'

'I said I'm fucking sick of getting hassled.'

Three plain-clothes coppers jumped out and arrested her for drinking on the street. After that, Lorraine, Beverly and Sadie spent four Saturday nights in a row standing about along there, taking down registration numbers. It scared a lot of men off,

51

thought they'd be reported to the cops, bit unlikely really, seeing how things stood with the filth, but the drivers weren't to know that.

The memories marked the territory as Sadie's because so much of her was connected with it. She crossed Amhurst Park. Out of Hackney into Haringey: one more corner. The nearer she got the slower were her steps; in years to come she would look back and think: this was the route I took, this what I saw, how I felt when I helped the woman off the bus, moved my mouth once more around English words. She began to save it all up like heirlooms for grandchildren.

Soon she would be walking in her street, where she paid rent, where she had a right to be. A train swayed past: the line only went to Liverpool Street. It was her railway line, her train, in a way that the beautiful orange corail never could be, cleaner, faster and more useful though it was.

She turned the last corner into Zinnia Street. The corrie on the other side told her the council's haste in pulling down the houses had not been matched by their speed at putting up new ones. This part of Tottenham was a grey labyrinth of corrugated iron where no street sign grew and only the abandoned wooden structures of last year's adventure playground provided any notable landmarks.

In Paris the houses came in all different shapes and sizes with flat roofs and yellow brick or grey slates and green railings. But life was mediated through French and she could not think it here on the London streets. It was such an effort of mind that it sounded more like a lie. It had been fun: leaving the city on a Friday night to camp in a cave and go midnight potholing; schlepping over to Nancy near the German border to listen to Frankie Armstrong at a jazz festival; nicking mazout from a building site to fire the boiler. But in Stamford Hill Sadie might do nothing and not feel she was missing out. For things were changing: women were unpacking rucksacks, no longer dossing in the backs of cars, getting wet when it rained, drying out in the sun. They were replacing sleeping bags with cotton sheets, buying the butter they really liked, hang the expense. They were consigning the day-to-day choices of habit, waking by reflex not wrist alarm, dipping crisp bread in bowls of milk coffee, gazing at the neighbours' shutters from the comfort of their favourite armchair. As Sadie looked round it suddenly

52

seemed that everyone in the world had a favourite chair. Were they digging in for war? A generation of nuclear emus. If you had ten minutes before the world exploded, where would you most like to spend them? Warheads: strong, silent, apocalyptic. Annihilating all that's made. A spur to protect hearth and home. If not for us then for our children: bootees on the barbed wire. The nice butter and the cotton sheets were not for the women who bought them but a bribe. Sadie spread the butter, helped choose the sheets, had apocalyptic visions herself which drove her not to the green thought of Greenham but down to the British Consulate to get 'right of residence' stamped in her passport.

She trudged on along the street with that special ache between her shoulder blades familiar to all who have nursed a rucksack over from Paris, and that weariness which comes from sitting for four hours outside the toilets in a crowded Corail. At times she could still smell the seeping odour of urine clinging to her clothes and hair, feel the icy wind cutting across her neck each time the train stopped and the doors opened.

As she jostled bulkily past people in the street she apologised in French, changing it to a muttered 'sorry' well after they'd gone. It worried her. And then it worried her that if she explained they would think she was doing it on purpose. But soon she was to be the old woman one set one's clock by, boring as burnt toast for breakfast.

The French trains were full of young men doing their year's military service. Sadie would start off vaguely sorry for them as they threw their bags up from the platform, mindful of friends' brothers who gobbled handfuls of speed for weeks so they'd be refused when the time came. No, not refused, reformed, strange though it sounded. But it was still wrong: military service stories were told laconically in French by young men with long greasy hair on white plastic chairs round a pepsi-cola umbrella. Unthinkable here where Sadie avoided speaking to men at all.

When they got out of the army the boys would wander, arms round each other's shoulders, drunk as peas in a pod, chanting, 'Zéro, zéro, zéro, zéro,' to the tune of Auld Lang Syne, the number of days left to serve. Sadie managed to remain sorry for them in an offhand way until one of them banged on the window or sat down next to her, grabbing her arm or her attention, and gabbled, 'Americaine? Anglish? Deutsche? Doyouspeak Eenglish?' Usually a mate called to them from the corridor and they went away again laughing.

Sadie had waited calmly at the Consulate, passport in hand, pretending the stamp was merely reassurance, not something she feared she might not get. She was called into a glassed-off cabin where she handed over her form.

'But of course you don't have right of residence,' the woman said. 'What made you think you had?'

The bomb dropped, the penny dropped, the glass cabin failed to shatter.

'Does that mean they won't let me in?' Sadie asked.

'How long did you want to go for?'

Colourless, odourless and stateless, Sadie disappeared into the armchair.

'They might turn you back at Dover,' said the woman. 'How did you get this passport? Her delicately ringed hand closed in on the little black book.

Don't take my passport away.

Don't take the floorboards away.

I'll fall, I'll fall.

I am afraid.

'My father,' muttered Sadie. She was born by chance, by sheer chance in New Zealand. Though she had spent her youth and infancy in London; her childhood in Africa. Her mother, while visiting relatives in Auckland, had fallen ill and had to stay a little longer, and Sadie, being big enough by then, had had no choice but to be born. No way was this interview a serious threat: she would contact her father, absent for years, hated and feared, and procure a copy of his birth certificate, but it was a sufficient jolt to confirm her suspicion that when people are busy protecting hearth and home, arms either linked or nuclear, they are warding off signs of deviance and the force of the Assumption is strong. Sadie must keep her father's birth date close to her at all times; he at least was man enough to protest and survive.

She passed the sub post office that stocked macadamias. It was an Indian family who ran it. No, she thought, not now. I shall save some stories for the days to come when euphoria carries me no longer. In her low truckle-bed in Paris where the metal shutters rendered the room lightproof, Sadie had carefully imagined each step, each stone, pausing to check that the colours, the smells, the unevenness of the pavement were each just as they should be. And her imagination seemed more real than the slow tired steps she now took. She tried to calm herself with the pain of the hardback in her spine, the smell of dust and petrol, the awkward introduction to Ellen whom she'd only known as a voice on the phone and a signature and who could not have been pleased to learn that she would have to find somewhere else to live.

In her eagerness at leaving for Paris, Sadie had hinted that she might not be coming back. Of course she'd written more recently, and Ellen had always said she only wanted the place till her course finished, but the flat would be full of her things and Sadie would have to give it time to get used to her being there again. A sobering thought, but she was re-entering real time after the rainbow bubble over Issy.

The rising excitement which she had not quite been able to suppress since leaving France began to boil over and sing to her: she was going home, home. Home! How soft it sounded, like warm sheets in the morning. Her own home, her flat. Soon her feet were skipping and bounding along the pavement, pebbles over a stream. She passed the pillar-box and began to laugh because it was red and then to cry because it was a pillar-box. A London pillar-box: red like buses and phone booths are red.

Sadie surveyed her street proprietorially as a baron his battlements after a prolonged period at court. One of the houses further on had piles of rubble outside.

Lowers the tone, she laughed happily to her rucksack. Council must have decided to rehab after all. Shirley and Martine's house was pointed orange, then came the Swanleys with their concrete yard and sparkling Cortina.

He was a right weirdo, thought Sadie. Paves the garden so he can pat the car from the front window.

Mixed with the lingering exhaustion, which was now so familiar it seemed more like a way of life, was the certainty that as soon as she did sit down she would break in the middle and be transported to Heaven to lie on a fluffy white cloud with the angels. Soon, soon she would collapse in a place where it would be safe to let go.

Only another three houses. So which was the one with the pile of sand and brick? Just as the anxious mother turns and sees a fire-engine parked in the street, her street, and through years of fearing the worst believes it to be outside her house and that the children, her children, are trapped in an upstairs room, only to be flooded with relief further on when she realises the fire is actually at the newsagents. So Sadie passed from the terrible fear: Oh my Bodd, they've knocked the house down! to the more impersonal: I didn't realise the Council had plans for this side of the street.

Unfortunately . . . tragically . . . her relief was somewhat precipitate. Somewhat precipitate? It was a terrible, an awful thing. To have walked so happily; to have skipped down those streets; to have been so eager that neither the long walk nor the back-breaking weight should slow her; for so long to have had one bright, one reassuring thought in the total security of her . . . her . . . it could no longer be called her home, to be thus vilely and utterly disappointed was a crime which should cry out loud at every tribunal in every court across the Assumption.

But she didn't own the house. Was British in passport only.

Sadie stared at the debris. It was impossible that it should be her house, yet there was the rubble and timber, the old bits of metal and brick piled high up, covering the path, tracing a dusty track into the house itself. The front window, a pretty bay with window-box and geraniums, was now a gaping hole in the brickwork without frame or glass as though a giant hand had ripped it from its socket. The steps, cracked and broken under the weight of countless wheelbarrows, had been replaced by a board, like a building site. Sadie's home was a building site.

The front door flapped, chained up with a huge padlock but the hinges were broken and it was easy to squeeze in round the side. Sadie's rucksack scraped the door frame. The bannisters had been pulled down leaving two regular holes in each step; the ceiling in the front room lay on the floor in sections. The joists were now all that separated the ground floor from the first.

Floorboards, Sadie muttered in an attempt to put words to the devastation around her. Why have they put the floorboards on the ceiling?

There was a small wedge of envelopes stuck behind the pipes in the hallway. It was nearly dark. Sadie's sense of time had stopped somewhere mid-Channel. The street light sent a furtive bunch of rays into the hall, creating more shadows than they dispelled, unwilling to leave the safe, open space outside and not a little reluctant to seal Sadie's misery by helping her read official notification thereof. Clutching the letters in one hand, her pack still on her back, Sadie climbed the stairs, shoulder to the wall for fear of slipping in the gloom.

On the first landing she felt in her pockets for ten pees to feed the meter. Patiently she fumbled each coin, calculating by weight, shape and size what denomination it was. But she was confused. None of the coins fitted the patterns in her head which were for francs, half francs and centime pieces. Anyway it would have done no good: the electricity was off at the mains. Was someone trying to save her from reading this proof of total rejection? The letters in her hand which she gripped with such a fever were surely from the Assumption.

Somehow she had slipped through its net all these years, but now it had caught up with her. It would mock her horribly, hideously, with the milk pure teeth of the righteous; laugh long and loud, open and free, and then it would tell her most courteously that people such as she might roam the world on their own, taking no one with them, asking no one for help, might have a reasonable time in Paris, Africa or Jakarta but should they ever try to settle down, stay in one place and have the audacity to call that place home, why then they would have to learn the hard way what their rightful place in this world was to be.

On up the stairs. Sadie's neck and shoulders were as tight as a block of wood. Mysterious forces seemed to be gathering inside her rucksack prodding, poking, slicing into her back. On the top floor she put her key in the lock. A simple, even an automatic gesture: the key in her hand, the dark hole at hip level; the barrel turning to welcome her. Inside was a mass of objects from which no order or category generated. A broken television set. No, two broken television sets: one black and white, one colour. A cot-rail. A spilled bowl of what might have been cornflakes. Dolls with no heads, teddies with no arms. They held no fond if grimy memories for Sadie.

'They must be Ellen's,' said Sadie out loud.

Her voice came up from her lungs, vibrated against her vocal cords and was chopped up between teeth and tongue to join the miscellany of things that did not belong in the room. What had happened to Ellen?

57

Sadie picked up some candles whose wicks were all either too long or too short. She could make no sense of anything. The letters were still clenched in her hand. White envelopes with her name on as though amidst desolation someone had been expecting her.

She slit open the envelopes with her nails, took the contents out and unfolded them. They were neatly typed on the white, headed notepaper of the Assumption. Sadie stared at the letters on the page. Some were large, some short, others rounded. Individually they stood their ground against the best of them but together they made no sense at all. Each word was spelled correctly, no more than one space between each word and two spaces after a full stop. All lines were parallel, double-spaced, the relevant points underlined. So there were relevant points? The very neatness of the letters stood as an oasis of tranquillity in the chaos that surrounded her until, inexplicably, as though endowed with a life of their own, the paper between her hands started to shake and rattle so that the lines ran into each other forming diagonal columns fanlike down the page.

When she had stopped trembling, Sadie stared again at the things in the room: the playing-cards (a ten of clubs, a three of hearts) the pile of paper doilies. They had more right to be here than she did. According to those letters Sadie Monash had been evicted in absentia more than a week ago but all property was to be stored until collected. This flat, her home, on whose carpet she now stood was unfit for human habitation.

'But Ellen?' said Sadie and the cot-rail and the cornflakes echoed, 'Ellen? Ellen?'

Ellen had poured milk on those cornflakes, had left behind that cot-rail. She must have called in the Environmental Health to force the landlord to do repairs. Sadie hoped she'd been rehoused.

So the Council had condemned the building and the landlord evicted his tenant. A neat, a fairy-tale ending. No house, no occupants. Ellen, never more than a brisk voice on the phone, a signature on an agreement now dead, Ellen had gone. Sadie shouldn't be there, the house shouldn't be there and every cupboard, every wall, every inch of lino exuded memories of Ellen. Sadie leaned against the wall with the curious feeling that she didn't exist. She wasn't wanted and her only rights to the flat were inside her own head because she called it home. It used to be the decisions that were difficult and now, having made one with triumphant clarity, it was picked up and taken out of her hands. She had been faithful to this flat throughout her stay in Paris: Issy she had called 'our house', but the flat was always home. She wondered, if she closed her eyes, would everything go away. Where to ? And would it take her with it?

She closed first one eye then the other. Her body swayed from side to side like the ferry. All around people were talking French, saying everyday things and there was a dead weight digging into her back. Pain, triangular pain, unchanging pressure. She opened her eyes. That awful pain, like a knife, like a compass point. All the way from Paris she had looked forward to that blissful moment when the H-frame hits the floor and your arms, suddenly freed of the rucksack, glide into the air like a shuttlecock from a racket, floating up to the ceiling. She had forgotten to take her rucksack off.

Forgotten. She had known, somehow always known, that if she kept the use of her faculties she would be all right. Not happy, but all right. The Assumption would continue to goad but she would keep on unless, until, she lost somewhere on the way some vital part of herself. Her eyes, perhaps, or the use of her legs. This was what she had anticipated and now it seemed it was to be her mind. She who had made her one big decision; had decreed that despite the endless wanderings of her parents she could choose to live in one place and love that place because she lived in it; could look calmly at photographs of France, Africa, Asia without any sense of envy; could expose that hideous wanderlust as a deep-seated inadequacy; she, Sadie, despite the pain and the weight had neglected to take her rucksack off. As though it held inside it a kind of momentum which would keep her going until it was safe to stop. But it would never be safe, and she would never stop.

She had no reason to stay but no energy left which would pick her up and make her go back out there where everyone spoke that strange language she used to call hers. She sank to her knees, shoulder sliding down the wall, and crawled towards the mattress. Then she curled up in a ball. The pack was now a comforting weight behind her, pressing against her like another sleeping figure and if the hardback still poked, its touch was as light as a familiar elbow which would move soon with a little snuffling grunt. If her rucksack was all she had she would accept

59

it like a lover, the Assumption might beat her in the end but she would not give in to it. She would sleep and morning would come, would fill the room with daylight and the things in it would just be a nasty mess. She would be angry with Ellen for not warning her, would talk to the Law Centre about her rights, write to the landlord, get rehoused by the Council.

She turned, slipped her arms from the straps and clung to the aluminium frame of the pack, burying her face in the rough red nylon. Then, all of a sudden, of all strange noises which might haunt a derelict house, the phone rang. Businesslike. It could as well have been a crowded office. Sadie listened for a while as one follows the call of a bird, not so much for its tune or pitch, as the soothing regularity of the notes. The tick of a clock, a heart beat. She staggered to her feet, steering an uneven course through the room, guided only by the steady ringing. She put her hand on the cold black plastic of the receiver and picked it up. A phone call exists to be answered.

'Hello?' she said sleepily into the receiver, registering only now that half the floor boards on the landing had been taken up.

'Hello? Sadie? This is Ellen.'

'Ellen? Thank Heaven. Listen, what the hell's happening? The place is an absolute bomb . . .'

There was a noise downstairs.

'Just a mo, Ellen,' she said. 'Someone at the door.'

Before she reached the bottom step she had seen the two figures in the hallway. How had they got the key? she wondered angrily, frightening her like that. Then she laughed at her indignation. There were no windows downstairs, no hinges on the door: anyone could get in.

'Hello, love,' said one of the figures. 'Not seen you before.'

'I live here,' Sadie claimed stoutly. 'What the hell are you two doing, breaking in like that?'

'Didn't need to break in, darling, window gave us a wide welcome.'

They seemed surprised to see her. Perhaps they'd been dossing here, knew the house was empty. The two figures looked at her, summing her up in the dark. Then they came towards her. Slowly, calmly, nothing pushy. They were between her and the door. She backed up the stairs, knowing she was trapped. They were in no hurry, simply followed after her. A young girl alone in a derelict house. Friendless, obviously or why would she end up here? No plan had formed in the shadows' mind save to follow the smell of fear and let the wild thing lead them to her lair. On the first landing one of them spoke again:

'We're looking for somewhere to kip.'

'You can't stay here,' Sadie flashed.

The creature was showing her claws and they weren't even sharp. Still she climbed the stairs, towards her own attic flat. Did she seek protection from her belongings? Would they speak out her right to be there? On the second landing she paused. She could dive forward now and lock the door behind her, for some reason the workmen had started at the bottom of the house: the top flat was basically intact. Her mind moved, skimming possibilities but the more possibilities it touched on the more fears it unleashed. In her mind she turned upon these assailants and forced them down the stairs; she rushed into her room and out on to the roof like a cat; she screamed a long loud blast to waken the neighbours. But along with the bravado came the awful consequences, clear as the fantasies themselves. If she hurt them their revenge would be terrible; if she leaped away they would know she was frightened and she might slip on the roof. Thus did her mind skip and hop, agile as a butterfly on a summer's day.

The silhouettes behind her bided their time, curious as to what she'd do next and how they'd counter it. The phone was still dangling. Sadie moved automatically to put the receiver back in place. The intruders shifted uneasily; they had not realised the outside world still had access.

'Don't call the filth, sweetheart, we were only looking for a place to crash.'

'There's nothing here, said Sadie. 'You've seen the house. It's empty.'

'Well, looks like we best be going.'

'Yes, yes, you must go. Get out of here.'

Sadie did not hear what she was saying nor understand why they went. Her legs shook. The footsteps echoed.

'Give us a light, sister,' one of the men called up the stairs. 'We'll be over the edge and break our necks in a minute.'

Sadie fetched a candle and left it burning at the top of the stairs. It dripped green wax along the bannisters. She turned

61

again to the phone.

'Ellen? she whispered softly. 'Ellen?'

But the line was dead.

They'll go down the pub for a quick half and they'll be back. They'll talk it over and they'll be back.

From the attic window she watched the two figures move away. Then she sat down on the cold lino floor. For the first time in the long aching years which had dragged her to the objecting age of twenty, Sadie realised you could die unless you made a conscious effort not to. The men would come back, lit up with booze. If they had stayed it would all be over by now. Perhaps. She watched the wax drip down the bannisters and dry before it reached the bottom. The flame flickered in the draught.

There were women she could stay with: Lorraine, Beverly, but she had relied on being back and feeling English before she ventured out again. No one knew she'd arrived. The thought of being met at the station made her quake, so quickly, so abruptly to be thrown from France to England. No gentle easing. She would have to speak English, be English immediately and with conviction. She was only good at doing what she had no investment in: instant rapport with strangers, a free drink thrown in because she had a nice smile. Now there was no choice. She must put on the pack once more and get to Lorraine's in West Bank before the men returned. She must throw herself on Lorraine's mercy, plead her absolute, abject impotence. She could leave no corner for Lorraine to say no.

And then? Well, Lorraine was out. Was, quite simply, not there. Might be back later. Might not. The closed front door said nothing. The bell was silent. It was like an endless endurance test and each time Sadie thought she must have passed, something else came up to hit her from behind.

'Well?' she said to the Assumption at large. 'What do you want me to do now? Cry?'

She would cry, at length and in her own time. She would cry so much she would never stop; cry so that the dam broke and the waters crashed down dry gulleys and uprooted trees, she would flood whole valleys with her tears, deafen nations with her wails. But not yet. She would fight the Assumption to the bitterest of bitter ends because she was hard, so hard you might push a drawing-pin into the sole of her foot and she would not feel it but go on walking. Down the road was Amhurst Park and the bus stop. She would go to Beverly's and there would be someone in because of Claire who was too little to be left.

London Transport has provided well for people with an hour to kill. You can wait for ages at a bus stop without seeming the least disreputable. No one would have guessed, looking at Sadie, that she was a homeless derelict, a lesbian, a foreigner. She was soon joined by a young couple.

'I don't know, darl, why don't you ask that girl?' the woman was saying to her bloke.

'Scuse me love, do you know what time the last bus goes?'

'Not a clue. I'm a stranger here myself.'

Both parties lapsed into foot drumming, finger tapping silence.

'Why don't we share a cab?' the woman asked brightly as one appeared round the corner.

Sadie had no idea how she'd pay for it but at least it would get her away. The whole place was laughing at her now, at the idea that she of all people might ask their love and protection.

They were a perky young couple: the man chivalrous, the woman chatty. His firm's car had packed up and he was highly annoyed because this was the third time in a week. Where was she going? Wandsworth? Really? They were going to Putney so it was just the right road. Sadie tried to stop glaring at the meter but it seemed to relax her mind, ticking numbers over. They were sure to split the fare two ways, couples always counted as one and she knew she didn't have it on her. Not in sterling. Could she wake Bev and borrow from her?

By now the meter had clocked up so much Sadie could not afford a third let alone a half. She would have to brazen it out.

'Stamford Hill to Putney,' said the driver, 'that'll be £12.90.

Sadie gulped. She didn't have it. Shouldn't have taken the taxi then, if she didn't have it. What would she say to the driver? She must say something now. Now. She felt sick. The smell of petrol, the windows rolled up, the two complete strangers sitting in the seat opposite.

'Honestly, if it wasn't for your bloomin' car we'd of been home hours ago,' the woman was saying.

Sadie heaved herself together and wondered what to do. The woman was looking at her, waiting for her to offer her share of the money. Sadie looked back at her and smiled and as the smile flashed at the woman it suddenly didn't seem like such a wasted evening after all. The trip through London had been fun, the woman was tired and glad not to have to navigate, her husband's firm would refund the fares, it was a beautiful night, those stars, that moon . . . Sadie's smile was fading.

The woman turned to her husband 'No need for her to shell out,' she said. 'You'll get this on the firm.'

The cab returned via Wandsworth and the cabbie must have caught some of the smile for he drove right into Bev's estate.

'Not a nice neighbourhood,' he said. 'Wouldn't want you roaming the streets.'

'No,' Sadie murmured and walked past the rubbish chute to the stairs. She held the rail and was incredibly and exhaustively sick, trod gently up to the first floor and knocked at Bev's door.

'Bev,' she called through the letter-box, hardly louder than a whisper, but Bev was used to listening for Claire.

'Who is it?' she called.

'Me,' said Sadie and fell into her arms.

'Sadie, sweetheart, what a surprise. Come in, let me take your rucksack off.'

Quercus had finished.

'We take your point,' said the Archangelica, 'but we disagree.'

'You see,' said Clianthus, 'Sadie is not the pathetic little wimp you imagine, nor is she without gifts of her own.'

'Oh yeah,' scoffed Quercus, 'she can hold her breath to a thousand, has double-jointed thumbs, can guess the suit of the next playing card with more than 65 percent accuracy?'

'You weren't watching were you? Twice already, two times . . .'

'I know what twice means.'

'Two times she has made use of this gift unaware of doing more than getting what she wanted.'

'You mean you knew her already? Why wasn't I told?'

'It's all in the Minutes,' said Clianthus.

'Ahem,' the Archangelica cleared its collective throat, 'we have decided that you willingly and directly intervened in the lives of the Huwomen, that you are more concerned with their problems than with your own and we therefore suggest you live amongst them.'

'We respect your concern for them,' added Clianthus, 'and we feel a spell on Earth will empower you to involve yourselves more directly without the awkward superiority endowed you by virtue of your Bodhead.'

'Is there anything more you want to say before you go?'

'I know you all have other things to do now,' said Melaleuca, 'but there's more to say, it isn't over yet.'

'More to say . . .'

'It isn't over yet . . .'

'There's some fresh evidence . . .'

'Conversations never end . . .'

'I think you ought to follow the story through,' said Melaleuca. 'I think you should see what happened next.'

'But why?' protested the Bonsais. 'You intervened. That the Huwoman in question was too wise to heed the intervention is in itself irrelevant.'

'One does not enquire into the fate of certain letters; one notes their theft and hopes the owner kept a copy. Whether they are themselves useful or worth the trouble caused is a subject of mere conjecture over a light loam. The consequence is not the point.'

'A young man picks up a brick and throws it. Does one not stop to ask: whom did he hit? It is not wrong in itself to throw. The consequence is all.'

'Young men? Bricks? Certain documents? Thieves?'

'It is not enough to intervene,' said Melaleuca. 'Some change must occur because of it. You must wait and see if the lives of those three women altered one iota because Quercus reached out and made that coin tails.'

'Knowing only too well the danger of understanding too much too clearly, that awful omniscient comprehension which binds your stem and disarms you, causing you in your sympathy to forget yourself, causing you to suspend judgement, empty-headed as dry straw, yet we did try to see it your way . . .'

'But Sadie's as much a part of my experience as the wind or the rain,' protested Quercus.

'We took your point,' continued the Archangelica, 'and we disagreed.'

'A fair trial.'

'A fair fight.'

'A bad loser.'

'It matters so much to you to be fair to us?' asked Melaleuca.

'We would not wish to feel we'd been unkind.'

'Then watch on.'

'Till when? When does it end?'

'Ah,' said Hakea pensively. 'Perhaps we cannot speak of beginnings or endings but only of clusters of heightened or lessened activity.'

'There is always fresh evidence.'

'Conversations never end.'

Unaware of this Boddly fixation the three women came and went, pursuing trifles and pettiness in the full insignificance of their lives.

'I think we should remember how this started,' said Buddleia from Polly's back garden, now so comfortably settled her removal would seriously threaten the ecosystem. 'In the beginning . . .'

'So there was a beginning . . .'

'She's been there all this time . . .'

'A mindslip . . .'

'An oversight . . .'

'A missing link . . .'

'You asked me certain questions, I was to exercise discretion, I wasn't to be pushy, I was to wait till I was told. "Go on now, Buddleia", said your Bodships, "find out why this women sins. Tell us why her friend left while another has troubles of her own. Explain her desertion of her studies, her mother's faith in the Highway Code. Tell us why she irons the sheets and why the stair carpet is blue." '

'Are these questions answered?'

'Some fully.'

'Some not at all.'

'I do not yet know why her friend left,' said Buddleia. 'Surely we must postpone our decision till our own purpose is accomplished?'

There was a silence.

'So be it,' decreed the Archangelica. 'As we put the wheels in motion we will wait till the tale is told.'

6
Hiccups

'Hello? Sadie?' said Polly. 'I was wondering are you still interested? I mean, would you like to move in?'

'Really, Polly, really?' said Sadie. 'Oh, I was sure you'd say no. I couldn't see it in colour at all.'

'Move in? Oh that's wonderful,' shrieked Kim forgetting that her housemates might be listening. 'Oh Polly, I can't tell you what a relief.'

Polly looked at the living-room furniture and thought maybe it wouldn't feel so big if there were more people to share it.

Kim moved in with a van; Sadie moved in with a rucksack. There were hiccups.

'Tell me now,' said Polly, 'what is it you do?'

'Nothing,' said Sadie. 'And you?'

'I'm er, working on a PhD.'

'Wow,' said Kim. 'A real one?'

'Well it's still rather theoretical. I mean, I haven't actually written anything yet.'

'Ah,' nodded Kim wisely, 'I'm a bus conductor myself. So if one of you wants to be my spouse I can get you a free pass.'

'Mmm,' said Sadie, 'I never pay anyway.'

And it seemed then to each that she had nothing in common with the others.

Then there was breakfast. Sadie usually slept through it which left Kim and Polly alone together. When Kim neglected to clean the butter knife before plunging it in the marmalade, Polly would ask was that what she did at home. Kim would reply: yes, when she was treated like a lodger. Polly would ask what she meant by that and Kim would say Polly still made all major decisions about the running of the house and seemed incapable of communal living.

'You expect us to share bills equally when we don't earn the same money,' Kim would say.

'But if we did it according to income, you'd end up paying most,' Polly would protest.

'Oh it's not just money,' Kim would spit. 'You get the best room in the house and the phone extension's just outside your door so you can have private conversations while me and Sadie have to do it in the corridor.'

'I spend more time at home than either of you and I'm forever taking messages. Some days I can't sit down but the phone rings.'

'And all the furniture in the house is yours. Can't get to the bath tub without falling over a heavy oak chest,' Kim raged.

'You could try switching the light on,' suggested Polly drily.

'And the food you buy. When it's your turn to do Sainsbury's you get real butter, meat, all the most expensive stuff.'

'Well, Sadie likes butter and I haven't noticed you refuse a chicken dinner.'

'And then you insist on brown rice, which means going all the way into Brixton, because our bodies need the roughage. You're so fucking contradictory.'

'What a dear little Puritan,' Polly would tease. 'Like everything hunky-tanky, would you?'

'You can't say that, Polly,' Kim would object. 'I think we should talk about it.'

Soon the arguments went underground to resurface as unspoken hostility and obsessive interest in each other's eating habits.

Every morning she pours herself a second cup of tea, Polly would say to herself. She never finishes it. It always goes cold, one or other of us knocks it over and I clear it up. Kim drinking tea was not a pretty sight. She would pick up the cup in both hands and proceed to slurp, yes slurp down the contents. Polly had tried doing the same herself to show how annoying it was but Kim didn't even seem to notice.

Kim eating a full breakfast, however, was far worse. More scope. First she would flood her muesli with milk (and they only got two pints a day) then she would crunch it with her mouth open: champ, champ, champ like a horse. When she swallowed it made little gurgling noises in her throat. Was she under the mistaken impression that she sounded sweet? Polly yearned to stretch across the table and place a light hand under Kim's chin to encourage her to close it while she ate. Sometimes Kim would think of something to say just after she'd filled her mouth and, being too impatient to wait until she'd finished, would spray it all over the place. Polly would wipe wet hazel-nut sludge off her cheeks and wish it wasn't too late to teach Kim table manners.

Kim hated Polly. Worse even than she hated her driver and that was saying something. He would pull away from bus stops before all the passengers were on board and old women, children and push-chairs would stumble over each other and she would have to ring the emergency bell as if it had all been her fault. Her driver was simply oblivious to all other concerns save his own desire to return to the garage and play poker. A single-mindedness which in other spheres might have been commendable. But Polly, Kim was convinced, was a polar bear. They had blue tongues and were motivated by pure malice: killed for the love of killing, leaving their prey untasted on the ice.

Under Polly's gaze breakfast was torture. Polly drank a refined cup of black coffee, or, sometimes, only a glass of cold water: 'Must cut down on artifical stimulants . . .' but she took a perverse pleasure in watching Kim eat. Kim would search for something to say to draw Polly's attention away, begin to speak but, overcome with nerves, would end up gabbling incomprehensibly into her bowl. What's more, Polly was always throwing Kim's tea away on the grounds that she never drank it. 'Don't get a chance. You whisk it away too quick.' And, anyway, Polly never washed her own muesli bowl. She would sip genteelly at a few spoonfuls, sigh, and say it was just too filling, put it back in the fridge for later . . . where it stayed all day until Kim came to wash it and had to scrub away at the thick gunk which stuck like yesterday's chewing gum. Polly went on about Kim's tea but couldn't see the muesli in her own bowl. Kim liked the expression but daren't try it on Polly who had absolutely no sense of humour and anyway preferred Sadie.

'Polly,' said Sadie one afternoon when Kim was at work, 'let's go for a walk.'

'Oh,' said Polly, 'I have to prepare a class for tomorrow.'

69

'Do it tonight.'

With mixed feelings Polly went. Glad to be out in the open, wary of emotional trauma. Was Sadie clearing the way for an in-depth discussion of her psyche? They took the bus to Putney and walked down the river to Kew. Sadie was no more outgoing than usual. Soon Polly settled into step beside her, gazing at the pink and white blossom which seemed to have come up overnight. Occasionally she wondered did she and Sadie see the same things or was Sadie lost to the willows, the yellow green of the grass, the knotted roots which looped like veins down the river bank.

'Roots,' said Sadie with sudden enthusiasm as though her thoughts came too quick to allow more than a brief bulletin on their progress. Despite her silence, however, it was Sadie who took charge. She knew what bus to take, which path and where to stop for tea. Polly could wander freely.

And so they arrived at Kew. Pagoda, greenhouses, stands of trees, gardens. Sadie looked at the walled garden. Immediately her eyes were seized by the red glare of the roses, the white, brilliant carnations, the sticky colours of the wild, rampant pansies. The different shades rushed towards her, dragged her around, chasing here a light purple, there an orange; tracing the line of leaf and stalk. It was exhausting. Nothing stayed still longer than the flick of an eyelash but commanded her cesselessly to compare and contrast, return and continue. Straight lines, curves, angles: flowers that looked like paper; flowers that looked like plastic; flowers whose colour changed half way. Just as she thought she knew how it fitted together a breeze would stir and all proportion would softly blur; a bee would buzz and demand consideration. Sounds. Sadie had forgotten sounds. Buzzing, twittering, leaves, voices, footsteps, her heartbeat. The trees looked like a river the way their leaves kept rustling and babbling; as the branches waved towards each other a hundred fish leapt and bounded.

'Pretty whimsy,' she said out loud.

'What are you thinking?' asked Polly, an intrusion usually reserved for actual or would-be lovers.

'It's so demanding,' said Sadie.

'Yes?' said Polly.

Sadie looked at her, wondering was it worth the effort.

'Like a children's playground,' she said. 'The seesaw bumping up and down, the swings soaring, roundabout spinning: from any one the kids might fall and hurt themselves. I feel responsible.'

'I know what you mean,' said Polly.

Sadie doubted this.

'Like it's all set out just for you,' said Polly, 'and you must be appreciative, not miss a nuance.'

'I like Kew,' said Sadie, 'because it's so ordered. All those name-plates. Like a graveyard. But this garden disturbs me.'

'It's a riot,' said Polly.

'A civil disturbance,' said Sadie.

'Mere anarchy is loosed upon the world,' said Polly. 'My mother was afraid of anarchy. She lost God, you see, turned her back only for a moment and he was gone. Seemed to have fallen into such disrespect, derision even among her friends and neighbours that she searched around wildly for something else. Something with clear rules, international observance and retributive justice. She found the Highway Code.'

'Oh no,' said Sadie. 'It disturbs, but it fascinates me too. I'm not like Jane with her shears and her pruning-knife.'

'Her hedge-clippers.'

'Her secateurs.'

Sadie gazed again at the garden and suddenly began to laugh. What did she see?

'Oh Polly, it's so funny,' she spluttered.

Polly looked about her.

'What do you see?' asked Sadie still laughing.

'An English country garden, I suppose,' said Polly. But what was funny? Did Sadie see the African bush or the dry park of a mine town?

'Your heritage,' pronounced Sadie. 'You see the well-thumbed pages of your bedtime stories: Beatrix Potter, Milly Molly Mandy, what it means to be English. I know, we had those books too, only our mother had to tell us what foxgloves are, robins and laughing bluebells. I wrote a poem for school: Page 13, Theme number 7, 'A Summer's Day', (our textbooks came from England too). It's all about ice-cream vans and dandelions. In Zambia we didn't exactly have summer, just hot, dry or rainy.'

'But I'm Irish,' said Polly softly, 'not English.'

'Oh,' said Sadie with exasperation, 'Kim then.'

'I doubt it. She never left London except on school trips, and then she said it was a good day out but there were no toilets and she never quite liked to take her shoes off. I imagine very few people feel calmly at one with these flowers.'

'Then why don't you say it? Why don't you all say it? In Africa I knew the names of countless English flowers I had never seen, and those I had around me, that I lived amongst: the water pistol blossoms we pulled from the tree to squirt each other; the ones that dropped down many-coloured that we gathered up for petal gardens; the ones that smelled like a toilet; the ones you could eat, I had no words for and could not own, could not recognise, did not see.'

'What do you see then, Sadie? What makes you laugh so angrily?'

'Look around. You see the red glare of the roses, the white, brilliant carnations, the sticky colour of the wild, rampant pansies? And it turns you around, tosses you about and makes you dizzy at the thought of so much richness, the wonders of creation, these plants quietly getting on with it, year after year, with tree-root tenacity?'

'Yes,' said Polly.

'Then look again. What is that hard round metal poking out from beneath those glorious rhododendrons?'

'It is a wheelbarrow,' said Polly.

'And what wispy line, that hairy parasite on the climbing roses?'

'It is a piece of string,' said Polly, 'it trains the stem to the lattice.'

'And that small woman there in brown, bending attentive to the lawn?'

'It is a gardener,' said Polly, 'and she grips the handle of a mower.'

'I see hedge clippings,' said Sadie, 'and neat borders and litter bins. I see wooden benches and sprinklers and toddlers pushing prams. This garden is no more natural than the grey smudgey stamp in my passport.'

'In Ireland,' mused Polly, 'the flowers are not different from here. The colours maybe, maybe the green is blue there whereas here it is yellow, but I don't think so. I don't think that's it. For the landscape gardeners covered Ireland with ha-has much as they did in England.'

'I went to Wales with Lorraine once,' said Sadie. 'The coach climbed higher and higher and I began to feel sick. We were staying in a little stone cottage and I opened the bathroom window to get some air. A great stony hill rose sharply up in front of me with goat paths and rocky outcrops and for a moment it was Swaziland. There were the two peaks: Kamhlaba and Elangeni, and this was the rondavel covered in purple bougainvillea; away over to the right would be Mrs Hemp's cottage and down there the stream and the secret garden. And there was the stream! And that flat rock where I used to read letters from Llonka, and chips of wood because Alan had been stoking the boiler; and the frangipani and the gumnuts and the donkeys and the pool at the bottom to swim in and the aloes and the protea. And the day it hailed so hard it took the roofs off the huts in the valley and I collected hailstones and carried them in my flippers for Alan to have in his cocktails. The day the stream flooded and they left the car at the bottom of the hill and my mother took her shoes off and forded the water in her evening dress. But that smooth black stone, what was it? Slate perhaps, blue-grey. And that road over there, where did it lead? Had they built it while I was away? But there was nothing up there, the rondavels were the last house on the mountain. I stared. There were lots of roads. And houses, a council estate, a church, a graveyard. This was not Swaziland it was Wales, and Wales is full not of mountains but of roads. Roads, roads, roads.' Sadie looked round as if surrounded.

'Yes,' said Polly wistfully, 'England isn't Ireland either.'

'Oh it is,' said Sadie gloomily. 'Pretty near.'

'No it isn't,' said Polly, still serious, beginning to feel cross.

'But it is,' Sadie insisted. 'It's all England really.'

'I don't believe it,' said Polly coldly, 'I refuse to stand here and argue about whether or not England is Ireland.'

They stared at each other furiously, then grinned.

'What did you do though?' asked Polly tentatively. 'I mean when Wales had stopped being Swaziland?'

'What do you mean, what did I do? What techniques do I have for coping? How do I live with panoramic schizophrenia?'

'Sadie, what I like about you is your willingness to say how you feel. And what I hate about you is the way you assume you're the only one to have felt it.'

'You do that too, do you? See some kind of similarity, slip

into it so deeply what you see is the comparison not the original until something jars and you are caught suddenly, plummet down between them, all trust betrayed, both lost and trapped, and you don't know where you are or what is happening and your legs shake and you feel sick and dizzy and have to hang on to the walls or the chair leg in order not to be simply blown away. You feel that too?' Sadie was trembling with anger.

'Is that what you did?' Polly asked softly. 'Held on to the furniture?'

'No, I curled up in my sleeping-bag.'

'How sensible. I – I mean I suppose it's different but I like to live as if it doesn't happen to me at all and then it just falls on me and I don't know what to do. Not landscapes but activity, my say in the world, my PhD. I sit there and watch the blue line down my pen on to the paper. My blue vein, my anchor, and I dare not lift the nib from the page nor look round further than the safe, straight edges of the paper.'

'And what do you do?'

'Do? I don't know. Cry. Nothing useful.'

Polly stared unseeing at a neat clean cut on a rose bush, elliptical in shape, light green, ringed. She could feel her shoulders shaking, felt small and grey, felt a hand on her hair, stroking, patting, an arm round her, Sadie holding her.

They walked on across the gardens.

'Marianne North,' said Sadie.

'Howmuch?' said Polly.

To the right of the path was a low house devoted to the permanent exhibition of the exotic paintings of that nomadic Victorian. Polly had never been there before. By themselves they were rather sticky and anthropological; Polly's mouth filled with an array of endless silken orchids. But Sadie's commentary opened them up into real places: flowers that reminded you of your mother, trees you climbed in as a child.

'Christ thorn, Polly, look – with the long prickles and the red berries. My feet were like pincushions from falling into those things. Oh and grenadillas, a mouthful of sweet slimey seeds. Those trees there are casuarina. Monday hung me a swing in one but the sap hurt my eyes. Oh and oleander and bougainvillea.'

Sadie was like a child in a sweetshop who cannot decide which to settle on.

74

'England must be difficult,' Polly said to her, 'after living in one of those paintings.'

'Yes,' said Sadie, 'the sun and the space. It's like having to learn everything again but different.'

It was more than that, her life was not a picture, but she did not know how to say it all.

'Wet gravel and windy trees,' Polly was saying, 'that's how I remember Ireland. Not the accents so much or the people.'

'No,' said Sadie, 'it isn't the people. It's not like missing your friends, although of course you do. But it's frightening to see two things at once. There's an oak and you think tree, and then what you see is an acacia because that's what tree means to you.'

That was true, but there was also the sense of not being allowed to say acacia, unless there was a painting in front of you.

'Like living in a metaphor,' Polly suggested.

'Maybe,' said Sadie, 'but the Assumption has rules on which metaphors are permissible and mine always seem to stand outside. I mean, the metaphor isn't the problem.'

'You could try breaking the rules.'

'You don't recognise them? Polly, they're your rules.'

'And yours,' Polly reminded her, 'because you respect them.'

'What does she mean, "There's an oak and you think 'tree', but what you see is an acacia"?' Quercus exploded as Sadie showed Polly *The Maids of Honour* and the two women ordered cream teas.

Polly felt unexpectedly weary and a shock of great sadness hung over her still. In London one lived mostly amongst concrete and the occasional tree – planted by an environment-conscious council, carefully caged against footballs, netted against birds, and pollarded in summer so the buses could get past. Big cities offered a welcome sameness to the foreigner. Only Sadie, it seemed, refused to play, and reminded Polly that she did not wish to be absorbed into a grey cement block either.

'How can she possibly mistake me for an acacia?' Quercus went on indignantly. 'They are light, elegant, fluttery, whilst I . . .'

'Yes,' Meleleuca interrupted her, 'I can see it's a problem. But you see, what Sadie really means . . .'

'What Sadie really means,' Hakea interrupted in her turn, 'is what Sadie has said. Trouble is, we don't understand what she means.'

'I feel like re-rooting myself and bursting forth in front of her,' Quercus raged, 'me, a solid pillar of the community to be vulgarly confused with one of those jittering wattles oozing with wax and furry with pollen!'

'So what do you make of it?' Melaleuca rounded on Hakea.

'Without us plants to recycle their air supply, of course, they'd lose their vertical and turn into moss pretty damn quick . . .'

'Not a bad thing if you ask me,' interjected Quercus inevitably.

'So I suppose they must mind what happens in the world . . .'

'We know they do. Look how anxious they are about the weather. That's why we have to be so careful when we regulate the water rate,' Melaleuca continued sounding more and more like two-thousand-year-old rock-lichen-the-learned. 'Take their greetings: where you or I would ask of an old friend, or even a mere acquaintance, who they were rubbing petals with, expressing the hope that their days brimmed with pollen, their nights with sweetest resin, these Huwomen offer, in tones hushed and trembling, "It's getting quite overcast, I'm afraid it's going to rain." '

'Yes Melaleuca,' sighed Hakea, 'are we back then in the nursery, still trained to some dry stick? These things we take for granted, but what if we were wrong?'

Polly leaned back against the chintz cushion of her chair. The flames in the grate flowed and flickered like water over rocks. A real fire. Sadie had conducted her to this chair, knowing she would like the fire, would appreciate the delicacy of scones warm from just baking though the coffee was poison. And Sadie was a coffee drinker. Before, Polly had been irritated by the great gush about Africa. Sadie's tone of childish wonder struck her as disingenuous: she was neither that young nor was it that recent so must not the immediacy be false? There seemed to be no questions in Sadie's mind, no uneasiness. She spoke of the flowers as if they, in all their undoubted diversity, were the entire population of the country. Was Sadie really oblivious to the racist nature of her life there? 'Monday hung me a swing in a casuarina tree.' Who was Monday? 'A Black servant, clearly, and his name, a white man's joke. And then Sadie lumped the whole of the British Isles together as if she saw no difference there either.

A woman arrived with a tray of tea and a plate of cakes. Polly pulled her gaze away from the flames to see Sadie looking at her.

'My turn now,' said Sadie, pouring the tea, thanking the woman who brought it. 'What are you thinking, Polly?'

'Arrogance perhaps,' murmured Hakea. 'Gigantic arrogance to assume that they are obsessed with us merely because *we* are.'

'One pot plant to every room,' countered Melaleuca, 'and what with the atomiser sprays, the soil thermometers, the bio leaf shine, we're treated like little household gods.'

'We see what we expect. Just now Sadie was talking to Polly about plants.'

'Well exactly.'

'But as though it were allowed. A trifle. A nothing.'

'How perfectly horrible.'

'In Hortus, at the least hint of bother, someone calls a water rates meeting to discuss the Huwomen and avoid a fight.'

'I was thinking about your stories of Africa,' Polly replied. watching the butter melt on her scone so she could put on another layer, to hell with cholesterol. 'They sound like yesterday, as though you hadn't catalogued them yet but let them tumble out.'

'As if? Calculated spontaneity?'

'Not weary. Not like you'd told them a hundred times before.'

'I haven't.'

'It's all you've talked about today.'

'My excitement bothers you? You want me to have aired my views elsewhere, arrive here with sophisticated finish?'

'I'd like you to have some views!' Polly rejoined crossly. She liked Sadie's freshness. ' "You're so unjaundiced, my dear," who can say that?'

'Views, opinions, the well-educated man can converse on any topic?'

'Well, what do you think, Sadie? What you talk about are the bloody flowers. Of course you didn't live in *South* Africa, but everyone knows it's the same all over. I mean it's still a racist regime. I mean we're talking about imperialism, aren't we? And you benefited from it. You can't say you were too young to be responsible. It's a liberal luxury to ask to be taken on your own merits, simply as an individual. We all know that.'

'As it seems we all already know everything, there is no need for me to add to the pile.'

'But you actually lived there,' insisted Polly. 'I'm sure you have things to say.'

'Good, then perhaps we can dispense with the Lenin prologue.'

'Whatever are you suggesting? You know if you were Black . . .'

'But I'm not, and you're not.'

'No, I'm Irish and Kim's working-class English and that's different again, yet you lump us all together simply so that you stand out.'

'But I do stand out, Polly,' Sadie replied, 'and so do you and so does Kim in other ways and how the hell is any of us ever going to talk about those ways if we have to do a coverall speech every time about recognising everyone's oppression?'

'You come from a white racist regime, Sadie, I mean you just can't say that you are in any way oppressed.'

'I'll say whatever I bloody well like.'

'God, you're so childish.'

'Probably, but then I'm nearly twenty years younger than you so you're going to have to put up with it. As well as all your unrealistic ideas about the good you can do me.'

'Sadie, belligerence is no more charming than petulance.'

'Listen Polly, I recognise it. Of course I fucking recognise it. Even I know more about it than you do. But I am sick to death of tapping these little plastic tokens on the table as if we were having a real conversation. It's like a bloody game of monopoly. You serve me with racist South Africa – often that's a trump card with such emotional force no one can go on playing . . .'

'But you return with British Nationality Laws and hadn't I noticed what we do to Black people here . . .'

'You sidestep that you're Irish.'

'And you throw Irish neutrality and possibly my class position back at me.'

'Then we say that we are both lesbians and so it is different for us.'

'And so it is.'

'Yeah,' said Sadie. 'I have friends in Jo'burg, a lesbian couple. Mpala, the Black woman, has to pretend to be Netta's housemaid. Netta of course is white. Oh they live together all right, very cosy, nice climate, only when they drive anywhere Mpala has to sit in the back of the car. Couldn't share a seat with a white woman even if she does share her bed. You see Polly, I do know this, I recognise it all right. It is disgusting and wrong and I am part of it, but I want to say other things too, otherwise it simply isn't real.'

By now the pot was empty and the scones were finished.

'I think I'll make a move,' said Polly. 'I have to prepare this class.'

'Sure,' said Sadie. 'But I was talking to you not issuing a Press Release. You don't have to hunch your shoulders as if someone were judging your every word.'

'Oh dear,' said Hakea, 'do you think they can see us?'

'For certain,' said Melaleuca unbothered, 'but they don't know we can see them.'

Kim was on early shift that day, which meant starting at six, but she was home again by one. The house was empty when she got in and she heaved a sigh of relief. She thought she might clean the windows. Once the dry rags and the wet rags and the windolene and the soapy water for the frames were duly gathered together and she in her old squatter's boiler suit was sitting half in, half out the kitchen window, she began to rub away at the grime with a vim and a vigour which were in no way diminished by having already seen her way through an eight-hour day. For a while she gazed unseeing.

'Well,' she said at last, to no one in particular, or perhaps to the lilac buddleia, 'what do you think?' And as the only thing in sight which showed any sign of having heard was this same precociously blooming shrub, which waved slightly in the breeze as if asking for particulars, she continued by addressing it directly.

'Tell you what, Buddleia,' she said, 'two waves for yes, one for no. You on?'

Buddleia waved twice.

Kim laughed at the coincidence.

'Okay then. Now, what do you think I should do? Here I am, all comfy cosy in a nice lesbian house and . . . oh, by the way, do you think Polly and Sadie are going to get off with each other?'

Buddleia waved twice.

'Mm yes, so do I. Well if I'm going to be living with a couple here, am I necessarily better off than I was in the mixed house?'

Buddleia waved her branches emphatically so that some of the petals fluttered softly to the ground.

'I see,' said Kim. 'You think it's good for women to live together?'

The branches waved again in great commotion.

'So you're a woman-identified bush are you? Good. Now, my problem is, who am I going to get off with? Do you think I should lunge at the first opportunity just to get the bloody thing over with?'

Buddleia waved once.

'No, you're right. It wouldn't be fair. But who wants to sleep with a first-timer? They'd suspect me of awful things: experimenting, intensity, fickleness, earnestness, being clumsy in bed. Perhaps I should keep quiet till I had at least slept with someone?'

Kim glanced over to Buddleia but she remained quite still.

'You see what I really want is a great passionate affair which will take me over completely so my whole life changes because of it.'

Buddleia was unmoved.

'Like Polly and Margot.'

Buddleia rustled expressively and if it had been possible for a bush to raise its eyebrows that surely must be what Buddleia did.

'Trouble is, how'm I going to meet someone like Margot?'

Buddleia fluttered just the tips of her twigs.

'Well I don't know what you mean by that,' said Kim. 'If you're going to disapprove I don't know why you can't do it out loud.'

'I can only respond to yes/no questions. If you're going to

change the ground rules it's only decent to inform the other players.'

'You should have told me you could talk,' Kim said sulkily.

'You were too busy telling me I couldn't,' Buddleia protested.

'Well, how did Polly meet Margot anyway, since you know so much about it?'

'She advertised. Or rather, she answered an advert.'

'And she makes out like it was the biggest fucking romance since Elephant met Castle. So Polly found Margot in the Small Ads? What put the idea into her head?'

'Oh, Hakea probably, she likes a vicarious adventure. But do you actually have anyone in mind?'

'No.'

'Then what's all the fuss about?'

'Well the time comes in a lesbian's life when she feels like she has to go out and DO it. Besides, the spring is coming. I can't live on credit forever. It's not just about hating men.'

'You don't have to convince me, dear. I always thought Humen were strictly for procreation till I came to live here. The things you hear over the washing-lines! Anyway, I think it's meant to be fun. Sex. Initial enthusiasm is a great help in the more awkward stages.'

'Right, Budd, I'll remember that.'

'Now if you were wondering how you would ever repay my kindness . . .'

'Yes?' Kim asked politely.

'You might just remove that nasty rain-barrel. It encourages gnats and all sorts and they frighten off the butterflies.'

'But they won't be hatched till summer!'

'Pays to think ahead.'

'What happened on the buses today, Kim?' asked Sadie while Kim took off her uniform and hung it on the coat-rail she had wheeled home from Brixton market.

'Such a funny conversation I overheard,' Kim replied bouncily. Her place in Sadie's affections at least was established. Sadie would drift into the room and sit on her bed while Kim chatted, checked her pay-slip, or watered the plants.

Polly put her head round the door and asked to borrow the baby bio, catching the end of Kim's remark. 'Good God,' she said, 'do conductors listen then? How embarrassing.'

'So go on, Kim,' said Sadie, 'embarrass us.'

'Well, these two women got on while we were stuck in traffic at Hammersmith Broadway,' Kim started looking at Sadie, aware that Polly was listening too. 'They were chatting so loud I think the whole bus heard them.'

'And,' said Polly, 'what did they say?'

Now Kim turned towards her. 'One of them was telling the other what happened last time she caught the bus. "So I asked this young fella did the 73s stop there and had he been waiting long. That was all I said, right. But when the bus came along and I got a front seat all to myself he came and sat next to me. Completely empty bus, right, but this geezer has to sit next to me. I ask you."

' "Bloomin' cheek," said the other.

' "WellImean, I didn't say do the 73s stop here and would you like to come back to my place?"

' "Been waiting long and let's do the bathroom blue."

' "What time is it and let's call the first one Sarah."

' "Lovely weather, about the decree nisi . . ."

' "Good morning, do you want to be buried or cremated?" '

Kim experienced a little difficulty finishing the story as the urge to laugh overtook her halfway through. It was infectious: Sadie hugged her knees and spluttered while Polly rushed to the loo. They spent a long time afterwards adding phrases of their own.

'I think it's going to rain and why don't you go defend the Falklands?'

'Got a light? Let me tell you about vasectomy.'

'Is today the eighth and would you like to leave me your kidneys?'

One day when it was very hot they went to Box Hill for a picnic which Polly cooked, Kim carried and Sadie looked pleased about. An odd threesome but all threesomes are odd unless one of them is three years old. They took the train from Waterloo. Polly brought her book, Kim climbed the hill and Sadie took all her clothes off and lay in the sun. For a while it was very pleasant.

'You know people can see you from the hill?' Kim informed Sadie.

'What people?' asked Sadie. 'You?'

'Gracious!' exclaimed Polly looking up from her book. 'Why've you taken your clothes off?'

'I like it better this way,' Sadie shouted and danced off along the river bank.

Kim stared after her. 'What's up with her?' Kim asked Polly.

Polly shrugged and went back to her book. When Kim caught up with Sadie she was on her knees scrabbling at the moss with her nails.

'Where's the concrete?' she was saying. 'It must be down here somewhere under the ornamental earth.'

'This is the country,' Kim stated flatly. 'There isn't any concrete.'

'If it is the country,' said Sadie, 'then where are all the hippos?'

And she laughed and laughed and Kim laughed, but not as they had laughed before.

'Is the tale told?'
'Is our purpose accomplished?'
'Not yet. Not yet.'
'We must do a proper job.'

7
Penknives in the Park

It was 5.30 a.m. Kim battled against warm blankets and the smell of sleep, brushed her long hair and struggled into her clothes. The jacket was regulation grey but the trousers were her own. London Transport issue seemed to date from the land girls: zips at the side, baggy in front. That's what they gave you on the training course but on her first day Vivienne, at the garage, had told her:

'You don't have to wear them, love, just because they're there. Try slipping into something more comfortable.'

Kim checked the change in her pockets. Notes on the inside,

fifties top right; tens and fives went together but separate from twos and ones.

'If he hands you a fiver,' Vivienne had said, 'you say "five pounds" straight out then neither of you forget when you're counting change. Worse thing is when they convince you you might have made a mistake.'

'But I might.'

'So might God Almighty but she ain't sayin' nothin' is she?'

Kim yawned. Before starting on the buses she'd never quite believed in 5.30, though it seemed there were other hours more exotic still: 4.15 say, or even 3.28. She went downstairs and was groping for the light-switch when it dawned on her slowly that the lights were already on and she was not the only person alive at this far-off corner of the clock, for there was Sadie chewing soberly on a piece of burnt toast and reading yesterday's paper, intimating that she and 5.30 were old acquaintances.

'Hello,' said Kim with the awkward heartiness of one who had hoped to breakfast alone.

'Morning,' said Sadie looking up from the paper. 'I couldn't sleep.'

Kim nodded. To some people 5.30 was an imposition then, not a joyous discovery.

Though Sadie knew Kim was not pleased to see her, her arrival was nonetheless a relief. She wondered how soon Kim would have to rush off and hoped that, being new, she still woke earlier than necessary. Kim's excitement annoyed her and she envied the good night's sleep but she wanted to talk about her dream, be assured that that's all it was.

'I had a nightmare,' she said softly, looking up at Kim from the charred remains of the toast.

'Oh,' Kim grunted, realising in a communal house even 5.30 had to be shared. 'I'll make tea and you tell me about it.'

Sadie was silent.

Well, Kim thought, I offered.

'I have it often,' said Sadie, 'though the details alter.'

Half Kim's mind was trying to remember fare stages.

'I'm riding up a hill on my bicycle coming home from Peckham. The night is warm and there's no wind. I've had a good evening. I'm excited because it's so late and so empty. I'm riding up the hill. It's Dog Kennel Hill, very steep. I feel powerful, unassailable. Soon I have to slow down, change gear.

84

I start to pant. I begin to notice my thigh muscles. I am proud of them; they show no strain and will push as hard as I bid them. I look up to see how much further it is to the top and am tempted to get off for a rest. My breathing is heavy. I notice a group of boys up ahead. They are young but I am frightened. I pedal harder. My legs hurt. The balls of my muscles ache. I want someone to let down a rope so I can drag myself up by the arms. One of the boys jumps out. I am knocked off my bicycle. I feel relieved. I don't have to go on pedalling. The boys are all around me. One of them has a penknife. One of them has a compass. We used compasses in school to carve our boyfriend's name on the desk. I didn't have a boyfriend. We used penknives in the park to carve our boyfriend's name on the trees. I didn't have a boyfriend. When they carved my back I was a school desk. When they carved my forehead I was a tree in the park.

'I open my eyes. I am covered in bandages. Slowly, carefully, Beverly unwinds yards of crêpe from my body. I wait. She screams. I look round. She tries, too late, to cover me. I have seen the mark in the mirror. The small of my back, between the shoulder-blades, is branded with a flaming NF. My fingers reach for my forehead and I tear at the pad with my nails. I fling the bandage to the ground and in the mirror I see a triangle with neat edges, the point towards the ground. It is pink. I look at Beverly and she too has that triangle on her forehead and you, Kim, and Polly and Lorraine and a whole line of women stretching as far as the eye can see.'

Now it was seven a.m. The morning was no longer young. Kim walked to the tube for once glad of the long journey. Sadie's dream circled her brain, whispering, repeating: 'a triangle with neat edges, the point towards the ground'. The wish to be annihilated, become the power of the oppressor. And pain? 'Branded with a flaming': Sadie had not mentioned pain. 'I am knocked off my bicycle. I feel relieved.' Now Kim's brain filled with images from sex shops the bus passed every day. Women beaten or in chains. 'When they carved my back I was a school desk.' Why couldn't Sadie have turned over and gone back to sleep? As Kim walked she wanted so much to think about mist and empty streets, the routed silence of the city. Her brain filled instead with fear.

At Stockwell station Kim sat opposite an ad for the film *Butterfly:* 'innocent as a child, seductive as a woman', and was no longer angry with Sadie but with the man behind the poster who said women liked violence, said it so loud even Sadie believed it. Kim wanted to run through the gaping tunnels of the Victoria Line, felt like shouting: 'Take me to your leader, I wish to shoot the man in charge. If you own the streets, you wake up at 5.30, it's the dawn of the world, you can claim it. If you're a woman, you wake up at 5.30, nothing's changed.' Well women weren't going to change, so how about the streets?

But all too soon came Seven Sisters Station and Kim had to run up the escalator, show her pass to the ticket collector and clock in at the garage. All day she thought about Sadie and Sadie's dream. She worried about her: that bare room with scarcely more than a sleeping bag and a rucksack that she hadn't unpacked, as though she was afraid she would not be staying long. Kim had decorated her own room first thing, so relieved was she to be living among lesbians: turquoise and black, very flash. And it wasn't as though they hadn't offered to help Sadie. You'd almost think fresh paint was against her religion. The more she thought about it, the more powerless Kim felt. By midday she wanted to phone home just to check Sadie was all right, only by the time she'd convinced herself she didn't mind looking silly, it was too late to find a phone box that worked.

At the end of the shift she left the money and her ticket machine for Vivienne to check in and rushed off down the tube. Again she heard Sadie's voice, that slow careful speech as though English were difficult to master. 'A whole line of women stretching as far as the eye can see.' Women, thought Kim to herself, women. The tube arrived, Kim got on, casual as a passenger, but her mind was seething, marching. In it she was joined by other women, Sadie, Polly, Vivienne, they were walking the streets of Soho.

Women, lots of women, dressed in purple, green and white. Whistles, tambourines, bells. Luminous paint and burning torches; screams, hoots, catcalls. A parade, a carnival not a march. Three young girls smearing tomato sauce on hot dogs.

'What's it in aid of?'

'Any woman who has felt afraid on the streets at night.'

'Too right,' shout the girls and join in.

Old women coming out of a theatre.

'Are you worried about getting home?'

And they went along too. The narrow streets roared as they passed; they filled the dark alleyways. Two hundred of them, two thousand of them.

'Curfew for men not women.'

'Men off the streets.'

'Excuse me, sir, are you on your own? Only it could be dangerous with all these women about.'

Some women had scissors, some women had shears, boldly they strode to the men who were watching.

'Click go the shears, boys, click, click, click.'

'Snip go the scissors, painful but quick.'

'Oh no! Not that. Bit literal, isn't it?'

'Don't think "spread 'em darlin" would win prizes for subtlety.'

On into the backstreets bright with two-thousand watt bulbs. Red and gold arrows blinking on and off, pointing at women naked, women handcuffed. Men queueing, watching, strolling past the displays. Torn nighties. Red and gold. Red and gold. On and off. Dirty raincoats. No, clean. Nice white shirts, open-toed sandals, lacoste vests. Relaxed. Sauntering, reading the notices.

'Warning: Explicit material.'

'Did she really die?'

'Likely to offend.'

Already the singing can be heard in the streets. Dancing girls? Naughty nymphets laid on by the management? Women, real women walking off the posters, off the walls. Lips, thighs, breasts coming towards them.

'OK girls, come and get me.'

Middle-aged men, felt hat with a feather, standing in the middle of the road, arms open wide. Welcoming. Contemptuous. Despicable. Scarcely heard above the noise, scarcely noticed. But the women are tired of scarcely hearing. Scarcely noticing.

'Hsssss,' they roar like a gas jet. The dancing changes to running, they chase after the middle-aged man: felt hat trampled underfoot, feather squashed in a puddle. The sex shops and cinemas let down their iron curtains. The man is cornered in a doorway. Behind him is an array of crotchless knickers, inflatable dolls. The man cowers. Meanwhile . . .

Meanwhile the streets are covered with stickers.

'Women are angry.'

'It is because you have done nothing.'

'Yes, we are castrating bitches.'

And then the sirens, the loud hailers, the baton charges.

'Police protect pornography.'

Managers in respectable shirt-sleeves watching bravely through the glass. Women beaten, thrown into vans. A movement through the crowd, pushing, shoving: situation under control. Out comes the manager. 'Get them to clean this muck off.'

In rush three women through the open door, tear stuff off the shelves, throw it on the floor.

'Kim, come back we'll never find you.'

'Kim, come back, you'll get arrested.'

But still she rushed forward and from the shop came the sound of plate glass smashing, echoing through the air. For the issue had never been so clear and Kim in her certainty was omnipotent. Powerless to understand the intricate workings of the Assumption yet Sadie covered in bandages was a diamond cause to fight for. A brick might bounce back and hit a woman in the stomach but Kim used her ticket machine swung from the shoulder-straps. The shock jolted through her like a rifle kick. The glass rippled and fell like ice melting. She stayed only to drop a lighter on the pile. The blaze was immediate and danced with blue skipping sparks like paraffin. Explosions rang out as off aerosols.

'The spray that makes men last longer.'

The work of a moment.

Fourteen women arrested, nine injured. One sex shop gutted, two screens covered with paint, foot-long tears in the fabric. As Kim broke the glass, but before the shop could catch fire, her hands were reaching for her latchkey. Kim was home. She would see for herself how Sadie was. Fourteen women arrested? she thought as she fitted the key in the lock. Bloody conscientious fantasy. No. Their cases were thrown out for lack of evidence. By now she was inside the house so the injured would have to wait.

There was a light on in Polly's room; the rest of the house was dark. Kim put three cups of tea on a tray and took them upstairs. She pushed the door open with her hip and walked backwards into the room.

'Tea up,' she said and stopped.

Sadie was sitting on the floor hugging her knees and calling to herself:

'Sadie, Sadie, Sadie,' rocking back and forth with a note of desperation.

Polly sat on the bed watching, hands hanging limply in her lap.

'Sadie!' Kim shouted, putting the tray hastily on the ground where the tea slopped aimlessly about. 'Polly, why don't you do something?' Kim asked angrily.

'She's been like that for hours,' said Polly in the voice of complete exhaustion.

'She's hiding,' said Sadie. 'If they find her they'll put her in the cupboard with all the other Sadies but she peeped in behind their backs and there aren't any Sadies in there, only . . . only cockroaches! And they rustle and run about but softly so you nearly can't hear them. Everywhere, everywhere there are cockroaches: big, brown, shiny, squish, squash. They fall off the lampshade into the bath and they run up the folds in the curtain, and they walk across the wall leaving little yellow blobs. Only the ants cleared them out though the Luanshya Public Health tried and tried. They made everyone go out while they set roach bombs but the roaches just hid in the cupboard till it was over. The ants came while she was asleep. She lay in bed and something pattered across her face. She brushed it off but it came back. Again, again, again. She flicked it off but it came back till she put the light on and the whole bed was alive with little ants. Her mother said the swarm must be on the move and next year when the ants came the family would have to sleep in the duck house. But,' Sadie leaned forward and lowered her voice, 'the duck house is full of fleas and there are lizards under the rocks, legofirons sleeping in the sand and little flying insects in the mangoes.'

Kim looked at Polly. Polly shrugged.

'What mangoes, Sadie?' Kim asked. 'What cupboard?'

'No need to shout,' said Sadie. 'She can hear you perfectly well.'

Outside the branches of the buddleia scratched at the window.

'A few nights later Sadie started screaming, short shrieks which varied little through the hours: 'Kim, Kim, Kim' with shrill eyeless terror. To which Kim replied unheard. They took her to out-patients, the doctor in charge gave her tranquillisers and advised her to get more from her GP. Kim and Polly wrote down the week so that Sadie never had to be on her own, but with no idea how long this was to last, whether Sadie would get better or worse. At first she seemed only miserable, would wander around the house unable to settle, collect all the dirty mugs from the bedrooms and forget what she was going to do with them. A look of pain and horror would come into her eyes as she realised something had gone. She shuffled her feet, stopped mid-sentence in a croaky, whining voice and wrung her big hands awkwardly. Her height seemed to emphasise her aberration. Her movements were jerky and desultory as if they would never quite reach their destination.

When Sadie spoke it was with the same explosive articulacy with which she had talked about cockroaches, half deeply private, half oration so that Kim would catch herself doubting Sadie's sincerity. It was a selfish, childish game, this madness, an excuse not to get up in the morning. Angels went crazy, mere mortals went to work. And Polly was completely duped, like a fascinating game they were playing. But then Sadie would start plucking her knicker elastic like a two-year-old and in the chore of coaxing her to dress warmly at least if not decently there would be no time for reflections on sincerity.

Polly was too wary of the State system to allow Sadie into its hands without a fight: its values which smelt of methylated spirits, its welfare kindness which asked that you participate in your own reformation, its codes which protected the powerful from their power. ECT, to be used only in extreme cases, like when patients are too dopey or relatives too desperate to refuse. Rows of metal beds and shell-shocked inmates in night clothes to lend them the status of illness.

Kim's shifts regulated their lives: as soon as she got home Polly retreated hurriedly to her room with a thermos, closed the door and hoped for a few hours' escape into the world of Dorica Maud, subject of her long-unwritten thesis. But still would come visions: Sadie curled behind the sofa, eyes covered, back to the wall so that nothing could get her from behind; Sadie making weird connections, drawing everything up into a huge symbolic net, herself caught at the centre. Polly felt she could do nothing but carry out her promise to sit with her till Kim came home. Kim was so good at it, would bring out two pairs of scissors and a piece of black hessian, and calmly start cutting up lengths of wool from jumpers she'd bought at a jumble sale. Then she'd move the threads of hessian apart and loop through a length of wool. Sometimes Sadie helped with the rug making, other times she watched the rhythmical movement from the sofa, her fingers stroking the cat.

But Polly had nothing like that to offer. She was not a calm presence with a purpose and she could not get away for eight hours a day like Kim. It was exhausting keeping up with Sadie, you could not relax one single minute. Though Sadie hotly denied any leaning towards solid dependability, Polly was somehow still taken in by her height, even her sullenness Polly had seen as merely wayward, unconventional, and interpreted as confidence in Sadie's own way of doing things. There was surely no charm now in this shambling wreck.

Life continued thus uneasily for three weeks. People came by to help: women from Kim's old house which was near enough to drop in; Sadie's regretfully generous Beverly, but she had Claire to look after and Stockwell felt a long way from Wandsworth. The most conscientious were Suzette and Jane. Jane would get Kim telling stories of life on the buses; Suzette always seemed to have a literary point she was burning to discuss with Polly. A sense of enormous relief welled up in the house on the weekend when Suzette and Jane were due to visit. Only when they were there could Kim and Polly remember they had lives unconnected with Sadie.

However weary, irritated or upset Kim and Polly felt they never showed it to Sadie. They didn't dare.

'You can't shout at someone who doesn't know what she's doing.'

'I'm sure she does. I'm sure she has some control.'

'But it seems to cost her such a lot.'

The doctor who'd seen Sadie at out-patients hadn't mentioned a shrink, only tranquillisers.

'It'd be sheer madness to put yourself in their hands;' said Kim, 'like planting electrodes in your brain.'

'What about therapy,' Polly suggested, '– a feminist therapist?'

'Feminism,' Kim thought. It was the thought she took with her for the bus that day. But, as always when she was trying to be serious, her brain got frightened and shied off. Feminism seemed like a long time ago: the pink triangles had turned into double women's symbols; abortion marches were no longer a must but a concession. Once it had meant equal pay and making demands on men, but that was before, when she still lived in the mixed house. Kim thought about the Women's Centre she had tracked down and visited, unsure of her position now she was a lesbian, unwilling to be born again.

It was at the top of a very tall building where the heating was paraffin and the armchairs looked like they'd chaired a lot of meetings. It wasn't the empty paint-tins or the age of the furniture which turned her away: they made it seem well-used and necessary. It was the feeling of intimacy, that the women all knew each other and were there for a purpose. Somebody had asked her would she like to address labels and for the whole afternoon she had copied out names and addresses on to rectangles of sticky paper of women she had never met and never would meet. When she had got down to the bottom she had rolled the reel of paper into a neat ball, replaced all the name cards in the drawer and slipped off quietly down the stairs. She was unlikely to get to know anyone like that. It said in the newsletter you weren't allowed to advertise for lonely hearts but failed to mention that the correct way of doing it was to say you wanted to start a discussion group, even if what you wanted to discuss was why you felt so lonely and does anyone else feel the same, in which case could you meet up afterwards and make love? With Sadie needing so much attention Kim felt more isolated than ever.

One weekend when Suzette and Jane were down, they sat out in the garden the first sunny day and discussed what Sadie should do. At first Kim and Polly felt resentful: weren't they doing enough already? It had seemed wrong to pile on the agony, put Sadie into a perspective of folk-tales; then, suddenly, it was a tremendous relief. The remotest, batty great uncle who walked himself into exhaustion was deeply and rewardingly interesting after the protective silence they'd been guarding.

'She needs professional help,' said Jane. 'It's not the eighteenth century you know. Some of these places are very good.'

There were recommendations for sympathetic psychiatrists, places you could go and just rest. Everyone seemed to have a story to tell of a lover, a friend or a relative who had gone mad and got better.

'When my aunt . . .' Jane began.

'Who had eight children,' Suzette supplied.

'When my aunt who had eight children sank too low to think straight they popped her in a clean white clinic up on Hampstead Heath. The only treatment she had was to wander in the gardens and chat to the practitioner once a week.'

'What practitioner?' asked Kim.

'Christian Science,' Suzette answered. 'Jane's aunt is a Christian Scientist.'

'You know,' said Jane, 'no pain, only lack of good.'

'But Sadie's not a Christian Scientist,' said Kim, 'she doesn't have a practitioner and she isn't bad, she's in pain.'

'When my friend Renée had a breakdown in Dublin,' said Polly, 'they gave her three doses of ECT and she forgot all about it. Trouble was, she forgot everything else as well.'

'What do you think, Sadie?' asked Jane.

'Oh leave her alone,' snapped Sadie. 'Why can't you leave her be?'

The three of them had gone on, waiting almost for divine intervention, for Sadie to make a move which would be recognised now that no one listened to her words; a last appeal to go away somewhere, that she need no longer exercise restraint for fear of frightening her friends. The luxury of screaming till she was hoarse, daubing shit on the walls with no witness but the nurses with their strong calf muscles who expected that kind of behaviour anyway.

Why didn't they contact some alternative support group before Sadie, before she, before it all got so awful? Because they knew so little about it? Because when they phoned it was engaged and then a wrong number and they were given a different number and anyway in August everyone went on holiday? They tried to do the right thing but Sadie had seemed a little better and in the end they thought best do it through a proper doctor. By the time they found a therapist, there was no way Sadie was going to get to North London once a week.

It was warmer now and they sat out in the garden most days. The buddleia was doing well and its purple flowers welcomed them. Polly watched as Sadie began scratching at the ground with a stick, like a baby, like a chicken, like an idiot. Polly hated herself for watching, hated Sadie for being crazy. As Sadie pounded away at the ground, Polly wished she would kill herself and get it over with. No she didn't. She didn't. She looked around quickly in case someone had heard what she hadn't said. At times, Sadie was perfectly sane and Polly did not know how to react. Now Sadie lay in the sun motionless and absorbed as though watching the warmth of colours inside her eyelids. Polly imagined them: brown, purple, red as the clouds passed; wondered how long till she hit Sadie.

'Stamford Hill to Putney,' said Sadie aloud and Polly listened for she seemed to be making sense, 'that'll be £12.90. But she doesn't have it. Shouldn't have taken the taxi then, if she didn't have it. What'll she say to the driver? She must say something now. Now. She felt sick. The smell of petrol, the windows wound up. Two complete strangers sitting in the seat opposite. Dizzy. Sick.

' "I feel sick."

'She tells the driver she feels sick. she never had to tell her mother. Sometimes she just opened the window and then it would get caked in with the wind and the dust and Monday would shoot it with the hose from the dam. Once he left the back window open and all the seat got wet.' Sadie laughed and grew calmer as though the memory were pleasant.

'You see,' she said expansively to Polly, 'from Stamford Hill to Putney are all the car journeys I have ever made. The long drive from Luanshya to Mbabane — how rusty the names sound now no one uses them. Five days in a car. Everyone together. Blankets on the floor, bundles on the roof. We slept in it too, like camping, only better. That's what my mother said but Mrs Atkins who lived on the farm through the casuarina hedge that made my throat swell, said nothing was quite like camping and nothing could ever be better. But that was because she was very old and tough as old boots and walked the seven miles to Luanshya once rationing started. Sometimes the car stopped for me to be sick, sometimes for someone to wee. Hugo, my brother, threw the potty out the window when he was only meant to be emptying it. The roads were dusty and if another car passed everything went orange. We leaned out the windows and sang and the wind was hot. We quarrelled and our mother told us stories while we waited at the borders and our father in a khaki suit and knee-socks went into little white buildings with his brief-case. Sometimes we stayed in huts and we got wet at the Victoria Falls just by the water that sprays out and there was a rainbow stuck in that spray as if something could be happening right there in mid-air. Like climbing out the window of the plane and sitting on the clouds. I felt safe in a car that was going somewhere because the driver had to stay at least until we got there. In Livingstone there were monkeys and bush-babies that screamed and pulled your hair with long thin fingers like chicken legs. The Kariba Dam was nothing; just big and concrete and lots of water but afterwards it was another country. In Bulawayo there was a photo of Ian Smith on the wall and he said you could teach an African one thing but when you tried to teach him something else he forgot what he learned first. I wasn't sure which Africans. If it was Monday and Edwina who worked on the farm, or Gideon and Kenneth who came to talk to my mother, or Audrey and Mwela who went to school with me and were my best friends except when Audrey ganged up with Hugo or Mwela had to look after the little ones. But Ian Smith was a whiteracistbastard and he called Africans that word I still can't say, that word that begins with K and has two ffs in it, that the Atkins said was worse for an African than cunt or cock or anything and we said it to Monday just to see and Monday belted us one. Then he went off into the bush and we thought he was frightened of what our mother would do when we told on him for hitting us. But she screamed:

' "Who told you that word? It's those bloody little Atkins, isn't it? Well they're filthyracistbastards (which is what she said about Ian Smith) and if you ever say that word again I'll tan the living daylights out of you." ' And our father said:

' "Oi'll tear out yer liver and loights and Oi'll spread em across the wall till yer own mother don't know yer." (Which is what he said when we hadn't really been naughty.) But our mother didn't say anything to him. She told Edwina to find Monday and she dragged me by my hair into the bush. She tried to grab Hugo's but his was too short. Then she said to Monday:

' "My children have come to apologise."

'But do you know, my father sacked Monday and sent him away with a reference saying he wasn't very good with children. Me and Mwela used to shower together with a bucket by the tap out the back. When we took our clothes off Mwela burst out giggling, patted me on the bum and sang:

' "White spoon sugar," which was written on the sugar packets. I started to sing, "Black, black coffee," which wasn't the name of anything but it was all I could think of at the time. So I said we should shower in the house with hot water next time. Afterwards my mother took me aside and said:

' "I don't think Mwela should come in the house, your father thinks it will upset the servants." '

'So when I saw the photo of Ian Smith in the hotel room in Bulawayo I was sick. But it might have been the cereal for breakfast. In South Africa there was a Bible in every room even the toilet where no one stays long enough and anyway Gideon said you should never read the Bible because that was all they gave you in solitary and what would you do then? I had to share a room with Hugo so I read out all the names in the phone book under S for Sadie. Somewhere we crossed the Limpopo and there were hippos in it. There had been hippos before, on the Marlin farm, and my mother was pleased. She said:

' "Oh I love a hippo. I do so love a hippo." '

'You see,' said Sadie, summing up, 'I lived there, eleven years of my life, and it is no use tying it up neatly with slogans as though that could somehow neutralise it.'

Polly nodded. 'After I left Gerard,' she began, 'I threw out all my photo albums but as I didn't empty the waste-paper basket they were still there at the end of the week. With cautious fascination I relented. I turned over page after page: me and Ger swimming in Glendalough; watching the hare coursing at Blarney; Gerard explaining the British Abomination outside University College, Cork. As I examined them I reflected that I hadn't changed so very much and I decided to keep those photographs rather than write off my own past as belonging entirely to my husband.'

'As though you were only there because of him,' said Sadie.

'Carefully I cut round his unsmiling face. In every one he was gazing at a point just above the camera, setting off his troubled eyes to best effect. Oh, the monstrous arrogance of the man. I cut round him closely and obliterated him from the picture. It still left a gap but no more than my life at that time needed filling.'

'That's what you do while you're still furious,' commented

Sadie, 'in the end his face is your memory same as the rest of it.'

'You're so right,' sighed Polly.

For barely the second time since entering the house Sadie smiled. Polly had a stream of hazy, soft, smooth, warm, liquid thoughts starting with the calm of lying in the sun, stretching out, lazy. Then not so lazy, kissing wetly and the kiss spreading, the wetness spreading, the warmth growing, heat.

Sex! thought Polly blatantly and for the first time in her life did not confuse it with hunger. She looked at Sadie lying out in the sun under the buddleia and remembered the first time Sadie had smiled, the day they went to Kew Gardens, Sadie's watchful vigilance. Polly was filled with the very simple desire to lie down on the grass beside Sadie and kiss her. Sadie watched with wide brown eyes, waiting for her to make up her mind. There was really no reason not to. No reason not to? Was Polly mad? Only a few hours ago Sadie had been scratching at the ground with a lolly stick.

'So what?' said Buddleia. 'People doodle. It helps them concentrate.'

'But it would be so, so . . .'

'Nice?'

'Irresponsible!' said Polly.

Sadie was still watching her. Polly sat on the cushions under the purple blossom. The sun was hotter now and there was a warm laziness in the air. Sadie stretched her long backbone and stood up. She bent over Polly and whispered, 'I'm going to sweep you off your feet,' and she put her arms round her and pulled her close. Polly had the distinct impression that all this time it had been Sadie who was looking after her. They lay on the ground together, the massy shrub protecting them from prying neighbours. Sadie pulled off Polly's clothes. At least that must be what happened. Polly was conscious only that she wanted Sadie to stroke her skin and that the layers of cotton and cord somehow got in the way. Sadie's body was big and expansive, soft flesh exposed in the garden. Polly felt immensely beautiful. For a while Sadie lay next to her smiling quietly. Then she began to stroke the inside of Polly's fingers, smooth out her tired hands; she ran one nail along Polly's arm and played over her lips. Polly tried to kiss the fingers but the hand moved away. Sadie's fingernails touched Polly's body, reminding it of how it felt, how it fitted together. Sometimes

97

frightening, sometimes agonisingly slow. Polly breathed more and more heavily, moved her legs slightly apart. Sadie's hand swept down over Polly's breast, her nipple, her clitoris moving neither slower nor faster than before. For a moment Polly felt sick, like a head massage, like science fiction, as though she did not quite understand what was going on. Then she pulled Sadie down on top of her, held her head in her hands, kissed her. She was surprised how soft Sadie's mouth was, how hard they kissed each other.

'Well,' said Sadie at last, for the sun's shadows now chilled the garden and they were both tired from licking and sucking, smoothing and caressing: pleasure was unified in a low hum. 'Well, shall I make a cup of tea?'

'Mmm,' said Polly, 'hot, strong and wet.'

And they sat out a bit longer, until the cool of evening turned cold and the shadows lengthened into night. Polly was busy with the evening meal, stirring rabbit stew while Sadie chopped onions, when Kim's key jangling in the lock let in the world and reminded Polly that Sadie was ill, that she was looking after her and that the fiery heat of the afternoon, the extreme gentleness, the kissing so hard it numbed was a horrific seduction of innocence, a betrayal of trust.

Kim walked in rosy-faced, picked up a raw carrot and munched it, asking for news of their day. Polly bent down to the fridge, muttering about the weather. She would never be able to look Kim in the face. She could not bear to think of what she had to tell her.

Sadie looked up happily, asked Kim was she tired, would she like a drink? Supper would soon be ready.

'Had a good day, Sadie?' asked Kim, pleased at the difference in her, though some days Sadie did seem perfectly all right.

'Wonderful.'

Polly cringed behind the Kenwood. In a way it would be easier if Sadie told Kim herself.

'Wasn't it warm,' said Sadie. 'Do you feel the heat on your bus? I imagine you standing at the back to catch the breeze as you go round corners.'

'Yes,' said Kim, 'and hiding my ice lolly in my back pocket when the inspector gets on.'

'Polly and I lay outside all day,' said Sadie.

'It's nice you're feeling better,' Polly interrupted. 'Watch out now, this stew is hot. Kim would you put a mat down?'

Sadie began to explain to Kim about Africa. 'People don't want to hear about it,' she said, 'they don't like to think there are things they can't understand. They only want to talk about London, but I won't live my life as if I was born yesterday.'

It reminded Kim of the Women's Centre: addressing labels, feeling she had no history as a lesbian and therefore no history to speak of.

After dinner, Polly escaped to her room, said she was neglecting her studies. Kim went up to give her a cup of hot water.

'Well, what about Sadie then?' she asked, playing with the anglepoise on Polly's desk.

Sadie went up the stairs, anxious now about Polly's motives, wanting to reassure herself. The door was open but before she came to the study she heard voices. Kim must be in there. Sadie hung back.

'She's happier,' said Polly vaguely, in answer to Kim's question, studying her typewriter cover, unable to look Kim in the eye. 'But maybe it's the calm before the storm.'

Now Polly had had a chance to think about it, no longer bowled along by Sadie's charm, by her own desire never to allow Sadie out of her sight, her need not Sadie's, she realised that Sadie's tall silence was vital to her, that Sadie's rare words answered questions Polly had not dared formulate. And every kiss, every passionate touch was a desecration. Why had she not been pleased simply to learn that Sadie wanted her and then waited till Sadie was better? Something about the day, the heat, the purple blossom. She must have known it was all wrong.

'The calm before the storm.' Sadie heard the words and quailed. All the time you yearn to know what it is they think of you, you watch their faces, their lips, their feet tied in knots under the table. Do they like you or hate you? Do they wish you'd go away? And then, in passing, as if it really wasn't very important, you overhear them talking. Talking about you. Saying 'The calm before the storm.' And you know.

Kim left the study and closed the door wishing Polly was more forthcoming, less wrapped up in Dorica Maud.

Sadie slunk back in the shadows. Polly closed her book and walked through to the bedroom. She turned the light on. Light flooded Sadie's eyes.

'Sadie!' said Polly. 'What are you doing here?'

'The calm before the storm,' repeated Sadie. 'You feel guilty about making love to me.'

'It . . . er . . . seems a little ill-advised,' stumbled Polly.

'Ill-advised?' said Sadie. 'It was wonderful. Besides it was me seduced you. You couldn't make up your mind.'

'I, oh hell, Sadie.'

Now Sadie was sitting next to her it was difficult to remember there were reasons not to touch her.

'You think I'm mad, don't you?' said Sadie. 'That I can't be held responsible. I wanted to kiss you Polly. I've wanted to kiss you for ages and ages. I wanted to make love to you and suddenly I dared and now you think I'm not responsible?'

'Sadie, I'm just afraid . . .'

'Don't be,' said Sadie softly. 'What awful thing is going to happen? I'd like to spend the night with you; we don't have to make love. We can tell Kim in the morning.'

'No!' said Polly, suddenly terrified. 'It's too soon.'

'If this is the calm,' said Sadie miserably, 'I dread to think of the storm.'

That night Polly couldn't sleep. She heard Kim go into Sadie's room to say goodnight and longed to go herself but feared that if she and Sadie were alone together in Sadie's room, she would rub her cheek against Sadie's, kiss her ear and neither of them would act responsibly.

Sadie lay awake in bed. Kim came in to say goodnight and asked her how she was. She said she was bored. She was bored: bored of Polly's scruples, bored of her protection. Her feet churned the sheets with frustration. She thought of cars again, being sick in cars.

Her father came to take her home after Lorna Rainbird's party in Battersea.

'Well Tosh,' he said. He never got their nicknames right. Hugo was Tosh; she was Sadie. 'We're going away darling. Somewhere beginning with A.'

'Aunty's,' said Sadie because it sounded like I Spy and with her father there was usually a trick.

'How clever of you. No, sweetheart, it's the name of a country.' And of course it turned out to be Africa.

Polly woke briefly in the night. It seemed to her that the

100

buddleia was scratching at the window, but perhaps it was just the wind.

Kim slept well; the leaden sleep of one who has given directions to a hundred tourists, climbed a thousand stairs, rung up a million tickets. In her dreams she pointed out the Post Office Tower, told an American where to get off, tried to reassure a distraught mother that she had not left her child on the bus, did not in fact have a child but the woman kept pulling at her sleeve, shaking her, waking her.

'Kim,' Polly was saying in that subdued, overcalm voice which fills you instantly with terror, 'I don't like to disturb you but I can't seem to wake Sadie.'

For a brief moment Kim panicked, could only wish it was too late to do anything. In a way it was what they'd been waiting for. The emergency phone call, the screeching brakes, the friend for life, the tense visits to a white-faced but slowly recovering Sadie. Kim was up in a flash spurred on by Polly's need of her.

Sadie was in bed. Kim noticed things very slowly. Pieces of glass on the floor. Red spots on the lino. As though the cat had knocked something over. Precious moments when it still might all be normal. Sadie always got a glass of water last thing before bed to take her pills with. She was very fond of the cat, it slept in her room at night. The pill bottles were still on the orange crate. There were red paw marks leading to the bed. Agatha, Kim's cat, was sitting there cleaning her back. Kim picked up each paw in turn to see what harm she'd done herself. It was almost incredible that she did not turn immediately to Sadie, a little bubble in time during which she must perform certain motions before she discovered what she'd already guessed. Agatha was perfectly all right. Where then did the blood come from? Kim stood and watched, unable to speed things up. Sadie's face nestled amongst the pillows: a grisly yellow with thick white lime coating her lips. She half opened her mouth and began to mutter.

Dumbly, Kim leaned over to listen. Polly pushed past her and slapped Sadie. Slap, smack, whack. She tried to wake her from what she hoped was a nightmare. Sadie waved her arms limply, so soft and smooth they were.

'Sadie wake up!'

Her lips fluttered, her pupils were wide and blank. Kim

101

blinked and the room flooded with explanation. The glass, the blood, the empty bottles, the scum on Sadie's mouth. Polly grabbed Sadie's wrists and turned them over, each was intact though the nails were black with dried blood. Sadie moaned and her restless movement slipped the sleeping bag from her legs. And Agatha, Agatha whom Sadie loved and stroked fondly when beseeching affection, Agatha licked neatly at the blood on Sadie's thigh. Kim stared. Sadie's thigh. What was that awful red hole in Sadie's thigh? Agatha's whiskers were frothy, the ends tinged pink. It turned its sweet pussy cat face towards Kim and its canines were like daggers. Polly seized Sadie's shoulders and shook her like a rug.

'It's a beautiful day,' she said, tight and squeaky, 'the kids'll be leaving their floaties on Kim's bus.'

They picked Sadie up and made her walk but she whimpered so much they had to set her down again, worried about her leg. Now Kim looked at the wound directly: a scab of blood sticking straight out, a yawning gash like someone gouging out earth with a machine, a piece of flesh, of butcher's meat, lay scooped up out of the body. The pills Kim could accept, painless and sleepy, but that someone could do this to her own body and not cry out, go on hacking till it came away. Why? Why did she do that? Kim felt angry. She had seen Sadie last night. She hadn't said she'd do this. She said she was bored. Bored, she said, not suicidal. It was awful. Awful, awful, awful. It couldn't happen. People didn't do this. Kim felt the blood drain from her own face and she leaned an elbow to the wall.

'Don't you dare!' barked Polly's voice, bringing her back.

Polly was slapping Sadie again and as Kim watched, the thought hit her like a wave which dumps you face first in the sand:

'I know what she's doing. She's dying. Right here in front of us: dying. How dare she?'

'I've phoned an ambulance,' Polly said intercepting her thought. Until it arrived they had to keep fighting. Fighting when there was nothing to do but yell at Sadie for being so bloody stupid and frightening them both so much.

'She heavy?' the ambulance men shouted and they carried her down, folded in the middle like a camp-bed.

She stayed in two days then she was discharged: pumped out, stitched up, sent back. Kim couldn't believe it. The cat on the bed licking Sadie's cut as if lapping a bowl of milk? As if cleaning her own wounds? That was sickening, an image Kim would never forget, but what happened next, though outwardly cleaner, neater and more reasonable was infinitely more difficult to cope with. Sitting at the doctor's with Polly and Sadie in green plastic chairs, the calm respectability of the surgery. Sadie's scar was wider than it would have been had it been stitched immediately and the edges were uneven. It frightened Kim to see it though Sadie was sure herself and as convincing as she could be that she had fallen on the glass and not done it to herself. But Kim and Polly had taken Sadie to the doctor's. Had deliberately wrapped her up warm and taken her down there.

They had sat saying coldly and repeatedly that they were not prepared to have her at home. Kim had imagined the doctor would take one look at Sadie and demand she be committed, that she and Polly could protest, murmur their fears and have them answered, let themselves be rocked gently by his persuasion and agree finally that perhaps it was for the best. She had thought they would be able to state conditions, be consulted over medication, visit the hospital, talk to the other patients. She was wrong. So wrong she had no idea what rights they did have. If they wanted Sadie to go into hospital they had to fight for it.

'But you're doing such a splendid job at home. She's obviously in capable hands.'

They had to show the doctor what it was doing to them, act out their little domestic drama and just maybe he'd do something for them. Their misgivings they must answer themselves in gratitude to the State for doing their job for them.

'Perhaps we can let Sadie decide,' said the doctor.

'It's crazy asking Sadie,' Kim exploded, 'obviously she'd rather be at home.'

'She knows what she wants,' said Polly quietly.

'What about us? Don't we have any say in it? asked Kim, appalled at her own selfishness, but somewhere in the background were Suzette and Jane telling them they must remember they had feelings too.

Sadie was picking the pens out of the Portuguese leather-holder on the doctor's desk, clicking each in turn and scribbling on a stray piece of paper. Polly watched her. Click, click, scratch. The doctor reached out a large benevolent hand, closed it over hers to stop the clicking and grunted:

'Hmm, Sadie?'

Sadie crumpled the slip of paper she'd been scribbling on. 'I want to go away,' she said.

Even after the doctor had agreed they had to wait while he phoned round for a place.

'You see really she should go back to Haringey,' he said with his hand over the receiver, as if Sadie were a complaint addressed to the wrong office. He smiled affably. These women didn't seem to know quite what they were about. It saddened him that they believed the NHS could do a better job with its impersonal institutions. Took away people's self-respect. What price generosity, sacrifice and regard for others if the State just blundered in and took over? Such admirable little women shouldering their burden, drawing strength from one another.

'Not incontinent is she?' he asked as he addressed an envelope on his desk.

Quercus looked round desperately at the other Boddesses but they shook their heads. This time there really was nothing they could do; there was no faith left in the three women for them to work on.

It was with enormous relief that Sadie looked round at the yellow walls of the hospital ward. She had tried to settle down, had tried to take someone with her and each time it was the house itself, the lover herself who rejected her. She could not fight the Assumption and win, for it insinuated itself into everything Sadie held dear. Here in this anonymous hospital she was as safe and unremarkable as a passenger on a ferry, a woman in a train station. She would give in now and go docilely back to where she belonged. They had come for her after Lorna Rainbird's party, told her alone in a taxi, using the wrong name, that she was going away. She had gone; she had made friends. Lorna wasn't there but there was Audrey and Mwela and they played together, sold chibuku by the roadside, beer Mwela's mother made; built catapults from car tyres, lorries of chicken-wire and coffee lids. But she and Mwela showered together, she invited her into the house. The ants came and ate the cockroaches, Monday was sacked. Then came another Africa, with mountains, and India, Malaya, Australia, and Sadie had nothing to anchor her save a slim black book, stamped in a hundred places, bearing the precious message: 'Holder has the right of abode in the United Kingdom.'

England, where nothing smelled right and all the flowers were different. They had African plants at Kew but so small and stunted Sadie never would have recognised them were it not for the name-plate at their roots. Already Sadie's plans were made: to buy a ticket and fly to Luanshya where the tarmac melts on the roads, the rain hits the roof in buckets and the steam rises from the earth with a hot, damp smell.

Polly walked on Clapham Common, that blank aimless wander where one notices nothing, stumbling, crying, till a rock, a log, a bench appears in the way and one slumps down scarcely conscious of the change. Kim had gone to visit Sadie, Polly hadn't dared. Nor had she told Kim, though it might have eased her mind. Instead she sat, and as the bench where she'd ended up was opposite the children's playground she watched vaguely as little boys bought ice creams, little girls squabbled over skyboats. A small child climbed, slow but determined, up the slide. Polly looked round. No one seemed to be with him. His hands clenched the rail, let go a moment and gripped higher up. Finally he reached the top and waved a grubby hand at his sister seated below. He would slip and fall. A baby on the roundabout crawled to the edge and tried to clamber down while the older children only swung the platform faster. A girl, standing on the swing, hurtled skyward. Didn't she know it was dangerous? The playground was full of hidden perils: height, speed, asphalt, concrete. Polly saw an array of bruises and broken bones, smashed skulls, torn thighs, a yawning gash, a piece of flesh, of butcher's meat scooped out of the body. Sadie.

Sadie would stay with Hugo and his wife. When she'd first heard of her brother's return to Africa to teach at their old school, she had sneered at his outdated romanticism. Was he making up for having missed the Spanish Civil War? But as she lay in bed and remembered Hugo's involved description of the rethatching of a hut, how many men it took, how many days, how the grass was arranged to be warm in winter, dry in the wet season, she was struck by his urgency to cram as much information as he could into one sentence, as though he could not crave her patience to sit through another. Then she remembered her own slow slide from urgency to impatience.

Hugo had stayed on at boarding school with their father when Sadie and her mother went back to England. They rented a flat above the South Circular and Sadie, coming straight from the last hut on the mountain, had sat at the window watching the stream of traffic, aghast at the noise, the fact that London never shut. At school the other girls envied her suntan but she was put in the bottom division because the teachers had trouble with her accent. In her rough-book along with the usual 'Sadie luvs Angela. TRUE' appeared the more threatening scrawl 'Whites out of South Africa.' 'But', she explained angrily to her imagined attacker, 'I never lived in South Africa. I have the accent of most English-speaking whites from the Congo down. And, anyway, what're you so smug about?'

After gym you had to have a shower unless you had your period. Sadie unbuttoned her white sport shirt and bra, pulled off her navy blue knickers and walked into the shower. When she came out there was a giggling silence and the gym mistress quietly handed her a towel. Sadie dried and dressed herself as quickly as she could wondering grimly what she had done wrong. She disappeared to the toilet to check if there was blood dribbling down her leg and stayed there a long time. Later she realised that the correct way to take a shower is to wind a large towel around you and get undressed underneath; you ask your best friend to unhook you, handing her the towel only after you are safely behind the shower curtain. Sadie was too stunned by her first experience ever to attempt another, and told the gym mistress she had her period on the rare occasions she didn't manage to skip gym altogether. Everyone's period was marked on the class register and the teacher usually recommended girls to see a doctor if they claimed one two weeks running. With Sadie she never murmured.

The girls, curious at first, now had official permission to treat Sadie with suspicion. Clearly she was different from them. When the whole class was kept in for detention for throwing paper darts, the girls protested at Sadie's inclusion: who'd throw a dart at her? 'Sadie, it's a matter of class, you know,' said the gym mistress, referring at last to the shower incident. 'Working-class girls live in much more cramped conditions than

you or I so they have to be more private about their decency.'
All Sadie learned from this interchange was that the teachers
thought her a snob and had decided to ignore her foreignness.
In a French essay she described how the river flooded and her
parents couldn't get across but had to leave their car on the
other side. She was told the story was meant to be imaginary
and anyhow the other girls didn't have access to such rich
cultural experience as she had. Everywhere she looked, people
were telling her to take a shower and laughing at her when she
took her clothes off to do so.

Not until Manju came to school could Sadie make much
sense of what was happening. Manju was the first of many
Ugandan Asians whose families had taken refuge in the Asian
community in Balham after their expulsion by Amin. Manju
was put in special English classes to sharpen her grammar for
British examiners. Usually if you took Special English it was
because you had difficulty reading and you were not offered a
foreign language.

'They make me so mad,' Manju confided one day. 'My
English is not good but my Hindi is excellent. I need five
O'levels to go to university and the blasted school won't even
enter my name for the exam. They don't need to teach me, I
don't require that. They enter me, I must pass.'

Manju and Sadie sat together through a class on African
Current Affairs. Manju was asked her opinion of the apartheid
system in South Africa.

'I know nothing about that,' she said. 'I am from Uganda,'
and the way she shut her mouth firmly with the corners turned
down Sadie imagined she was thinking of the race system in her
own country where Asians owned the stores Africans shopped
at.

'It's a trap,' she whispered to her friend. 'You'll get all
broken up telling them and they don't want to know.'

'I know that,' said Manju, tightly.

Looking back, it dawned on Sadie that Hugo had not
returned to Swaziland after college with any missionary zeal
about anyone. He had gone because England made no sense to
him, because the contradictions of being white and African had
to be lived out in Africa. Sadie's teachers had hated her because
in the tradition of British liberalism they were not allowed to
hate Manju.

107

So Sadie would fly to Johannesburg, take the train to Mbabane from there. And she would not have to explain about the hot springs, the wet velvet of the night grass under bare feet, smile benignly while her reluctant questioner scoffed at the impossible romanticism of a tropical flood.

People do not like to be told things they do not already know, so the African Experience has to be phrased in expressions already familiar to them: exotic safaris, colonial adventure, cultural imperialism – they liked that best. If Sadie spoke of the Zambian independence celebrations, the mass rally for UNIP that was held on their farm, the drums and the chants that seemed to sound round the clock for six months, someone would laugh about 'the heat, the flies and the drums' as though it were a Martini ad., something they could recognise and ridicule.

Slowly Sadie too had slipped into exactly that way of talking: facetious, clowning. At a party she met a woman who had been in Zambia the same time as she had. Because she was older than Sadie, her memories of what was happening were much more sophisticated. She nodded when Sadie mentioned Swaziland and said a lot of her friends' families had also moved there after UDI. Suddenly Sadie had a specific social context for something she had always suffered as part of her family's oddness. She'd met ex-colonials before, but English people did not like them to speak to each other and would change the subject, start off about their holiday in Hong Kong, the shocking poverty one saw, anything not to feel excluded.

'What were you doing in Zambia, Sadie?' the woman asked with interest.

'My father was making films.'

'Oh really, about what?'

'Documentary, for Anglo-American.'

'Mine shafts? Rock beds?'

'The one I remember was called "Land of Four Rivers." '

'Shots of little miners panning for copper in the Zambezi with Raj hats on their heads and American accents . . .'

Evidently it was simply intolerable that expatriates should speak to each other. Sadie would not stoop to explain that most of the miners were Scottish and if you panned for copper you were more than likely to contract bilharzia. Sometimes she joined in the picture of foreign oddities, embellishing it herself with touches of near realism. Always afterwards she felt as though she had lost her temper and trampled some delicate insect into the mud.

Heat, hot springs, the endless flower conversations with Polly, the lyrical mask of sincerity. The charcoal burners by the roadside, Moira at school whose family fled from the Congo when a hand-grenade burst through the window and fell on the mosquito net under which little brother Kevin was sleeping, the man outside Luanshya Post Office who charged tourists a tickey for photographing him pushing a twig through his nose: the horrific, piteous, lurid side of Africa journalists discover every year, blurred and flattened to meaningless, even, pulp. It was the flat picturesqueness Sadie wanted to counter, that simplistic, black and white vision which obscured anything real, complex or uncomfortable, any idea of change.

The six months up to Zambian independence was punctuated with mass rallies. A great wooden platform was built in the front garden of the Monash farm where the aviary used to be. During the weeks before, Africans began to assemble to attend the meeting, sleeping in respectful corners away from the house. For Sadie, young as she was, it almost seemed to be the election celebration itself.

There were chants of 'One Zambia, one Nation; one Nation, one Leader; one Leader, one Kaunda' but what stuck in Sadie's mind was the speech her father made.

'As a white man, I watch this movement for independence and Africanisation much as a bystander watches a fire-engine drive past in the street. I will certainly point out a short cut but I cannot drive the engine myself.'

She could not trust the English with his obviously pompous generosity, those white liberals sworn to mention South Africa only through gritted teeth as if that somehow proved their awareness of the problem. Sadie remembered that speech being quoted and requoted, not by the papers, she was too young to read them – but by her African friends, the servants, men who came to visit. It was their great powerlessness which made her cry, not the stupidity of a fire-engine when the fire fighting system consisted of earth and sand thrown into the bonnet of the car the time Hugo pulled the choke out and the engine went up in flames. People liked to hear about that, it fitted their idea of savagery, or native naturism; and Sadie liked to tell, she was easily side tracked. Water was scarce: drawn from the well, collected in rain barrels or fetched from Luanshya in tanks during the dry season. The electricity broke down each time the diesel generator cut out so that Sadie had learned to read by gaslight. If you don't expect anyone to listen, you grab at straws for things to interest them.

Monday had been sacked with references saying he was no good with children. You would have thought that in a place where half the house servant's job would be to pick up after the kids, it must mean the reference was worse than useless to him. The first time she mentioned it Sadie herself had been fooled, but as she thought, she remembered. For months after Monday's departure men would appear at the back door asking Bwana Monash how much he'd charge to write a reference for them. The incredible power of a pen in a white man's hand. Sadie's parents were good employers because where other farms hired by the month and sacked without pay at the end (and they never lacked for servants) Mr Monash paid for Mwela to attend the same school as Sadie, his wife drove Mwela's mother to hospital when she was ill, picked the men up from the townships on Sunday night if there'd been reports of rioting. One did not give a reference to a servant one had sacked, nor did one hire one without. If Bwana Monash said he'd point out a short cut, well at least he wasn't threatening to shoot every K—— in sight.

After that speech and the political rally '. . . in their front garden, Oma, practically on the stoep!' the Atkins children were forbidden to play with Hugo and Sadie, calling them 'K—— lovers; 'your mother spreads her legs for black Africans,' 'your daddy licks Kenneth Kaunda's bum.' Sadie thought about Mwela and herself, two little girls wandering arm in arm. Or rather she was wandering; Mwela was looking for the loofah tree, picking ground-nuts, hushing the baby on her back. Mwela spent very little time playing, it was more that Sadie found her activities a game. They were the same age, though Mwela was three years behind Sadie in school.

'Don't get cocky,' warned Sadie's mother, 'Mwela's cleverer than you are, only she hasn't had your chances.' What was Mwela doing now, a rural black girl with a European education? What had she done with her chances? Africanisation meant precisely that: there could be no white short cut because only Africans knew where they were going.

It was Polly and Kim that Sadie lived with now. She must force them not to laugh 'at anyone who can say the word Karoo with such an air of familiarity.' English people did not trust a sentence with foreign words in it unless they could dismiss them as either ethnic or elitist.

'Is she all right?' asked Polly hesitantly when Kim got back. 'Is she in bed? Do they let her walk around?'

'Why don't you go and see for yourself?'

'Well do you think she'd . . . I mean do you think it's a good idea?'

'Oh, for Christ's sake, Polly, what's the matter with you? Need my permission?'

'I just don't want to make matters worse.'

'Look, I'm going tonight, you could come with me. Only do stop behaving like an apologetic hangman.'

'Grief!' said Hakea.

'But with Kim and Polly, Sadie could be no stormier than the temperate English weather,' said Melaleuca.

'And we had to just look on and let it happen,' said Quercus.

'Until we get sent down to join them.'

'Yes, but meanwhile we can watch over the proceedings and keep them on the right track.'

8
Problems of Scholarship

Polly had walked a long time on Clapham Common, had thought a lot about Sadie and even more about herself. At times it all seemed her fault but she had to admit she was not that important, did not have that power, there were other things in Sadie's life besides her. Though she could not regret making love to her, she regretted not sleeping with her that night, that, yes, that she had turned over a hundred times. Sadie's soft 'Don't be afraid' and her own cowardly 'It seems a little ill-advised.'

So had it weaved and warped in Polly's mind until she knew that however much we care for one another we care for ourselves more. Though Sadie was in hospital, Polly was not; though Sadie was recovering from depression, pills and a six-inch gash in her thigh, Polly was not. Visiting hours didn't end till nine, Polly would go and see Sadie tonight. Kim said there was a garden with green railings where you could almost believe you were only there for the roses.

Polly took a cup of hot water to her room and closed the door, set the water down on her study table and watched the steam rise. She remembered how Sadie would hold a cup in both hands, hunched over as if to bury herself in the steam, remembered how unexpectedly big Sadie would look as she straightened up and said something calm and true. Polly saw again Sadie's wide face, her cheeks pink and damp from the condensing steam, only this time she didn't blank her out with a guilty shiver but let her speak.

'You've been sucked into that thesis by your own investment, Polly.'

How like Sadie to change the subject and to one that Polly was bound to find irresistible.

'If you prove they were dykes, so what? Is that the revolutionary statement – that other women were doing it before us? Why bother with fiction if you only believe men's textbooks? You could make it all up, you know, they have for centuries.'

For five years Polly had been working on that thesis. Though maintaining a fitting contempt, Gerard had always been excited by Polly's family. Would look them up in Debrett and be pleased they spelt his name right. Maud was a distant connection and Gerard must get hold of one of her novels to leave in the loo next to *The Communist*. He had, however, little faith in the power of idle curiosity for he always contrived to bring the subject up himself.

When her supervisor, Hyacinth, after a year spent agonising, had told her she really must narrow her field and if she could not yet state an author, couldn't she at least mention a century, Polly had brought out Dorica Maud. Hyacinth was greatly relieved, she had thought it was going to be Blake again.

Quite by accident, a signal failure on the Circle Line, Polly found herself taking the novel out of her bag and reading it. She was seated opposite a Polo ad. and between two Evening Standard readers when she began to giggle, that little half-smothered chuckle one makes to oneself in public places at a very private joke. She was hooked. Travelled three times round the line before she could put the book down and then she got out at the wrong stop. This had never happened to her before. As she walked through the white-tiled corridors, glided up past billboards and graffiti, she relived the story, playing each of the characters in turn. For weeks she thought about those women and her sense of loss when she finished the last of the novels (an event which occurred on a bench inside the Museum of Mankind in early Spring 197–, when Polly had ventured out in search of crocuses and been caught in a sudden downpour) was as real as Alexandra's on finding there was no more world to conquer.

'The Belgard Letty remembered was a cold, confusing building with real dungeons where they would throw you if you so much as touched the little houses made with matchsticks that people called "French prisoners" had built during the war.'

And there was Letty with her nine governesses, heartbroken when Nanny left, unconcerned when Ma and Pa went off to the war. Letty and little sister Hilda's life was filled with the tale of the superabundant Mercredi family and though they themselves were forbidden ringlets as common, the dolls had their hair crimped and curled every night. The two girls were so bound about by rules and restrictions that only the nursery had any freedom or attraction for them. The grown-ups played a deciding role in the affairs and ailments of the dolls that they would never have suspected. If Letty was summoned two nights in a row to the drawing-room to play the piano for company, then Teresa Mercredi's measles would prove fatal and she must die. If Ma's new governess turned out to approve of nature walks then the entire Mercredi family would have sponge cake for tea.

You could almost see the stone-tiled kitchen smelling of orange-peel drying out in the Aga, the tea-leaves that were never thrown away but saved scrupulously for the poor. Hear

113

Granny Frances explaining to a disappointed Letty and Hilda: 'Italian princes simply don't count.' Picture Letty with her Russian thinking at last she'd got it right only to be told: 'Our sort of Russians probably aren't going back. Better to wait before rushing into anything.'

Then there was that lovely scene at the school fire-practice where all the girls troop upstairs to throw themselves into the chutes let down from the upper casements. As each one jumped she was to shout out her name and the Latin mistress would tick it off the list. For the life of her, Letty could not entrust her own name to a void so she and best friend Dulcie swapped names and jumped together into the chute.

Dulcie was a frequent visitor at Belgard, often sharing Letty's bed. Though the governess always switched off the lights with the stern warning: 'No rootling!' unknown to the girls she defended their activities to their mother.

'Why it's only tickling, Lady Hardymount, and I'm sure it wouldn't be natural in growing girls not to giggle.'

Lady Hardymount must not have felt equal to the task of finding out exactly what made them giggle for she never enquired further. When Letty's periods had first started, her mother had acknowledged the event with a visit to the schoolroom and the cryptic injunction: 'Put everything in its proper place.' It was the governess who showed Letty to the boiler room and warned her to wait till old Rory had gone off fixing something before disposing of her napkin.

When she married, as heroines must, and went to look at Venice with her husband, Letty wrote to Dulcie that it was all a great disappointment. Dulcie could not decide whether she meant young Hector or the Ponte Vecchio. After a while, Letty's letters became more circumspect, no longer chatty lists full of petticoats and ink but brief health bulletins: 'Am feeling much more myself again', which worried Dulcie far worse she was sure than would have done a full description. One never knew, once it was all over, whether 'it' had been a sick headache, a fight with dear Hector, or a tonsilectomy. A trip to Switzerland to have one's tonsils out in the fresh mountain air rounded off a girl's education much more fittingly than a finishing school. Letty had to have hers removed three times.

Well, naturally, Polly became curious about this Dorica

114

Maud, distant relative, who had written those patently lesbian books which came complete with cautionary tale on the result of heterosexual coupling. Sleep with a woman and you giggle, sleep with a man and you have to go to Switzerland to have your tonsils out again. Clearly Letty, having explored to the limit with her dolls the great joy to be felt through the dependence of clinging creatures, was not about to raise young.

But Polly was not reading these novels for mere pleasure, her lofty aim was academic excellence and this it seemed was her undoing. Occasionally, and at their mutual convenience, Polly stayed in college after her seminar to see Hyacinth and give an account of reading matter to date. Often this meant a pleasant chat about one or other of Hyacinth's friends who had just published something seminal. That was easy enough. Sometimes it meant listening to the low-down on Hyacinth's lover's ingrown toe-nail. That was more difficult though Polly would try hard to imagine the pain and embarrassment such a common but well-concealed deformity might cause. Infrequently Hyacinth would ask how the writing was going. This smelt of betrayal though an apologetic tone went some way to mitigating the effect. Polly and Hyacinth had specially chosen each other on the tacit agreement that the student would not increase the work load by demanding time-consuming consultations, and for her part the tutor would avoid alluding to the thesis for as long as possible. 'I only ask,' Hyacinth was quick to add, 'because Professor Squawk is making noises. You need something down for the MA before you can convert to a PhD.'

With utter cynicism, Polly cobbled together a rough draft showing the development from the Victorian dying child (that feast of sorrow, the orphaned waif in an adult world) to an autonomous sphere of childhood and escape (Spyri's Clara and Hodgson-Burnett's Colin were permitted to get better) and the consequent modernity of Maud whose characters slipped in and out of childhood with less self-knowledge than good memories. This was already a distortion if not a lie, it was not Maud's view of children which excited Polly. It had done, however, for the MA.

Hyacinth smiled. 'Oh yes, yes,' she had said, flicking through, noting with pleasure that there would be few obscure references to check. After this, the conversation had flagged and both set to wishing the lover had a boil which needed lancing or at least a malignant verruca which might have been called upon to pad out the ten or fifteen minutes remaining before it would be polite for Polly to leave. A common sense of the value and privilege of scholarship having been established, Polly was free to go. But her life was closing over her head. If there had been any likelihood of Hyacinth sharing her interest it would have been nice to talk over the excitement, the frustration, the sense of looking again and again into the same pocket you already know to be empty. But Hyacinth would only sigh vaguely that it was all pretty pointless but nice to earn money while you did it.

'Nice to earn money while you did it!' scoffed the Bonsais. 'For Hortus' sake, this is not the Arabian nights, the Huwomen are not Scheherazade and we will not be cast in the role of executioner.'

'Perhaps Penelope would be more apt as an allusion,' muttered a dwarf cypress gnomically, 'since we never seem to get any further.'

'I don't know what you're talking about,' said Hakea factually, 'but I don't suppose that matters, does it?'

'My dear Hakea Victoria,' the Bonsais rounded on her, using her full name to remind her that she was a plant who ought to be a lot better up in the doings of her forebears, 'Polly, certainly, we agreed to look into; then Sadie and Kim sprang up from the roadside and demanded to be taken on board too; now each is opening up her suitcase and out are tumbling more white elephants than could fit in the proverbial phone booth.'

'Who the diggings are Letty and Hilda, let alone this Hyacinth woman?'

'If you're going to stall, you know, you should at least be fascinating.'

'Anyway, tell her to put her thesis away and close the book.'

The page lay docile on the desk. Polly slumped in her chair and stared at the slimy green covers of the Virago classics with their climbing roses and alabaster heroines, wondering would she ever have another thought, let alone commit it to paper. Had she held out and written only what interested her, those alabaster classics might even now be scrawled with pencil marks, that unblotted copy book might brim with observation.

But as she moved from her own judgement to what she imagined someone else's to be, someone of a different sex, a different orientation, she had lost contact with that earlier passionate Polly who rode three times round the Circle Line then to get off at the wrong stop. Sadie it seemed spun helpless from one way of being to another, Polly oozed back into the mould that had formed her. Urgency, a sense of urgency, that was what she lacked. What was so frightening about Sadie was how comprehensible her actions were. Polly must hang on tightly to the concrete fixtures of her life or she would fall apart as easily.

Though Sadie was in hospital, the no. 73 bus still ruled their lives. Time was no object to Polly's thesis seeing how she wasn't writing it and the creaky hours of night are as productive of the sort of hazy half thought of which she was capable as the frank glare of day which enunciates clearly that the reason you are saying nothing is that you have nothing to say. Kim would come home with apologetic humour and a tuneless little whistle after a day weighted down with change. They ate according to her bus schedule: she got home at two a.m., they had dinner at two a.m.; she had to leave at seven, the household rose at six. It was restful to leave these decisions to London Transport and no more fortuitous than the habit of a million Londoners of breakfasting at seven merely because they sign in at eight.

Today had been one of those rare occasions when their meal corresponded to a more or less normal time and could rejoice in the conventional title 'breakfast'. Food had become a focal point and Kim and Polly continued the routine. Sadie was at her best over a meal, responsible only for putting her own fork in her own mouth. Kim came home with a hunger that would have satisfied the most demanding cook and Polly was a great one. The sort with fifteen years marriage and a mother-in-law behind her. As a doctor, Margot had been obsessed with healthy eating and Polly too had become a straight-browed advocate of hot water and the Bircher-Benner path to a sugar-free old age. Underneath that cholesterol awareness, however, lay a heart that beat for Château Neuf du Pape and stuffed vine leaves. Her dietary regime lapsed under Sadie's depression: Like that fine layer of dust under the bed, thought Polly, – Margot's wearing off too.

She cooked rabbit and summer pudding, trout with new

117

potatoes or a light snack of oysters in lemon sauce. Buddleia was a fountain of knowledge, an expert on grouse, ptarmigan, ortolan, the salad to be served with each. 'The proper way to eat pheasant,' she told Polly, 'is to hang it for a week while the blood drains and the meat decays and the only solution to bluefly is a cool pantry and not to mind too much.' Possibly the high point in her career; though other tips proved more useful: never to buy yesterday's vegetables, that margarine is not butter and should be shunned in every culinary circumstance bar yellow jaundice, that sugar and salt are lazy flavourings best left to the individual palate. The sunshine which opens up the streets, purple blossom dropping in silence, Buddleia always reminded Polly that it is hard for a human to die.

'Tea or hot water?' shouted Kim at the bedroom door. Polly's study was always closed, against noise or cold, but if the bedroom was open she was neither worrying nor working and might welcome interruption.

'Tea please, Kim.'

Kim was still in uniform, must only just have got in. 'How's it going? reached page ten yet?'

'Kim,' said Polly seriously, swivelling around in her chair, 'a PhD is a slow internal poison which its victim has chosen of her own free will. It saps the sinews, drains the intellect, and exhausts the animal spirits. It is possible neither to complete it nor to do anything else. One is beset with a sense of deep and lasting failure.'

'Oh,' said Kim, 'then why do it?'

'Because it's so terribly important. The history of the world is the history of male struggle. Only in literature do we see what the women were doing.'

'And what were we doing?'

'Well, Dorica Maud was writing novels.'

'360 degrees.'

'Oh, there's always some charming cliché about a woman trembling for joy in the presence of her betrothed.'

'Mmm, hmm, my tea's getting cold.'

'Comparison with socks, that sort of thing.'

'Socks, Polly?'

'Oh, you know, a perfect match. But you see . . .'

Last wash was in thirty minutes, Kim supposed she could spare another two.

'The men are so frightfully dull. No one could get interested in them.'

'Polly, I have to go to the launderette. Anything you want doing?'

'Thanks Kim, not that I can think of.'

Kim pottered off again, filling Sadie's rucksack, pouring washing powder into a jar, pleased to have half an hour free while her jumpers stretched and her uniform turned the water grey in the shuddering revolutions of the machine. She would sit and watch and try to bring the past up to date with the present.

'Visiting ends at nine,' she reminded Polly. 'What time did you want to go?'

'About seven?'

Polly would march into the hospital with a fresh bouquet of buddleia and hug Sadie so tightly she would instantly recognise all the love and concern Polly wanted to express. Simple. Polly laughed. It was going to be a job of work. As she imagined the visit, the difficulty of touching when only sisters and lovers are permitted to kiss, she felt a well of anger at anyone who should attack her certainty.

'Dorica Maud's lesbian identity was her chief motivation,' she wrote boldly. 'In *Belgard*, for example, she is writing her own life.' But what would Hyacinth say?

'Bodd in Hortus!' exclaimed the Bonsais. 'Whatever Hyacinth would say, she can budding well keep to herself. What possible relevance could it have to Polly or Sadie?'

Oh bother Hyacinth, thought Polly, as she began to scribble notes for her thesis. What's she got to do with my life or the price of tippex? I've spent too long writing things for other people.

9
Biodegradable

While Polly was settling down after breakfast with her cup of hot water and her thesis, Sadie was wandering by the green railings thinking she would give Polly every chance to dissociate herself from the Assumption; and Kim was having a hard day.

Ten o'clock. The commercial vehicles were out, the roads were crawling. No time for anything but tickets, bus stops, passengers. Kim felt as though she'd been hibernating for the duration of Sadie's depression. Just as she had been trying to work out why she'd left the mixed house, once the flurry of acrimony was over, she'd had to shelve her own worries and concentrate on the daily problem of getting home on time to relieve Polly. Now as the bus drove past news-stands she leaned out to look at the headlines. Half the African premiers seemed to have changed since last she looked at a paper.

The bus pulled up at the Angel to a queue stretching in both directions. All the passengers made equally vehement claims to being at its head. Kim could make no comment.

'I'll have three upstairs and four standing.'

She must be the first 73 to come past for half an hour. The queue flowed in and spilled over with a bleating chorus of:

'What kept you? Too good a hand to put down?'

'I was before him; you tell him to wait his turn.'

Kim wanted to hold a public meeting; explain they shouldn't get pissed off with her, she was the bus that *did* come. And how did they like all being crowded in together with nowhere to put the baby buggies? Shouldn't they be writing to their MPs? But no one wants to be politicised by the first 73 for half an hour. Perhaps if the bus is passing Westminster there might be some hope of a mass exodus of dissatisfied passengers leading to a mass lobby of a surprised parliament. But the 73 doesn't go to Westminster and most people looked like they would really rather be at home. Which was what they'd been trying to do for the last half hour.

Kim organised her bus, priding herself on a smooth run. The long back seats were saved for pensioners and women with children; unattached laps were suggested to toddlers. She provided a running commentary of the sights, annoying for anyone hoping for a quiet think, but this was Kim's bus and she had to stay on it eight hours a day.

'Euston Tower. All done by mirrors. Bleedin' disgrace. Used to be respectable squats, now look what they've done. Oxford Street. Watch out for the old man telling you the evils of protein. Madam, is that a beef sarnie you're eating? Kindly desist.'

Next stop Marble Arch. When the commotion of grabbing parcels and infants died down, Kim's ear caught the imperious note of a whistle. There on the pavement stood a man with a suitcase, as unhurried as if he'd ordered a taxi.

'Phewit!' he whistled at Kim, motioning towards the case. The sound shrilled through a day's worth of patience with old women, kindness to young ones. Already her driver was pulling away though not everyone was on board with the regulation two feet on the platform and in the bustle for seats Kim found herself obeying the whistled command. Once on board the man insisted on leaving his case under the stairs despite the bomb warning and the bit about the conductor's discretion. Then he told her to look after it and went and occupied one of the carefully saved old lady seats. The cheek. The flaming bloody cheek of it: her bus, her routine, her authority. Kim fingered her ticket machine but the man was not a plate glass window. Instead she moved down inside, her face the image of duty. The bulky suitcase jiggled in the cubby hole.

'Any more fares?' Kim sang out as soon as the bus got up speed. Had to get the fares in didn't she; couldn't stand guard at the back. Lot of people be getting out at Knightsbridge.

As they took off round Hyde Park Corner the case, jogged by the sudden movement or perhaps Kim had been too rushed to position it securely – one should never leave these things to a menial – slid out of the cubby hole unobserved. Kim was busy checking passes by now and the man was drumming his fingers, staring impatiently out the window. When the bus changed lanes for Knightsbridge the case, tired of the darkness and eager for adventure, slipped off and bounced into the road like a wanton ball.

'My case! My God! For Christ's sake stop the bus, woman.'

'You what? Right in the middle of Hyde Park Corner?'

The cars behind made valiant efforts to avoid it but the catch had broken in the fall and the contents sprayed out into the road. Soon would come a juggernaut too high off the ground to be sensitive to clean shirts and stripey blue pyjamas. Crunch would go the shaving-mirror, clunk the shiny black radio, and the proud new lambswool dressing gown would wrap itself round the bumper. The man grabbed the bell cord and jerked at it wildly as if held by an electric current. It jangled like a fire-engine but if the driver wouldn't hold still for old ladies at bus stops, he was hardly going to pull over for some lunatic who didn't know the emergency code.

'Real live wire aren't you?' said Kim entering into the spirit of it. 'Next stop's a request. Remember to ring the bell.'

The man was a queue jumper and could expect little sympathy from the women on the bus. Kim smiled to herself, such total victories are rare. That the intimate possessions of a city gent should be strewn about the public highway and ultimately crushed seemed to her an incident as desirable as it was amusing. The whistle was amply avenged but her triumph smelt too much of the miraculous to be more than short-lived. Sadie and the mixed house forgotten, it had served momentarily to anchor her in the present.

Twelve noon. Split shift. You started at six and you finished at six and you had four hours to kill in the middle. Kim hated it, sat in the canteen longing to be putting the grey jacket back on, picking up the little attaché case and dealing once more with the public, so much more attractive than the busmen. Her driver reckoned the facilities for filling in the dead hours were better at their garage than at some but Kim would waste the first half hour wondering whether to go home. Most of the other women did, or at any rate she rarely met anyone in the canteen. She wondered where Vivienne went, the conductor she'd met the first day. While Sadie had needed looking after it had made sense to rush around in the break, buying nice things to eat, taking the kettle to be mended, but now there was no bustle only endless cups of tea till her mouth tasted like the ring round the bath. The men played pool, threw darts or bragged till the pubs opened.

'When you're on your own at the back, Kimmy, your best

friend's your ticket machine. Know that don't you? Swing it at a bloke's skull and you can bash his brains out; grown men turn into animals when you ask them to pay their fare.'

Kim smiled. She could think of other uses for her machine.

'Wouldn't attack her, though. She's just a kid.'

'All the more reason. They go for the women. Women and Pakistanis.'

'If a bloke won't pay, love, you don't argue, leave that to the men.'

Did they think she had to work on the buses before she got attacked? Perhaps it was good advice, leaving the men to sort each other out. Only they never did. And Kim wouldn't make anyone pay anyway. Just trusted to habit. Besides, on her bus, the old women would ask: 'How old are you duck?' because of her round face and long fair hair. They would offer her a peppermint and when someone turned nasty they would rise to defend her:

'She's only a young one.'

'Have to make it up out of her own pocket.'

'You pay your way same as we had to.'

It would be on the tip of Kim's tongue to protest she was very nearly thirty. But there it stayed. She did have a round face and long fair hair and she wasn't sure she wanted to give them up. On the bus often she would find herself staring at older women, at the powerful criss-cross lines on their faces, no longer soft like putty. But when she noticed her own lines were deepening she grew a fringe fearing to look her age because she would have to act it.

Kim put her cup down and wandered over to the notice-board, fingering the badge on her lapel. She stared blankly at the results of darts matches, lists of soccer fixtures. The men playing pool would piss down the fire-escape sooner than leave the game now. Kim found herself reading the rules of the snooker competition for the third time. Maybe she should get her hair cut. That man and his suitcase . . . why didn't she have anyone to tell? It would have made such a funny story. Her driver would only see it as one more notch in the war between the buses and the travelling public. Once she would have saved it for Sadie and Polly when she got home but what with all the commotion and them being so wrapped in each other there wasn't much room for telling jokes. She thought about moving out but was afraid if she left the house she simply wouldn't know any other lesbians. The buses were obviously not a favourite haunt. Though there was that woman with the badge . . .

It was Islington, the busiest time because the bus emptied and filled up again leaving a whole busful of fares to get in: all twenty pence shopping hops and no long stayers to fill up the seats. This woman had got on. Long grey hair, about Polly's age, maybe older: forty? forty-five? Jeans she was wearing and was it a leather jacket? A bit ex-hippy. She jumped on the bus and elbowed her way to a seat. Kim moved down inside and, resting her back against the heater, rapped a coin sharply to signal the bus off. From this look-out she surveyed the passengers. Then she saw the woman's badge. She had already noticed the woman. The only way to get a closer look was to ask for the fare which would be a pity as the woman, staring sedulously out the window, was evidently intent on non-payment. Kim stalled.

'All right, love, I've seen it,' she called to an old woman with a pass.

A tourist asked for directions.

'Chapel Market? Just coming up on the left.'

Now Kim was standing next to the woman's seat though the latter was still gazing out of the window. Kim was loth to do anything peremptory.

'I like your badge,' she said instead.

The woman turned slowly, wondering who was being addressed. It is unusual for a conductor to remark upon the clothing of her passengers. Kim took a closer look. It was the lesbian badge: two feminist symbols interlocking. At first she had thought it meant sisterhood: women with arms linked marching, but now she knew it was what real lesbians wore. She wasn't quite sure what she wanted the woman to do but she was pleased to have recognised her.

The woman grinned. 'You buy these things and forget to take them off.'

'Would you want to?'

'Well, it's not very good for the leather.'

A bit frivolous this, for a proper dyke.

'Would you wear it? asked the woman suddenly.

Blimey O'Reilly sweetheart, if you gave it to me I'd never

124

take it off.

'Spose I might,' said Kim.

'Here, try it.'

The woman unfastened the badge and handed it to Kim who fumbled.

'I'll do it.'

Kim bent over in the middle of a very crowded bus while a completely unknown woman pinned a lesbian badge on her uniform.

'Sorry to love you and leave you,' said the stranger picking up her parcels. 'My stop.'

Kim watched as she pushed her way through the passengers and jumped off the bus at the lights. Then she disappeared into Upper Street.

That too, Kim would like to have had someone to tell.

Six p.m. Finished. The afternoon had been worse than the morning. Thirty school children on a house outing each paying for their own ticket. Why the bloody teacher couldn't collect up their money himself. And those two students who kept explaining how inefficient buses are in terms of manpower, how London Transport should rationalise, go over completely to one-man operators. As Kim walked to the tube station she promised herself one uninterrupted half hour down the launderette that evening.

At the local launderette there was a large hand-written sign on top of the extractor saying:

'No persons may sit in this laundromat unless they are doing their washing.'

Someone had obviously anticipated her. She would take them at their word and bring her dirty clothes in Sadie's rucksack. Eighty pence a shot was a bit expensive for a mere half hour's thought but if you threw in a couple of clean shirts it wasn't such a bad bargain.

Kim rushed home, took Polly up a cuppa, asked if she wanted anything cleaned and rushed out again. The laundromat was empty except for one other woman.

'Scuse me, love, could you help me out with some tens for the drier. Clippie aren't you? Always good for change, clippies.'

'Sorry. Checked mine in, said Kim shortly, staring at the washing machine.

'Not to worry. Good excuse to buy a bun. Still open down the road are they?'

'Probly. Dunno. They seem to keep all hours.'

The woman disappeared out the door. Kim began to tug clothes out of the rucksack and dump them in the machine, checking pockets for tissues, unrolling socks.

'There!' said the woman sitting down again next to Kim. 'Bought a doughnut the other day. Took two mouthfuls, no bleedin' jam. Chased all over the doughnut looking for it, found I'd eaten the whole thing before I discovered there wasn't any. Well I mean. Couldn't very well take it back.'

'Spose not.'

'You ever thought of going for a driver? More money in it and they're taking on girls these days.'

'Yeah,' sighed Kim, 'I know.' Was it illegal to think in public? Had the government posted people in likely places throughout the land to ask inane questions at inopportune moments? She decided to reply and play for time.

'When I was on the training course I said I wanted to be a driver. They took me out to a bus, I climbed into the cabin and, truesgod, I couldn't reach the floor let alone the pedals!'

'That's an old one. Seats aren't chained down. You should have got them to move it forward for you.'

The machine had stopped. The woman pulled her washing out into a basket. A long scarf had wrapped itself snugly round the sheets. As she disentangled them Kim got a few quick thoughts in on the sly. Thoughts about working on the buses, about Sadie, about moving into Polly's house. She had told her housemates more about her previous home on her first visit than during the whole of the last year.

The mixed house. Big and cumbersome and no one ever tidied up. There were always people sitting in the kitchen smoking dope; women knitting jumpers for their blokes to wear to the next demonstration; gentle bearded men too small for their enormous motor bikes, making up songs about the price of rolling tobacco, saving their dole money for an electric guitar. Poignant really until you learned a cheque from daddy would make it all come all right. In the evening there would be a movement towards the pub or the flicks and the group that had been sitting round the kitchen table would re-form round pints of beer or take up a whole row to watch Easy Rider. They worked as gardeners in Kennington Park, summer story-tellers

126

or in government projects for the unemployed. Their politics were unproblematically socialist. The men ran crèches against sexism; the women went to conferences. It snowed they threw snowballs; the sun shone they threw luminous frisbees.

Kim's stuff was done. She lugged it over to the driers. The woman had discovered a bedspread forgotten at the bottom of her laundry bag and was still faffing around.

That big house with its enormous French windows, the iron steps down to the garden, workbenches and shelves everywhere because Riza had discovered Black and Deckers. The black-board next to the phone covered in messages so that everyone could tell the state of everyone else's lives: concerned mothers, absent friends, lovers who would say only 'Tell him it's me'.

'Here you are, love, I'll help you with that.'

The woman picked up two corners of a sheet to start folding. Kim shoved the rest of the stuff into the drier for another go.

'Thanks. Thanks a lot.'

'Terrible, aren't they, those machines,' said the woman. 'Never get anything really dry.'

'Hang em over the bannisters when I get in,' said Kim.

'I'm lucky that way. We've got a bit of a garden out the back. Smell much fresher when they've been in the wind.'

'True. Very true.'

'Would you keep an eye out for me sweetheart and stick some of this in when the light goes on?'

'Okey-doke.'

Four women and three men, two of whom by extraordinary upper-middle-class coincidence were called Quinton and there-fore known by their surnames: Willoughby and Jones. It was Jones who talked Maddy down when she'd taken more dope than she could swallow. When Kim came home drunk and roaring it was Lee who held her forehead while she vomited. Individual acts of kindness but they left their mark of tenderness and gratitude.

One night they heard on police radio that there was looting in Brixton so they went down to close up Willoughby's printshop. Though the sportshop next door got hit it seemed no one was plundering posters. They contented themselves with putting a bike lock on the door and boards up at the windows. Then they wandered back down Acre Lane. Someone had thrown a brick through the Christian Science Reading Room.

'Hey look!' burst out Lee. 'Right through the message of the day: "We have no rest, much joy and some ecstasy." Smash. Good but.'

Everyone laughed and they drifted along Coldharbour Lane. It had an odd feel to it: it was still light and there were people sitting in the oval but all the time the place was filling up, individual chases up and down the road, fights breaking out and stopping.

'It's a riot,' said one of the men from the Ritzy. 'You'd be safer going home.'

There was such a surge of anger and disgust for the police that it was difficult just to stroll off. The cops were always raiding the squats, creeping along the road whole vanloads of them, asking about bike insurance, abandoned cars or just wading in. Willoughby was stopped three times one evening coming home from work. Next day he went into Woolworths and bought himself a perfectly ordinary grey plastic rhinoceros. This he carefully wrapped in silver paper so that the next time the cops stopped him – what a surprise.

Now, to the sounds of total confusion, running in all directions, flames further down, the occupants of the house divided. Willoughby went off to watch, believing himself invulnerable, and came home two hours later having looted and eaten a Mars bar. Jones leapt off to get his camera. Chris and Kim walked home again slowly because it didn't quite feel like their riot. Chris's friend Milton said it hadn't felt like his riot either because he was Nigerian and lived in a bedsit in Streatham, only the National Front picking blacks off afterwards had failed to make that distinction. Lee had already disappeared and they assumed he was with Willoughby. Riza and Maddy were in Portugal.

Later there were phone calls to every conceivable place where Lee might have spent the night fearing to walk back through Brixton while the cops were still at large. No one could remember setting eyes on him. Kim and the others drank tea round the kitchen table and gossiped about which petite bomb-throwing stranger he might have shacked up with for the night.

'There we are dear,' said the woman, coming back into the laundromat. She went over to her machine.

'I bet you missed the little red light. Did didn't you? Honestly, can't ask anyone to do you a simple favour these days. Just too much trouble.'

'Gordon Bennett!' said Kim. 'I am sorry. I forgot all about it.'

'Too late now. Still not to worry. They do say bleach rots the fibres.'

'Oh they do. It does.'

'You're miles away. Haven't listened to a word I've said. You in love or something?'

'No.'

After Lee was finally allowed a phone call (that phone call which says with nerve-wracked clarity: 'I've been arrested. Can you get me a lawyer?') they had sat round an eternal teapot going over what must have happened, at what point he had left them, why no one had seen him go.

He was remanded in custody for a week and would appear at Camberwell Magistrates Court. His sentence seemed to depend entirely on what the papers might say about the riot: 'Inner City Frustration' and he'd get a fine; 'Mob Gone Mad' and he'd be sent down. With Riza and Maddy away the task of visiting Lee in Brixton fell to Kim and Chris. It was somehow understood that the men were very busy but would do what they could. Kim took on most of the work: brought food and clean clothes to the nick, collected Lee's stuff from the station, phoned solicitors, contacted character witnesses, organised legal aid. Her greatest success was persuading Lee's boss to keep the job open for him even if he didn't want to appear in court. She went to see Lee to tell him.

By a quarter to one a restless queue had formed in Jebb Avenue where the prison stands. They carried Chinese take-aways or bags full of Colonel Sanders chicken to give to the remand prisoners inside. A small wooden door opened like a cat-flap set in the main one; the queue filed in purposefully and re-formed inside to hand over food parcels and the name of their inmate. It reminded Kim of the Baths when you put your clothes in a wire basket and get given your number on a rubber bracelet. Lee's name was called, Kim went through to a long thin room with two rows of tables like a church fete and sat opposite her housemate.

Lee's nose was swollen, his lip cut. He seemed confused, kept contradicting himself, had hired two different lawyers by mistake. He was celled up with a German anarchist named Wilhelm who'd been done for wearing a billboard saying: 'The State is a Spectacle; Break the Glass.' He'd worn it for six months up and down the King's Road but only now had he been arrested. Perhaps they thought they'd found the outside agitator. Lee was more concerned for Wilhelm than about his own job:

'No one's been to see him, Kim, do you think you could phone his Embassy?'

Kim felt touched. So typical of Lee all bloody and bruised to be worrying about someone else.

He appeared in the dock Monday morning still confused, though his swelling was better.

'Bet they only kept him in till the bruises died down,' said Chris.

'Look at the copper, he's tarted himself up all right. Don't know why he put that muck on his face, Lee's brick caught him on the shin,' said Kim.

'Bloke hassles you, you chuck a brick at him. He gets you in a van with his mates and does you over. Fair do's hey?' said Willoughby.

'Unless one of you's a copper.'

'D'you think he'll get a custodial?'

'Depends,' said their barrister, apparently they were the only ones to have one. 'He hasn't any previous but they're sending them down like flies. Still, I suppose Lee's different from the others.'

Waiting for Lee to come up they had sat through three other cases: three youths on charges of obstruction, assault and robbery, all in Coldharbour Lane, all on the night of the riots. Took about fifteen minutes to hear the lot of them: conditional discharge, six weeks and three months respectively. Their stories were similar: they were young, male, unemployed and Black. Certainly, Lee was different. He was thirty-two, white, and his boss was holding his job open for him. Kim still remembered him standing in the dock, hands holding the rail, shoulders trembling, giving a quick look round to see if they were behind him. The magistrate gave him three weeks, half the Black youth's sentence though Lee had apparently much less reason for disturbing the very fabric of society.

There was little to say. Lee could not demand a longer term in the name of justice. How could Kim not be pleased that her friend and housemate would be out and home again before Riza and Maddy returned from Portugal? She thought about his shoulders trembling in the dock: vulnerable, innocent, child-like. And the three Black youths? Surely only middle-class white men can afford never to grow up.

Lee got out. There was a party. Riza and Maddy appeared tanned and avid listeners. Things went back to normal. Lee delivered clean laundry and picked up dirty laundry, stayed late after work stacking boxes. Willoughby printed more posters; Maddy sat in parks telling stories; Chris and Jones did their bit for the unemployed; Riza speared Crunchie wrappers and Kim thought about a job on the buses. There were riots in other parts of the country, ministerial visits, talk of a special enquiry. Kim slept with the window open and they ate dinner outdoors. It was hot. Kim could equally well imagine it all lasting forever or being bulldozed by the council. What she did not envisage was that the house would go on in its heaving irregular way but that she would be unable to stay there.

The present changed so quickly at times, it was hard to keep the past up to date. Kim's warm feelings towards the boys had to be cooled by subsequent events. What she thought they did as heirs to the hippy tradition she realised later was unthinking sexism: a word which was much stronger before woman hating became current. Lee, having hitched his way round the world, would never refuse anyone a bed. Some mornings Kim would go into the kitchen and have to climb over a sleeping bag to get to the sink.

'Fuck me!' a voice would exclaim. 'How many chicks are there in this house? The other geezer didn't let on when he brought me here last night. You his bird?'

The Ritzy staff had found him asleep after the late show and Lee had taken him home. An old story.

Kim shoved a couple more tens in the drier, smiling that their notion of sexual politics had meant treating people alike regardless of sex or sexual orientation. A kind of voluntary blindness. She wondered what Sadie would think if she related the two incidents to her. But it could not be the same now. Kim would never have challenged the house version of equality if something hadn't happened. It was just beginning to get cold again; the jobs in the park were over. Those still at work would come home anxious to know what had been going on in their absence. They toasted Sainsbury's crumpets over the two-bar, taped up the windows against the draught. Then, one day, Lee asked each of the women to come up to his room, one by one. As they followed him they had no idea he had made the same request of each of them. Kim was alone in the kitchen painting the putty round the new glass in the window, the kids from the street had broken it again. Lee leaned shiftily against the fireplace, looking down at his shiny leather shoes, and said:

'Um, Kim, I'd like to talk to you about something . . .'

She followed him up the stairs past the abortion posters, the Soho Nogo stickers. The electricity had shorted on the top floor, probably because the roof leaked, and Lee's room was lit by candles. Lee sat on the bed, Kim on the floor and from the dark, flickering corner of the room issued the following in a dull confessional monotone . . .

'I think yours is finished now, love. There are others waiting for the drier you know.'

Kim started as the rotating barrel rocked slowly to a stop. There seemed no end to the short intense scenes which materialised from her past. But what to make of it? And how not to block it out so that her brain slowly filled with dark corners into which she dared no longer look? She must not be so hard on the boys as to make them unbelievable nor describe the street of squats with such passion as to emphasise only their eccentricity.

10
Mock Gothic

Sadie sat on one of the orange armchairs in the day room, it was so low her knees came up to her chin. Her feet were in slippers, not that there was anything wrong with them, no one supposed there was, only a patient without slippers is like a policeman without a helmet and how should one know who to ask for the time? Tonight, Polly was coming and Sadie waited. The trick cyclist had taken her off most things and she was feeling remarkably lucid.

Polly pulled her coat on though it was a warm evening. She would have liked to have brought her thesis with her in its new green folder but the temptation to avoid conflict would be pretty high anyway without the possibility of taking it out to show Sadie. She contented herself instead with remembering that she was a person in a grey wool coat, in case the urge to identify with Sadie became too strong. Polly really could not wait for Kim any longer, she did not wish Sadie to think she was stalling. Down the road, through the gates, past the porter's lodge, into the foyer. She wondered what she would say. What do you say to someone you have committed for your own protection?

Up the stairs into Philodendron Ward, past two rows of beds facing each other like teeth, on into the day-room and suddenly there was Sadie, sitting calmly on a low orange armchair. Polly felt like the Catholic she'd been as a teenager, confessing her sins only to be told they were superficial and sketchy, she was insufficiently prepared, must give a better account of herself.

Though Polly flitted in and out of Sadie's brain, held earnest and tearful conversation with her, made love even so convincingly that Sadie woke up wet and wanting, hoping none of the nurses would come by before she'd finished, Polly's solid presence in her grey coat, buttoned to the neck, was more than Sadie had bargained for.

Kim had to stuff all her clothes into the rucksack so as not to keep Polly waiting. Some were still damp but she didn't have time to hang them out. Would do them no good to sit soggy at the bottom of the pack. Get covered in mould. Oh dear, always rushing. Hungry too. But she had promised Polly she would go with her.

'Oh no!' exclaimed Hakea. 'Kim's going to the hospital too.'
'It's okay,' said Quercus, 'Polly's already left.'
'Yes, but if Kim runs all the way she'll arrive only a few minutes later.'
'Poor woman, hasn't she enough on her plate: squeezed like a worn washer between those two?'
'It's no good at all. Given half a chance Polly and Sadie won't say anything more profound than "Hello, how are you?" '
'They have to be left alone with no diversions and an hour to kill.'

'Hello, Sadie,' said Polly.
'Hello, Polly,' said Sadie.
'Well,' said Polly. 'How are you?'
'Busy,' replied Sadie, 'busy, busy, busy and you?'
'Oh,' said Polly, 'I've been busy too.'

'They leave us no choice,' said Melaleuca.
'Tea and sympathy?' said Buddleia. 'Leave it to me.'

It was only just past seven, Polly couldn't be long gone. If she ran, Kim might even catch up with her. Was there a bar of chocolate in her pocket she could munch on the way? There wouldn't be anything at the hospital and she hadn't had her tea yet. Rather than sit there rumbling she'd do better to grab a sandwich before she set off. Kim cut two very uneven slices of bread, smeared them with marge and looked for something to put between them. Cheese? Tomato? Eating was one of life's little pleasures and you might as well enjoy it. Kim cut open the jar of gentleman's relish Polly had bought. Mmmm. Better. Then she sat down on one of the kitchen stools; if she ran all that way trying to stuff a sandwich in her face she'd only get hiccups. Or a stitch. Maybe it was better for Sadie and Polly to have a bit of time to themselves. When Kim had finished she wiped the crumbs off the formica table top and brushed them

134

into the bin. She really didn't feel like walking down to the hospital; she could have done with a hot bath and a laze in front of the telly in her dressing-gown. She didn't care if there was nothing on but panel games. Only you do have to do what you've promised.

'Buddleia!'
'She'll be off out again in a minute.'
'And Sadie and Polly have only had time to say nothing.'
'Calm down, busy Boddess, it's being taken care of.'

Kim was about to lock the back door when she noticed the cushions from the living-room lying on the grass. She wondered how long they'd been there. Didn't look like rain but you never knew.

'Cooee!' said a voice over the back fence. 'Just hanging my washing out. Didn't realise we were neighbours.'

It was the woman from the launderette.

'Oh!' said Kim. 'No,' said Kim.

'You ought to air yours as well. Still a bit damp wasn't it? Go all mouldy.'

'Yes,' said Kim, 'but I don't have time now.'

'Always in a hurry, you,' said the woman.

'I have to get to the hospital.'

'Friend of yours?'

'Yes.'

'Tall woman, big built, lives here?'

'S'right.'

'That who you were thinking about down the launderette? Clam shut and vacuum-sealed. Thought you must be in love.'

'So you said.'

'Hooty tooty! All right, so you're not. I was only trying to be neighbourly.'

'Thanks.'

'You can call me interfering if you like . . .'

'No, really.'

'But I'm just expressing concern . . .'

'Look, I was thinking about my life. The place where I used to live.'

'Want to talk about it?'

'Oh, you wouldn't understand.'

'Try me.'

'Well, I was trying to remember why I left.'

'Lonely? Isolated? You should learn karate, take up a manual trade.'

'Don't try so hard.'

'Amateur traumatics was it?'

'I was trying to reassess . . .'

'With your new feminist insights . . .'

'Piss off.'

'I'm sorry. Very sorry. I have this irresistible urge to interrupt.'

Pause.

Glower.

'I've been thinking about my life in that mixed house . . .'

'Seeing it all flash before you? Oh sorry! I am sorry, it just sort of slipped out. You were wondering how on earth you could have lived there?'

'No! I knew exactly why I was there. I liked it: the street, the houses, the people, even the men. What I don't know is why I had to move out. I can rewire a whole house so all the main appliances bypass the meter, I can take the seal off the gas without breaking it, I can locate and unplug a phone bug: of what use are these skills in Polly's house where the bills never reach the final notice? I've lived in South London all my life, so why does it feel like I know no one? I can't see Lee or the Quintons as people to hate. I remember them baking bread, sliding down the snow slope, sitting on the stairs crying into the phone, having to be passed out cups of tea. They were all right you know, weren't monsters, didn't rape us, didn't even noticeably earn more.'

'Well, you're easily satisfied,' muttered the neighbour, but she did manage to keep it to herself.

Sadie looked around wondering when Kim would show up. She wanted time to let Polly seep gradually into the realm of things that might be happening in the room.

Kim was taking her time, thought Polly. Perhaps she should have waited for her, hurried her along a bit. She and Sadie could have talked about the buses till they were ready to speak to each other.

Silence.

Polly: Could I get you some tea from the machine?

Sadie: I could go myself if I wanted any.

Polly: Of course you could, I was only suggesting.

Sadie: Fetch yourself some by all means.

Polly: I had a cup before I came.
       (Silence.)

Polly: What are you thinking, Sadie?

Sadie: Nothing.
       (Was it possible? Was it possible to live and breathe
       and be thinking nothing?)

Polly: You're so quiet. You've always been quiet.

Sadie: I talk a lot.

Polly: I hadn't noticed.

Sadie: That's because I miss out the middle bits.

Polly: You mean I don't listen?

Sadie: I mean you ask me what I'm thinking but you don't
       actually want to know. Of all the things you want me to
       think I'm thinking nothing.

Polly: Like what?

Sadie: You want to know if I'm angry with you, if I took those
       pills because you wouldn't sleep with me.

Polly: But?

Sadie: The nurses bustle round here telling me I was only
       calling attention to myself.

Polly: And?

Sadie: Well I don't say anything of course . . .

Polly: Of course.

Sadie: But I think 'only'? 'Only calling attention to myself'?
       What the hell is anyone else doing?

Polly: I expect they learn it on their psychology course:
       'dedicated suicides always get their man.'

Sadie: I don't feel I owe you an explanation.

Polly: Is there one?

Sadie: I forget. That's part of the problem really.

Polly: Large chunks missing?

Sadie: Very small pineapples only.

Polly: What?
       (What? Pineapples? Oh God! and Kim said she was
       better.)

Sadie: My little joke. Pineapple chunks. You see you really
       don't trust me.

137

	(And anyway how dare you think me mad every time you don't understand?)
Polly:	When do you get out?
Sadie:	Any day now. I'm a voluntary admission.
	(You should know; you brought me here. No, that's not fair. I did everything in my power to come.)
Polly:	You sound so bolshy . . .
Sadie:	Not at all how you imagined a drugged out loony to be.
Polly:	Sadie stop it. Say it or stop it. I'm pleased you're so bolshy. You're in fine fettle.
Sadie:	Just letting off steam.
Polly:	Oh don't let it off! We're always running out.
	(They laughed.)
Polly:	Sadie . . .
Sadie:	Polly . . .
Polly:	Cathy! Heathcliff!
Sadie:	Shane, come back!
Polly:	The silence surged softly backwards . . .
Sadie:	And we walked into the sunset hand in hand . . .
Polly:	In hand.
Sadie:	And how is Kim?
Polly:	Oh, you know, busy.
Sadie:	I know.

'Why did you move then?' asked Kim's neighbour.

'I was angry and it coincided with my period, but it wears off,' said Kim. 'There was five years before that when I just felt I belonged. Those years smooth it out. Make it seem like a bad hiccup in an otherwise gentle curve.'

'What hiccup?' asked the neighbour, beginning to get interested.

And Kim, hanging her washing out so that it wouldn't get mildew, punctuated by the movement of pegs into and out of her mouth, told her neighbour what she'd been thinking down the launderette . . .

'. . . So Lee sat on his bed and I sat on the floor and from his dark, flickering corner of the room issued the following in a dull confessional monotone:

' "For the last five years, in fact ever since you have known

138

me, I have been leading a double life. At home I have been the easy-going non-sexist everybod, ever-willing to help out at a crèche and do my share of the cleaning. I have always been most scrupulous in regard to my relations with the women in the house. I think you will agree on that point. I have treated you all, as far as possible, like men; and have come to regard you as my equals."

'I shivered at this point, realising how cold were the bare boards beneath me.

' "As you know," he continued, "I have been doing an evening course in adult education. What you do not know, however . . ." Here he paused as though reluctant to give up his hard-earned credibility sooner than necessary. All those crèches; all that washing up.

' "What you do not know is that after these classes, which were very good and very stimulating in their own way, I would wander round the cinemas of Soho, mingle with the other raincoated figures, and enter those dens of iniquity with the sole aim, I say the sole aim, not of research, would that such an excuse were open to me, but of watching pornographic films. Sometimes twice a week, sometimes only once a month. When you all thought I was working late I was in point of fact staying behind to leaf through magazines. Magazines I may say with which I would not dare to sully this house. I would read the rubric, unzip . . ."

' "Spare us the detail!" I interrupted.

'Lee waved his hand, strangely noble in his ignominy. "For my own peace of mind I must make a clean breast of everything. Surely you will allow me this one remaining comfort?" He made it sound like the last cigarette of a man on death row.'

'But Kim,' interrupted her neighbour. 'No one talks like that.'

'You haven't met Lee Holland.'

'He got to control the whole thing: when and how he'd tell you; picked the women off one by one; made you sit in his room.'

'That's what we said,' said Kim, irritated by the interruption, the suggestion that all was not quite as she'd said.

'If he'd asked to speak to you all together, in daylight or at least in the kitchen, you could believe in his sincerity, but you make it sound like mock gothic.'

'I make it sound like? You mean you don't believe me?'

'If you tell me it's true I shall have to believe you, don't have much else to go on. But I'd find it easier if Lee didn't sound quite so much like a penitent Count Dracula.'

'I left my house because of him. It's serious.'

'Then why don't you take it seriously?'

'Well, I suppose Lee didn't actually use those words,' said Kim, 'but that's exactly what he meant.'

'Why exaggerate? It doesn't have to be the worst thing that ever happened to anybody for you to want a bit of sympathy. Lee doesn't sound like the man you threw snowballs with.'

'But he wasn't,' Kim protested. 'He wasn't the same man at all.'

'But he was,' insisted her neighbour. 'If you make it sound like he wasn't, you're letting him off the hook. Tragic flaw or something. He can clean up your vomit and read Rustler. You have to hold both ideas in your head at the same time; if you wait for pure wickedness to shout out you don't get to say very much.'

'He looked like Lee,' said Kim, 'sitting on the bed cross-legged as if he was about to roll a joint, wearing the jumper Riza knitted him, but when he started off about working late and Soho, I thought – I am not really hearing this. This is something from a Hammer Horror.'

'So you remember what you heard, not what he said?'

'Well,' Kim began. But, such was the power of her mind to distance itself from what it found unpleasant, she stood in silence; sheets and pillowcases flapped around her like waves as she tried to unpack the weighted sentences she had used to describe Lee's confession which, once formulated, she had repeated so often that, as slogans hammer a shy and subtle truth so hard it is flattened to the dull ring of a times table, so Kim found it a draining task of concentration to remove the ready moulded words into which that dark upstairs room now flowed so easy and so snug, and grope for different words more stilted but closer to present needs. But oh the wild chaos of Sadie's garden where everything had to be admitted: colours, sounds, movement, her own heartbeat. Thump, thump, the sheets flapping, her heartbeat. Kim was far too sensible to stand for long contemplating her heartbeat, her navel, the power of words to freeze and gloss over. Present needs: to feel less isolated, to look at the streets of Stockwell and see not only how they were today but, simultaneously, all the other times she had seen them. And Lee. There was five years of him too: the fine layer of skin that rubs off and accumulates under the bed as dust, Polly's phrase; it might rub away but you couldn't shake it off.

'And you?' Kim's neighbour prompted. 'Were you supposed to feel endlessly tolerant and forgiving? Lee sounds much worse if you try to understand him, there must be so many of him about. What did you do?'

'Went down to Riza's room.'

'And?'

'Found she and Chris had had exactly the same experience.'

'But they didn't tell you before?'

'No. There was this feeling that they should respect Lee's confidence, let him tell me himself.'

'And that was that? I can't believe this.'

'No, that wasn't that. That never is. They were going to speak to me afterwards. I think this was the first time we really thought of ourselves as women; despite all the marching and the conferences we'd always felt somehow that other women were priorities.'

'And, once you'd realised you were women . . .'

'Don't be so snotty. I was shaking when I came out of Lee's room. I was alone. I thought he was going to say he raped women or killed children. I suppose he did that on purpose so that pornography would come as a relief, but the way he spoke – it was like, like he was doing it in front of me. It was awful. I kept wanting to giggle, pretend it didn't matter, see it his way. He made me feel guilty, really, because you know when I've looked at pictures like that it turns me on a bit too. I didn't ask him anything though, I was afraid he'd tell me.'

'Like a shot,' said Kim's neighbour. 'But what were you saying about being turned on?'

'Oh don't get heavy.'

'No, straight out. What did you mean?'

'Well, I thought it was because I'm a lesbian. That Lee might be sweating heavy duty remorse but really he wanted me to say I found porn exciting too, then we'd be in the same boat: both turned on by women, both turned on by porn.'

'I think it's terrible, said Buddleia, forgetting for a moment who she was, 'absolutely terrible: not only do men have the resources to hire women's bodies for sex but they can creep right inside women's minds and force them into sexual reactions which disgust them and which women then have to hide and feel guilty about as if they were uniquely perverted or accept with bravado because anything's better than self-hatred.'

'Thanks for the authorised version,' said Kim.

'Do you disagree? Do you think I've got it wrong?'

'I don't disagree. I think me and my bus came to the same conclusion during the rush-hour somewhere between Tottenham Court Road and Oxford Circus. I also think Lee's candlelight confession didn't leave me much room to theorise.'

'And the other women? What did you do?'

'We talked. That's what we did. Talked and talked. Whenever there was more than two of us alone together it became a meeting and the men would sidle off shiftily. Chris said we shouldn't be surprised at Lee, that's what men were like. If it hadn't been him it would have been Quinton or Quinton. I asked how she felt about that, seeing as she slept with Quinton. She said did I think this was the first time it had occurred to her? Did I think heterosexual women were collaborating with the enemy and if so why hadn't I mentioned it before? Riza said would we like to fight about it afterwards. After what? I asked. After what? I said we could manage to be angry without claiming to be surprised; we didn't have to be shocked to be horrified. I didn't want to bother with men whether they were all the same or not. Why hadn't Lee spoken to the other men if he felt so bad about it? Maddy said she hadn't finished living with men yet, that she liked Lee and the Quintons and if Lee said he wanted to give it up, mightn't we try to believe him? It must have been very hard for him to tell us knowing how angry we'd be.

' "And we are angry," I said, "they can fuck off."

' "But it's the middle of Quinton's exams," said Maddy. "We can't just chuck him out. And I don't want to live in a house where he'd feel he wasn't welcome."

' "He isn't welcome," I said.

' "Shut up, Kim," said Chris. "We don't agree with you, all right?"

142

' "Anyway," said Maddy, "we can't blame the Quintons for what Lee's been doing. They probably didn't know anything about it."

' "That's not the point," said Chris. "Whatever we say to Lee we say to all men."

'I looked at Riza who'd hardly said anything and who was in an awkward position seeing how Lee was her bloke. I also looked at her because there was always a moment during house meetings when everyone waited to see what Riza would say. She would keep quiet through the uproar then put to us what our positions were and state what she saw as the main points of conflict.

' "I can understand perfectly why Kim wants to chuck the men out," she said. "I was very shocked when Lee first told me and I warned him then if he didn't tell the rest of you I would."

' "When was that?"

' "When we first started sleeping together. He made a clean breast of everything." '

'Makes a habit of it, does he?' commented Kim's neighbour.

'That's what I thought,' said Kim, 'though I was angrier with Riza for not telling us than I was with Lee for telling her.'

' "You got off with each other a year ago," I said.

' "That's right, Kim," said Riza coldly. "Was I supposed to call a meeting immediately and tell all the women what Lee is like in bed?" '

'Riza was your friend,' said the neighbour slowly.

'Was,' said Kim, 'my best friend. We went to school together. It was through her I moved into the squat. When I told her I was a lesbian she introduced me to these two gay blokes; we used to go to clubs together. Sometimes she came to keep me company. We danced together mouthing the words of the songs: "Tap three times on the ceiling if you want me"; "Do you wanna touch me there? Where? There. Oh yeah!" She said she liked gay bars because no one tried to pick her up.'

'What happened at the meeting?'

'We started again. We obviously weren't going to chuck the men out and it seemed best to stick together.'

' "Let's tell them we want space for ourselves," Chris suggested.

' "Like a women's night? When?"

' "On demand."

' "On request, surely."

' "Oh no! We couldn't ask Quinton to leave if he was in the middle of revising."

' "Fuck Quinton."

' "I do and I'm not going to stop just because you . . ."

' "Just because I . . ."

' "If you start attacking me you know this could get very nasty for you, Kim."

' "You mean I'm a nasty pervert and you need Quinton more than you need perverts like me?"

' "Kim, calm down, Maddy didn't say that."

' "Didn't have to did she?"

' "I'm sorry, Kim, you know when you talk about Quinton that's very threatening for me."

'So we started again.

' "We could ask them to go out one night a week. If it was a regular thing it wouldn't be too much hassle."

' "But where would they go?"

' "Who gives a shit?"

' "Obviously Maddy does or she wouldn't have asked."

'And again.

'Where would this search for unity end? Did I want to live my whole life at the lowest common denominator?

' "Kim, I get the impression you're angry about much more than just the pornography?" Riza tried.

'That used to be what I liked most about her: how she could throw things open and let you speak your mind. Only we'd let off steam so often together about the shit we got from the boys that I wasn't going to start off all on my own now as if they were my personal, maladjusted problems. There were other things, like the stupid jokes: Quinton saying gays were socially isolated, either they lived in bed-sits or they had rooms in mixed houses. Partly I could see what he meant: gays are isolated, I was isolated but partly he was saying we should be grateful, I should be grateful, to be allowed to live with him. Only I hadn't really thought enough about it to bring it out there and then.

' "Just the pornography?" It was Chris who took Riza up on that; I could never work out where Chris would stand on anything.

' "I know it's horrible," said Riza. "But we can't meet the

144

men and tell them they must move out. We have to discuss it all the way round, leave some part of our minds open to the fact they aren't going to."

' "They aren't if we give them any option," I said.

' "Well I think it's more than pornography," said Chris, "if you get down to it. I'm sick of Lee's mate Robin calling me aggressive and telling dirty jokes."

' "I'm tired of him bringing odd blokes back to sleep when we don't know who they are . . ." I began.

' ". . . or even that they're in the house," Maddy finished. "I think Lee should face up to the fact that even if he isn't sexist some of his friends are."

' "I hate the way Willoughby always drills hooks just too high for me to reach. When I use the bottom shelves for the saucepans he says no one wants to bend that low," I said.

' "You know he calls me midge," said Maddy, who's about two inches shorter than me. "I started calling him Tyrannosaurus and asking did he have a brain in his hip and he got all huffy and said he was average height for his race."

' "Blimey!" I said. "Whasat make me?"

' "And the fuss they made when we asked for Lil-lets on the house!" said Riza.

' "Had to have an electric razor to make sure they weren't losing out," said Chris.

' "And those crèches they run," Maddy and Riza chorused, "– only, most women ring during the day and we end up doing the organising."

'Despite our abysmal failure at demand, we found we were very good at complaint. After a week of women meeting on staircases, in the kitchen, on the bath tub, the women agreed to meet the men. The men said they were shocked about Lee. We said we weren't. They said if we wanted him out they would understand. We said we didn't. We said we wanted all of them out once a week. They said that was ridiculous, this was their home.

' "And anyway, what would we do?"

' "Form a men's group," was Chris's scathing suggestion.

'Then we said we were starting a taxi fund out of house account in case one of us was stranded or scared to use public transport. They found that much more palatable.'

145

'This story's all about men,' said Kim's neighbour.

'S'right,' said Kim. 'It's my story. We felt we'd got something sorted out: that the men should challenge each other's sexism, that Maddy and Quinton wouldn't roll about the floor of the common-room, that women needed time to themselves.'

'Like a lifetime each,' said the neighbour.

'Minimum requirement. No, it was better after that. Like something had been stated. Only when I took a bath I'd lock the door, whereas before I'd never bothered. If I went up the stairs in front of Lee I'd remember what he said about a pornographic vision and think "that man's looking at my bum".'

'So you moved out?'

'Read Polly's ad. (she owns this house); felt so defensive the day I came round here, I was sure she'd be put off.'

'But she wasn't?'

'Apparently not. Though I'll never know what made her decide.'

'Buddleia,' whispered Hakea. 'It's safe now. 9.30. Visiting time is over. Polly's just putting on her coat.'

'Hang on, I'm still talking to Kim. Did it go all right?'

'Yes. Sadie and Polly exchanged enough of the right kind of regret and reassurance for love and sex to be re-established.'

'Excellent.'

'Actually, Sadie was so keen to describe to Polly things she'd remembered from Africa and Polly was so intent on telling Sadie about Dorica Maud that the grand reunion was pretty perfunctory.'

'Spect it'll rear its head again later.'

'Spect so.'

'Sorry, love. I was miles away. What made who decide? Oh, Polly. Perhaps it was divine intervention.'

'Divine intervention? Felt like that to me, I can tell you. After it blew over all anyone wanted was for things to go on as before. The men felt left out, wanted to know what we'd been saying about them and it began to seem like it had all been my fault. If I didn't want to live with men, *I* should move out not them. They felt fine about me.'

'Evidently not or they wouldn't suggest you leave.'

'I still see them occasionally. Monday night is men's night so

146

only the women are in; and they were very helpful when Sadie was depressed, used to come round with croissants and we'd breakfast in Kennington Park. But I still feel angry. Nothing happened after I left, you see, nothing. They all sit down the pub together, just like the old days, take up a whole row at the Ritzy only now they watch *Not A Love Story* instead of *Easy Rider*.'

11
Axioms one, two and three

'Hello?' said Polly's voice. 'Have you been Marie-Celested?'

'I'm here,' Kim shouted. 'Out the back.'

'Communing with nature?' asked Polly, appearing in person round the door.

'Hanging the washing out. Smells much fresher with a bit of a breeze running through it.'

'What happened?'

'I got hungry. Sorry I didn't make it. Were you both on your best behaviour?'

'Don't believe Sadie has one. No, we were ferociously polite for a while, till I gave in and got cross.'

'Mmm. Patch things up did you?'

'Oh, Kim, you never know. It was a bit difficult to sit there discussing it in the middle of the hospital with the trolleys rattling past. I just wanted her to know I cared about her but no one can go on being sympathetic forever and somehow I got to saying how I resent looking after people. I kept thinking this was hardly the time or the place, but she would keep asking.'

'Had she no home truths of her own to dish out along with the apple pie?'

'Not really. No. Mostly she wanted to know what had happened . . . what she'd been like. She'd look at me with a kind of suspicion because I knew something intimate and touching about her that she had no knowledge of.'

'Yes, she did that with me too. It's nice to be able to trust someone, but she has no choice about it.'

'It must be awful. Losing such an important part of one's life.'

'Only know about it from what other people say.'

'I told her what I could but then we got side tracked.'

'Well you couldn't very well do it all then.'

'I got frightened actually. It was a bit like my friend Renee in Dublin; you remember, she was at school with me and Suzette. She was having terrible problems, I mean really dreadful, went mad I suppose, and . . .'

'She's the one they gave ECT?'

'She's all right now, oh you know, married, job, two point four children, but when I saw her, mind you it was a long time ago, she said she hated not knowing what had happened. That she feels a year younger than she really is because she has nothing to show for having been eighteen.'

'Oh, Polly.'

'Mmm. After that it got rather "my turn", "your turn". I rambled on about my thesis and Sadie said she thought she'd be coming home soon.'

'Oh dear. I didn't realise she was contemplating not coming back. I can't imagine the house without her.'

'It's so odd, said Polly. 'Whenever I think about, well, about killing myself, mostly I see it in terms of pain. Whether my chosen method will cause those around me sufficient suffering whilst minimising my own. But . . .'

'Yes,' Kim nodded. 'When Sadie was, was dying really, it seemed more like she just didn't want to go on doing it any more . . .'

'That what she wanted was the end of Sadie; nothing to do with any of us.'

'Only we wouldn't let her. We wanted her alive.'

'It's hard to have much faith in someone who might decide again that none of it is worth it.'

'Yes,' Kim nodded again. 'When I imagine her now, the first thing I see is that terrible cut on her leg.'

'Kim, do you think she'll even remember I went to see her?'

'Of course she will. Well I hope so. When the drugs wear off.'

'I keep thinking I'll look up and she'll be sitting there on the step, a cup of coffee between her knees, and we'll all go on as before.'

'She was beginning to get bored, wasn't she? Oh hell . . .'

'What is it?'

'Just that the night before she took those pills, that's what she said. "I'm so bored." Makes me shudder.'

'One of those things it'd be nice to forget. How are you feeling? You look all in.'

'I feel as old as one of those skeletons that turns to powder if you so much as blow on it. But I don't really want to go to bed. I'm a bit afraid I'd have nightmares.'

'What about?'

'Blood, arms and legs, stumps . . .'

'Eyes, being hunted, moving house . . .'

'Yeah, all that. Usual stuff.'

'Let's sit in the living-room. We can put the fire on.'

'It's not cold.'

'I'm perished.'

Kim carried the cushions, Polly unearthed a bottle of medicinal vodka and stretched out on the long sofa. Kim curled up on the floor. It was very cosy. She took the cool glass Polly offered her and said comfortably:

'Tell me a story.'

Polly laughed and set down her glass. 'Once upon a time, a long, long, long time ago, something happened. Only no one was sure quite what it was, and because it all happened such a very long time ago, they decided to wait till they knew just a little bit more about it.'

'They all knew really,' said Kim, 'only they wanted to see did anyone else.'

'They knew all right, but it wasn't safe to say . . .'

'Watch the wall my darling . . .'

'Just ignore him, dear . . .'

'You won't feel a thing, love . . .'

'I'm sure they didn't mean to.'

'Only your imagination, no sense of proportion, paranoiac distortion . . .'

'When you awake you will remember nothing . . .'

'Only your imagination and the wind through the leaves.'

'But,' said Kim, 'if paranoia is thinking they're out to get you when they're not, what is it when you can't see that they are?'

'Pay attention, it hurts like hell, of course they meant it . . .'

'It's called a loving mother,' said Polly, 'faithful wife, his lesbian housemate, a socialist woman.'

'What?' asked Kim.

'Margot used to say, "A woman who sees the answer in socialism must secretly believe she's a man." '

'Well yes,' said Kim.

'Ah,' said Polly, 'wisdom in hindsight, but it's a pretty pervasive one, that one. So much nicer to think men blameless and trapped.'

'It's what they think themselves.'

'I'd like to tell Margot she's right. I think she should have the satisfaction.'

'Mmm, why don't you? Where is she?'

'Back in Dublin. She moved out. You know that.'

'Yes but why? What happened?'

'Oh, it all seems a long time ago now.'

'So you think you'll wait till you know just a little bit more about it?'

Polly smiled and shrugged.

'No, but straight out, Polly, why did Margot leave?'

Straight out.

'Do you hear that? asked Hakea trembling. 'Quercus, do you hear what Kim has asked? It is the last of the questions.'

The last, last, last of lasts.

'Don't panic,' said Quercus. 'That was only the question. The answer might last forever.'

'Why did Margot leave?' Polly mused. 'It's a long story.'

'Oh good,' said Quercus.

Kim snuggled her back into the cushions. Polly poured out the vodka.

'Basically, I suppose, because we went to Ravenglass.'

'Ravenglass, Polly?'

'You know, Lake District: Crinkle Crags and crampons.'

' "Nowt up there but scenery" ', Kim quoted. 'You had a holiday tiff?'

'You could call it that. I never rowed. Nor my mother before me. I suppose you could say it was Margot taught me how. In the end we could have done them by numbers, and even then

150

they were so similar they wouldn't have reached double figures. Number seven: How can you have anything nice to say about Jane when I can't stand her? Number nine: Why are you so silent? Don't you care that I think you've been mean to me? I found I got quite adept at it while Margot retreated into logic.'

'How irritating. Did you think you'd got away from it all only to find you'd brought it with you, without the supports of daily life?'

'The reverse. Margot and I had been living together for five years, seeing each other every day, sleeping together every night. I would save things up to tell her in the evening, things I wouldn't think of telling anyone else. Oh not grave secrets; simple things that she would understand, get the point instantly because we'd been talking to each other for five years. Suzette complained that Margot meant more to me than anyone in the world, certainly more than she did. I nodded, secretly amazed that it was possible to put Suzette's name in the same sentence as Margot's without the very corner stones of grammar writhing in their foundations. As though comparison were possible when what we were doing was unique. Margot was half of me. Half of all my conversations even with myself.'

'But didn't you ever get bored, go off each other, get off with someone else?'

'She did, I didn't. Couldn't. Didn't want to. Didn't want anyone that close unless it was because I loved them. Otherwise I would have to pretend it wasn't happening, like an internal examination, like sleeping with Gerard.'

'All that for Margot.'

'It seemed to me something I knew about the world. That's why it was such a mess with Sadie.'

'Because you don't love her?'

'I like her, and I fancy her. That surprised me.'

'Well, what's the difference?'

'I don't know. I told her I didn't love her and she said it was a pity, but she loved me and she wasn't going to stop saying so just for my benefit.' Polly paused, realising she was relating not answering.

'I think the difference is I admired Margot, I was desperate for her to approve of me.'

'And she didn't?'

'Oh, you know how it is. I was a lesbian and I was going to

change the world for women just by staying in bed with Margot. She'd been doing it longer, was steadier despite her "bad taste", knew already where she stood in the world and what she could do about it.'

Kim considered. Did she know how it was? Staying in bed so far with anyone had been awkward and unlikely. 'No,' she said slowly, 'I don't know about that.' Kim imagined feeling explosively possessive, passionately interested and felt again that it would be much easier to be convinced that way, than have to think out consciously and at each instance the way women were kept down by men.

'But I'd like to,' she added.

'Yes,' Polly nodded, 'I think everyone should have it at least once. The feeling that the world will give way to you because it is so obviously a good thing.'

'What?' asked Kim.

'Being a lesbian,' said Polly, 'I thought . . .'

'Oh yes,' said Kim, 'I was listening, only I suddenly wondered had I disappeared off on a track of my own.' For other women, presumably passion and analysis ran blissfully side by side, Kim thought. 'What happened in Ravenglass?' she prompted Polly, lying down again, awaiting a long story which would give structure to her own thoughts.

'Oh, it was Margot's idea. She got terribly efficient, phoned around, booked someone's father's country house, arranged to pick up the keys. Quite out of character, usually she preferred to be distant enough to criticise. I thought she was working at our relationship because the alternatives frightened her.

'The house was a lovely old stone cottage that the owner was fixing up to retire to. Spent his summers doing the double glazing, stripping old paint from the doors. There was a stained-glass panel above the staircase which filtered the most eerie blue, gold and red light in the late afternoon. It was all chintz and leather armchairs, real fire in the drawing room, electric toaster in the breakfast room. Upstairs was like a youth hostel with two rooms full of double bunks and a third, the master bedroom, with a double bed and an electric blanket. An intelligent mix of creature comforts and rustic charm. And books everywhere from the larder to the coalhouse, old yellow hardbacks, the complete Penguin crime, Swallows and Amazons: dusty scenes from someone else's childhood. The breakfast room was lined with prints of Eton College.

'The man who delivered our coal gazed around the kitchen and said his grandfather had lived in the house when he was a little boy. As the cottage was basically three up, three down I imagined no one but the current owner had ever called the front room the breakfast room, but what with the prints and the college blues, the name stuck. I felt uneasy about being there because of course I didn't approve of second homes, but Margot was so proud I didn't want to quibble.

'We moved in for the summer. I spread my books out in the breakfast room, Margot took over the drawing-room. It was our plan that I should get on with my thesis and she would complete the article she was writing on women's health. She always used to say my thesis was a great pity if not a complete waste of time; why were all these women academics clamouring for the right to study what other women had done and not getting on and doing it themselves. "Feeble," she used to say, "I call it downright feeble." She was always more politically active than I was. Rushed around shouting and breaking things when that was what they were doing; writing letters and reading poetry a few years later; and now that everyone seemed to be specialising, I asked her was she thinking of becoming a women's health expert.

' "No! I don't want to be any kind of expert. I am a doctor and I know something about health. This article's about ageing because I am going to get old and my body's going to weaken and I want to think about how it's going to do it. Do you really not understand? I'm doing this because it's *necessary*."

'Axioms one, two and three. Whatever I do is a great pity if not a complete waste; whatever Margot does is *necessary*, and whatever happens I am not going to understand. Still, the first week and a half was marvellous. We slept in the master bedroom with the electric blanket. I woke at eight and picked the mail up off the mat, made a cup of tea and went back to bed. Margot woke slowly, stretched and rolled towards me still warm and floppy with sleep. Usually we made love. Throughout that first week and a half, though our lives were immensely regular with boiled eggs, toast and marmalade for breakfast at nine, elevenses at a quarter past eleven, cheese sandwiches with tomato and a slither of onion at one, coffee and a piece of fudge at four, supper at seven and maybe a little walk to the estuary, through the rhododendron wood or simply to the railway bridge, there was always the chance pat on the shoulder, the brushing past over the dishes or the sudden glimpse through the window which would well up and land us back in bed with all our clothes off. Margot complained that when she woke up from a nightmare and snuggled towards me for warmth, I was always colder than she was. I wondered why she expected succour even from my sleeping body.

'We wandered at dusk, which seemed to last for hours. It was June and the sun didn't really set till ten. We walked through the little streets of the village, imagined buying the B and B, got chatting to the women who ran the post office, which doubled as a general store. We had an unspoken code of conduct which allowed splashing in the estuary with gumboots but not paddling, for the lofty white towers of Windscale belched smoke as we watched. We joked that the guards on local trains carried Geiger counters. I've forgotten now why that was funny. Margot made up a whole story about it for me. If we were walking in a field with cows in, then the slightest nervousness from either of us was sufficient to veto the project. Margot was sure once that she saw a bull and we both stood stock still on a stile for a full ten minutes peering at an animal in the distance, trying to make out did it have balls or udders. When we realised what we were doing we fell about laughing and went home a different way, not at all shamefaced at being cowards.

'The rest of the time, you understand, I was sitting cosily in my room, Margot in hers, reading, writing and thinking, watching the bread van deliver to Mrs Barge next door, the District Nurse visit Mr Johns or simply the fritillaries out front bobbing in the breeze. Margot had come here several times and knew the place quite well, said it gave her special pleasure to come here with me. She showed me an entry she had made in the visitors' book. Just an account of a day's walking and climbing but five years before I knew her, like a private diary. The owner of the house was well known and liked in Ravenglass and people would ask us how he was, where were his sons and what were they doing now, questions which Margot would endeavour to answer. An insight into a heterosexual past I was almost unaware of. I was the one with the husband.

'One morning I heard the mail flop onto the mat and I slid

out of bed to open it and put the kettle on. There was an envelope addressed to "Present Visitors", which I assumed to be a bill for the milk. "Dear women," it said, "Kerry tells me you are already at the cottage, so please don't feel you have to leave or anything. I arranged with Rod that I would come and stay for a week mid-June but apparently he didn't tell Kerry. Anyway, not to worry, Kerry says you'll both be working and as I'm coming up to go walking we shouldn't get in each other's way. I plan to arrive Wednesday on the 2.30 from Barrow, if you'll be out just leave the key for me under the chopping block out the back. See you soon, Al."

'Oh God. So Margot had double booked. Why didn't she check anything? Why hadn't she found out for sure no one else wanted the cottage? Kerry was impossibly vague about arrangements, of course one should have asked Rod. And now this man was coming to upset everything. I drank my tea in the little courtyard out the back. So nice to sit in the sun in my nightie out of doors and wonder about the thick green moss which grew in soft lumps all over the coalhouse roof. Then I put a man in the courtyard. Immediately I was aware of my bare feet and flimsy clothing. Even if this was the type of man to respect distance and go for long walks, still he would expect evening civility, if not cocoa, and intelligent conversation where he could laugh gently at me and Margot to show he had nothing against us. No doubt one of Rod's peace buddies, soft-spoken, affable and concerned, but oh I don't like men. I don't like them. Here were me and Margot writing away, metering out the day into secure regularity, breaking very occasionally to go into the other one's room and answer a question posed that morning but not yet suitably resolved. Calm, purposeful and intense, we had agreed on this small world together, and now one of those idle creatures who moved in their bodies as if they were cars, no give in them, and every scratch would rust, was going to walk easily into this courtyard, pick the key up from under the chopping block, and make himself at home in our lives. Didn't they have enough already?

' "Good morning darling," said Margot, putting her cold nose in my ear, a gesture guaranteed to send shivers. "Do you know cow elephants greet each other by putting their trunks in each other's mouths and hunkering up against each other?"

' "Really?" I said dryly. I'd read the article too, it was in the

155

colour supplement.

' "I hope I'm not intruding on your early morning dust bath," she continued, "I've heard a dose of sand is very good for ticks and parasites."

'Before she could tell me how to clean plates with gravel, I handed her Al's note.

' "Oh good God," she said when she'd read it. "Well this is awful."

'I was pleased she got the point so quickly.

' "Well, I suppose we'd better take that trip on the Ratty we've been promising ourselves."

' "What?"

'It would take twice as long to discuss what to do if Margot was going to be flippant.

' "Well, he's coming tomorrow, and I doubt either of us will do any work knowing today is our last."

' "Oh, don't exaggerate," I snapped, "we'll have to move everything around that's all. If you bring your papers into the breakfast room, we can leave him the drawing room. Anyway, he says he'll be out during the day, so it's only the evening."

' "For a whole week!"

' "Yes, but it is only a week."

' "Only a week with a strange man wandering in and out of the kitchen making cups of tea and leaving the loo seat up?"

' "Well, what do you suggest?"

' "There's no question, Polly. I can't write about how men treat old women once they're no longer sexually useful with one of the fuckers hanging up his coat in the hallway. We'll have to go back to London."

' "What do you mean, go back to London? This is your stupid fault for not checking with Rod. You got us this place through your men friends. You can hardly declare ardent separatism now."

'The gate of the courtyard waved on its hinges and I could see the estuary and the boats, the cows browsing up to the water's edge, the hills climbing into the distance. A perfect picture postcard of a scene, framed by the arch of the outhouses. I did not want to leave.

' "We discussed this when I made the booking. I told you I wanted to come back, if it was available, because of coming here so often in the past."

' "Let's move to Muncaster guesthouse, then," I suggested. "It'll be fearfully expensive but I do feel if we stay up here I am going to be able to get on with this thesis."

' "It'll be full this time of year – school holidays, they're swarming in."

'Eventually we agreed to ask the women at the post office if they knew of a house with a summer let.

' "It's nice up here," said Margot, "but I shan't be that disappointed if we have to go back to London. My article's just about finished, and I was beginning to rattle around."

'She said it casually, as if to cheer me up, but it confirmed my nagging suspicion that she was getting bored, that she did not like the narrowness of our life together, and being away from the daily distractions and demands was showing her just how narrow it was. She was furious with me for suggesting we put up with this man for the sake of staying where we were. She had taken the house because she could get it for free and she believed in lesbians enjoying men's luxuries. Any hint of a condition and she'd be off. This was all directed at me as though I had failed her in a way she had always feared I might. Well, I thought if we were going to get on to the rights and wrongs of it then surely the house should be shared. We were in the business of borrowing luxuries, what gave us the right of sole possession?

' "Seems a funny game to play," I told her. "What made you think it could ever be without conditions?" I never understood why she jumped around telling men they were bad and wrote papers about being woman-identified. Distinctly contradictory.

' "That's because you've made your snug little compromises," raged Margot as we packed our suitcases and slid them down the stairs. The stained glass flashed bright blue in her hair, then yellow over her face. "You think because you live in Gerard's house and your word is respected as academic that it's possible to deal with men. If it's all pleasant and above board then they'll keep their bargain. Gerard can take his house back any time he wants and if ever you write anything that is the least bit threatening, i.e. feminist, you'll see where your reputation is trampled. Why don't you try writing for women for a change, or at least for yourself?"

' "And you haven't compromised?" I flung back, picking up my papers and shoving them into folders every which way, guilty proof of a pact with the devil. I struggled with my typewriter case but the catch was broken so I left it on the table and looked around for string. "You live with me in my kept house; what kind of grimy bed sit d'you think you'd get if it wasn't for your hospital salary? You think doctors show a proper respect or even kindness to their women patients?"

' "No, no, no," said Margot, as if she'd been corkscrewing around and around in her own mind, "but I do treat women with respect and I don't write things I don't mean."

' "So you keep your own nose clean."

'The suitcases were now piled by the front door and Margot looked round agitatedly for something else to clear up. I was rummaging in the drawer of the hallstand as Margot moved towards the breakfast room; I knew exactly what she was going to do. I looked up in fascinated horror to confirm this flash of foresight. Seeing only my typewriter on the table she seized hold of the handle and picked it up purposefully. As she lifted the case I protested, "Don't, Margot," but not loud enough. Where I deliberated and pondered, she always dived in, heedless of consequence. Reckless, I thought. The typewriter fell out of the case with a crash, tumbled heavily over and lay dented on the stone flags.

' "You've broken it!" I screamed at Margot. "My typewriter, you've broken it."

'Suddenly I burst out sobbing.

' "It was an accident, Polly," Margot said. "I'm sorry."

'Of course it was an accident, of course she'd broken it, and of course she was sorry. But I knew it meant she was going to leave me.'

'Why, Polly?' asked Kim.

'Why?' echoed Hakea, Melaleuca and Quercus.

'Why?' puzzled Buddleia in Polly's back garden. How does a woman know her lover is going to leave her? Why does her lover leave? Buddleia craned her trunk forward, sprouted a frond or two to concentrate on how Margot might answer. But Margot was not the type to answer. Throughout various scenes of fury and bitter weeping Margot would be at first silent, then circumstantial and occasionally abstract, but never did she give the reason why. Both women agreed later that it was because they'd gone to Ravenglass, but, as they could hardly blame the

158

geography of the place, they fell back each time upon a narration of events.

'You were picking up your typewriter and checking out the damage,' Margot would say, 'when Al knocked at the door. We were each in a great state. You, because you couldn't make the L work, me, because I was going to have to tell you that if I ate one more cheese sandwich I'd shrivel up and atrophy, Al because she was a day early and knew she'd hardly be welcome.

'So Polly'd had enough,' said Hakea.

'So Margot was bored,' said Melaleuca.

'So everything was Al's fault,' said Quercus, '– all boils down to sex in the end.'

For Quercus, nosier or more perceptive than the others, had watched Al leave the station and find her way to the house. As soon as Al was near enough for Quercus to see she was a woman, it was clear also that there was going to be trouble. When Al knocked, Polly was hammering away furiously at the keys of her endangered typewriter and Margot was staring glumly at the cases by the door. Was that really all, then? That small pile, so neat, so easy to fold and pack away. Into which thought stepped Al, with a spring and grace of movement no brief nervousness could quell. The door opened behind the suitcases, 'I'm Al,' said a grey-haired woman in sneakers. 'I know I've come at the wrong time, but I'm sure we can work something out.'

Her voice seemed to introduce a world of unforeseen problems which would set Margot reeling and which only Al could solve. It occurred to Margot out of the blue that perhaps an affair was what her relationship needed and perhaps Al was the woman to have it with.

Buddleia grew forward a day to where Polly and Margot were standing in a phone box opposite the estuary yelling at each other. It did not seem to have occurred to either of them that they would be more comfortable outside. Or perhaps Polly hoped she would get more out of Margot if she left her no room to sidle. They had gone to phone Lancaster and find out the train times to London.

'You're the one who wanted to go,' Polly was saying. 'What do you mean you've changed your mind?'

'Neither of us would have thought of leaving if it hadn't been for that note. And now that's cleared up there doesn't seem any reason . . .'

'It is not cleared up. We now have a stray woman skulking round the house. It makes me nervous.'

'Al hardly skulks,' Margot protested lightly. 'I think she's a sweetheart.'

'Clearly.'

'What are you implying?'

'You said it.'

'Look, Polly, it's only for a week and she's out during the day.'

'I seem to remember saying those self-same words only yesterday. This is quite a turnabout.'

'But Al's a woman!'

'So? What's the difference? She's still an intruder.'

'It makes all the difference in the bloody world. Have you no politics whatsoever?'

'The difference is you fancy her,' yelled Polly. 'I don't see where the politics come in.'

Margot herself wondered where the politics came in, but come they did. Polly was what she would have called an apolitical socialist: similar to a liberal but more sentimental if the class you were championing was not your own. It was difficult to reflect on these things whilst confined by the walls of a phone box, though one could gaze longingly through the little panes of glass at the boats on the estuary bobbing up and down, listen to the seagulls and the mooring bells. In the street, a white bubble car drove slowly past and Margot had a sudden flash of a long series of these locations for straitened conversation: the front of a mini, the bath, a shared sleeping-bag in a one-woman tent. Polly believed it, though, was grating in her sincerity because, except in a very personal, direct way, she did not think in terms of women. When she left Gerard and awoke in Leamington Spa, Polly was a lesbian, but she still thought she was a person. It had always worried Margot that before she came on the scene, Polly had sold papers on the streets, believed in workers' control, had opinions on the power of multinationals. Things she'd only ever talked about with Commies. She seemed to have no vocabulary, no words for seeing women. Marxism was sex-blind, and so was Polly. She had kept that word 'socialism', cradled it, rocked it privately. As she tried to make sense of what politics Polly had, it seemed

160

to Margot that as the people Polly mixed with were less and less likely to hear her word as she meant it, so the word went underground, became less solid, more magic. She might take it out under the covers, like film from the back of a camera, and use it as an explanation, but as she rarely did so out loud, Margot could only suspect its existence. Polly's attitude to the threat of Al's arrival confirmed all Margot's suspicions, but still gave her no lever to air them. Polly's latent socialism told her property should be shared and apportioned according to need, despite personal preference. Her dormant feminism did not leap up to counter that fear of men was not preference but preservation.

'So that was it?' said Hakea. 'Polly and Margot had the row to end all rows because Margot thought Polly should have just known it was impossible to share with a man.'

'No, that wasn't it; that can't have been it,' moaned Melaleuca, fronds fluttering as she realised the Bonsais were beginning to grin with a menacing, uprooting noise.

That's it, then, thought Sadie, as she lay in bed in the dark. I'm a voluntary admission, I'll volunteer my way out of here.

'Come on, Polly, push,' urged Quercus. 'Your big chance: "my unhappy past", "how I was crossed in love and found feminism". Anything. Just keep it going till Sadie gets home. As long as she stays in the hospital I have visions of them trying out a Wonderdrug.'

Sadie was lying in bed thinking about colours.

'When Al turned out to be a woman, it wasn't just my politics in question,' mused Polly whilst Kim lounged on the floor in what she hoped was companionable silence. Actually, the vodka was slowly coating her tongue with fur, perfectly pleasant but tricky to articulate.

'Margot and I decided to stay on in Ravenglass and inevitably, because she'd finished her paper and I was still engrossed in my thesis, she spent a lot of time with Al.'

The thing about having a bare room to go home to, Sadie

161

mused, is that you can co-ordinate from the start. Really she should go and look at flowers; they got away with some amazing purple and yellows, orange and blues by virtue of being natural. But it is difficult to see colour in the dark and how could she tell what shade the lintel should be when she could not remember how the light fell upon it from the window? The most sensible thing was to go home. Besides, there was something she wanted to tell Polly.

Throughout Polly's description of the last weeks at Ravenglass, Kim could not help thinking, despite the tone of impending doom, that some of it must have been fun. Walks over Muncaster Fell to the castle with lots of little wildflowers to recognise and name; cream tea by the Roman ruins; the promised trip on the Ratty, up the valley and on to Crinkle Crags. If Margot was going to go gallivanting, Polly had no choice but to gad about too. The best way to break sexual tension was to water it down into friendship; maybe Al and Margot could be tamed by her constant presence between them. Until finally it was more than she could bear and she flung the situation at Margot.

'Are you coming with us to Seascale tomorrow, Polly?' Margot asked one night when they were undressing. 'Or do you want to stay home and study?'

'Well, which would you prefer?'

'It's as you like.'

'I'm asking you what you want.'

'Polly, I really don't mind either way.'

'You used to mind. You used to mind an awful lot.'

'Oh, for Godsake, do we have to have a row about it? A five-minute train ride.'

'It's not just a train ride, Margot. If you want to spend the day alone with your precious Al, you'd better say so.'

Margot was silent.

'Well do you? Is that it? You do, don't you. Tell me, Margot.'

'No. Don't be stupid.'

'I'm not being stupid. You don't care about me any more. I know perfectly well what's going on.'

'Nothing's going on. And I do care about you. For Chrissakes, aren't either of us allowed to get any sleep?'

'So, convince me. If you care about me, convince me.'

'Ye Gods!' Margot exploded. 'Will you listen to her? Makes up a whole story for herself about my unrequited passion and then asks me to convince her it isn't true.'

'You mean it isn't unrequited,' snapped Polly.

Margot got out of bed and stormed round for a dressing-gown.

'Where are you going? asked Polly icily.

'To sleep next door, there's plenty of spare beds you know. I don't have to stay trapped here with you.'

'What do you need a spare bed for? I'm sure Al's quite willing to share everything she has with you.'

Sadie slid out of bed and put her clothes on, was soon fully dressed except for those stupid slippers. Baby blue with a pom-pom. At every step she would be conscious of her feet. Let alone stray policemen who would think her an escaped lunatic. She sat down again and as she stared disconsolately at the woolly balls on her toes it seemed to her that she heard the Bodhead speaking, offering words of advice.

'Sadie,' said the voice, 'Sadie, if you were to look in the nurses' locker I believe you might find a paper bag. Open this bag and in it you will see a pair of shoes. Sensible brown shoes, with low heels, a bit too big for someone's sister.'

'Oh, but she might be planning to try them on,' said Sadie, 'might already regard them as hers.'

'I think not. They have been in that bag for six months now. Four times were they nearly thrown out. They are, you see, a size nine.'

'Size nine?' repeated Sadie. 'Why then, I think they were meant for me.' And she went to try them on.

Sadie had assembled her property and was about to set out for home when she thought perhaps it'd be a good idea to let someone know she was off. There would be forms to fill in, and there is really nothing worse than being told to delete where inapplicable when you've no idea who it might apply to. Sadie would delete herself. These places were run by filing cabinet, sombre grey vaults. She would spare everyone a great deal of trouble if she simply removed her file.

The night nurse stubbed out her cigarette then rinsed the ashtray. As she got up to check the patients she noticed a figure

163

standing over the files. Bloody would be, wouldn't there. Now there'd have to be an Incident. Then a Report. And possibly an Inquiry. Already she could hear the subterranean grindings of the administrative machine starting up, shunting forward on its parallel tracks, puffing itself to its own inexorable conclusion in the face of which both nurse and patient would be bound in secret complicity. From people who lived and breathed and frightened each other they would become mere providers of information. The nurse walked calmly over to the cabinet, no point getting excited.

'Well now,' she said, 'and what are you doing here?' Cassandra Monash, the tall one.

'Oh,' said Sadie simply. 'I couldn't sleep.'

'Come on back to bed with you,' said the nurse. 'Should be grateful. I'd give anything for a nice lie down.'

'Ironic isn't it?' smiled Sadie.

The smile hit the nurse full blast, like a featherweight behind the eyes. Her resistance was low. Soft pillows, an eiderdown, floating, floating, warm, fuzzy.

'I'm off home, now,' Sadie explained. 'There's a message I have to give Polly and I want to make a start on my room.'

'Home,' repeated the nurse contentedly.

'I've wound up my record cards so you won't have to bother about that. Just say Dr Boothroyd discharged me.'

Dr Boothroyd. What a wonderful name. How marvellous to be discharged by Dr Boothroyd.

But in fact Margot did not then sweep out of the room in relief and hurt pride. She had not thought her interest in Al was so obvious. Also she had left her dressing-gown downstairs and would have had to leave the room naked. Which would have embarrassed her. Instead she slumped back down on the bed and, heaving a great sigh, turned her back on Polly and made to sleep.

'I turned over to the wall,' said Polly, 'but I couldn't sleep. I could feel Margot's body beside me stiffened into a knot. She didn't want to be there. We tossed and heaved in turn for a while, quiet and contained so as not to disturb the other. In the end I suppose we dozed off. I dreamed I was in the middle of a busy crowd of people, Brixton market perhaps, and at first I thought everyone was just getting on with their shopping, not

164

paying me any mind. Then I realised as I looked that their faces weren't simply turned away from me, they were blank, featureless, they had no faces. Their faces were somewhere else. And I was convinced suddenly that no one loved me. I was walking in this blank crowd buying light-bulbs, squeezing avocados, just like everybody else and I knew that they didn't love me, not simply because I wasn't the right one for them, but because of an insufficient degree of lovableness in me. I jerked awake at that, but it was not like waking from dreams of falling or nakedness, because I woke up into it. Margot did not love me any more. I felt a rush of awful, despairing tears and it was me then who left the room to sleep next door. I cried all night, literally, till dawn.

Sadie straddled the hospital gates. The sky was violet like Kim's eyes. (Perhaps that was the colour for the lintel.) She gazed upwards and saw, she could have sworn she saw, a gleaming, glittering, lustrous shooting star; a real bobby-dazzler and so bright she would have sworn she saw it had it not been followed by a second and then a third. For whilst one might in the face of heated argument maintain that on such a night, the sky being violet, upon gazing upwards, hazardously perched astride a gate, recently released from hospital, that one had seen a shooting star, yet it would stretch belief to breaking to claim that one had seen three. Sadie kept them to herself.

'So that's why you asked Margot to leave,' said Kim, 'because she didn't love you any more.'
'No,' said Polly wearily, 'I think we just got sick of the sight of one another. I knew how many spots she'd squeezed, she knew how often I went to the toilet.'

Sadie waited a moment on the doorstep before entering the house. Kim and Polly were in the front room knocking back the vodka. She wondered what it was quite that she was going to say to Polly, but it was clear to Sadie that what Beverly had provided was a safe place to cry. Perhaps Polly wanted that too.

So, thought Buddleia, all that talk of politics and passion, of women quarrelling in phone booths. Polly is upset because Margot's mean to her. Margot has always been mean, simply she has been mean now for longer than when she first offered to put shoes down the middle of the bed. Buddleia sighed. She had grown very fond of Polly's garden, the gossip over the back fence, the butterflies which flapped about her like lovers. She drew breath and repeated once more the questions asked of her before the water rates began.

'Find out why this woman sins.'

'Tell us why her friend left while another has problems of her own.'

'Explain her desertion of her studies; her mother's faith in the Highway Code.'

'Tell us why she irons the sheets and why the stair carpet is blue.'

'Well now,' chimed the Bonsais in their nasty little voices, raucous only because they were many in number, 'in reverse order: the carpet is Gerard's, the sheets Margot's and the Highway Code more popular than God. Polly left her studies because she didn't feel they were hers and Suzette had problems of tenure in Leamington Spa. Margot left because Polly knew how many spots she'd squeezed and finally Polly despaired because she'd learned what it meant to be bored.'

No, thought Clianthus.

No, thought Buddleia.

No, no, no, thought the three who were condemned to depart.

What a travesty.

A parody.

A farce.

'Is this wrong, then?' protested the Bonsais. 'Have we not quoted Polly herself?'

This time there came no answer. There was no answer but everything Polly had said. And Kim and Sadie; about the pernicious power of slogans, thick white paste daubed liberally to conceal fine detail.

'What we started is now finished,' the Archangelica waved loftily. 'Banishment must begin.'

'But what is its term?'

'Its duration?'

'When will they be allowed back?'

'Boddesses Hakea, Melaleuca and Quercus are exiled forthwith from the Boddom of Hortus to the Land of the Huwomen.

There they are to stay and live out their lives as bodies not Boddesses for an unspecified period of time which will end either with all Eternity or the spoken consent of the women in whose lives they interfered. Boddesses, you are under oath not to speak of Hortus, the Archangelica or the Bodhead to anyone outside these confines.'

'But if we cannot tell them what we want, how are we to solicit their consent?'

'You cannot. Theirs must be an act of spontaneous charity as yours was, you say, an act of spontaneous intervention.'

Thus were the three bad Boddesses dispatched to the far-off land of the Huwomen with no idea of their reception nor quite where they would end up. As they hurtled downwards their trembling leaves fell, their roots shrunk, their trunks lost their bark and they were left bare and unprotected. They must carry their lives with them as a snail carries its shell.

The rest of their assembled Bodheads meandered back to the meeting discussing sub-zero temperatures and whether they were ever justified. Clianthus however still lingered.

'Buddleia,' she called softly, 'I don't like it. The Bonsais are too impatient, always thinking on a grand scale; they've no time for the little things.'

'True,' said Buddleia in agreement. 'They've forgotten me up there haven't they?'

'So it would appear.'

'Then I think I'll stay put a little longer. Finish the season as it were.'

12
Three Leopards (of which one is a tiger)

'Sadie?' called Polly, opening the living-room door through a vodka haze.

'It can't be,' said Kim, coming up behind her.

'Hello,' said Sadie, still standing in the doorway.

Kim and Polly stared blearily, too tipsy to be startled. There was a commotion of hugs and welcome-homes but it was not till her eyes had taken in the forty-watt dimness, her shoulders recognised the low ceiling that Sadie could relax enough to kiss Polly and Kim again properly, feeling the bulk, the warmth of the body in her arms.

'I checked out,' she explained.

'Did they let you just leave?' wondered Kim. 'I mean, it's not a hotel.'

'Oh,' said Sadie nonchalantly, 'must be why I didn't nick the towels.'

The others laughed uneasily.

'It's weird,' Sadie continued in a more serious vein, 'like an abortion, perhaps. Such a big problem that you decide you can't cope any more. And then it's lifted but you go on wondering where it went.'

'Only back a minute and already discussing metaphysics in the hallway,' said Kim as Sadie leant against the bannisters. Kim remembered with irritation Sadie's habit of continuing out loud whatever had been going on in her head. Were they meant to feel grateful for this familiarity? Run alongside, breathless for each pearl?

'For Heaven's sakes,' said Polly, 'whatever are we thinking of? Come on into the living-room. Sit down. Let me pour you a glass of vodka.'

The three exiled Boddesses arrived on Polly's doorstep only moments after the front door was shut.

'I think it's when your friends decide they can't cope with you any more that . . .' Kim petered out, hiding the end of her sentence in the bustle of moving into the living-room.

'A definition of madness?' said Sadie, upon whom consequences were rarely lost. 'Maybe. When I felt bad, there was no room for remembering I'd ever felt anything else. As though the rest were an illusion of pleasantness, rare bubbles of enjoyment, placed with impeccable timing to keep you from despair.'

'Placed by who?' asked Polly as she reached into the corner cabinet for a third glass. 'You'd have to have some belief left to imagine someone watching over you.'

Sadie shook her head. 'Despair is lack of hope,' she said. 'It can co-exist quite peacefully with a belief in the infinite power of wickedness.'

'Here,' said Polly, handing Sadie a glass. Her own despair was too raw to have grown more than a healing layer of perspective. 'We've been celebrating,' she added. 'Margot may now be spoken of in tones neither awed nor acid. Put your bag down and have a seat.'

Sadie sat. She spread her legs out before her and stared at her bare knees. Kim, absentmindedly, was dunking a biscuit in her vodka. There was a long jagged tear on Sadie's thigh, like a faded rip in a shirt, mended and forgotten. Sadie felt a sudden twinge of rage. Then nothing. She looked up warily at the others; there was horror there, her horror, and she would piece it back together with their help because it was their horror too.

'There was something I was going to say,' she said.

'Probably just the drugs,' said Kim. 'My mum gets a bit vague. Bustles off to the bank then forgets was it a deposit or a withdrawal.'

Sadie knew they were angry. Expected something. An explanation. She crossed her legs to keep the scar from view. That only drew attention to it.

'You look like you were mauled by a leopard,' said Kim at last, breaking the silence.

'In Stockwell?' laughed Polly. 'How romantic. You're thinking of the hot damp of the torrid zones.'

Sadie looked at her. 'Have you ever seen a leopard?' she asked.

'Hardly,' said Polly.

'Neither have I,' said Sadie, 'but there was one on the farm once.'

'A real one, with stripes?' asked Kim.

'That's tigers,' Polly corrected her.

'Yes,' said Sadie emphatically, 'a real one. One day, Monday, one of the servants . . .'

'You had servants?' said Kim.

'Of course we had servants,' said Sadie. 'Black servants.'

'And you can talk about them that coolly?' said Kim. ' "Of course we had servants, quite a few actually, this was Africa, don't you know." '

'How do you want me to speak of it? With tears in my eyes and sand in my mouth?'

'For starters.'

'You don't take it seriously. Any white person who tells you they lived in Africa is telling you they had servants, whether they make this clear or not.'

'Yeah, okay,' said Kim, 'but you don't have to rub it in.'

'Not talking about it is a way of rubbing it out.'

'I s'pose . . .' said Kim, 'like Polly said about her salary. That when she started lecturing she found herself with ten pounds an hour and thought everyone should know that that's what lecturers get paid. Even if it did sound like boasting. Only I don't know, I still don't want it rammed down my throat all the time.'

'But it's completely different!' burst out Quercus, who could not for the life of her see that they were in any the better position now, in terms of Huwomen contact, peering in at the window than staring down from Hortus. 'If Kim too had lived in Africa, then as a white woman she would have enjoyed the same privileges as Sadie, whereas . . .'

'Whereas you are taking up all the room at that window sill, Quercus,' Melaleuca said sharply, 'and neither Hakea nor I can see a thing.'

'Nothing to see,' said Quercus. 'The three of them are telling stories again. Exactly the same stories each has told already only as they never listen they probably don't even realise that

170

they're talking out loud.'

'Do you think we've arrived six months ago?' suggested Melaleuca. 'It's a long journey. So, this is the first time . . .'

'No,' said Quercus categorically. 'Hutime is a measure of change and as far as I can see nothing whatever has altered.'

'Yes, well, I want to see for myself,' squeaked Hakea, elbowing Quercus out the way.

'Have it your own way,' Quercus sulked. 'I could tell you exactly what is happening without even looking.' And she proceeded to tell three stories, which might very well have been the ones the women told. 'Sadie is describing how Monday, the farm overseer, came to talk to her father. Said there'd been a leopard in the night. "Mbwele nono"*, he called it, a little leopard. It had eaten all the turkeys. "Mbwele nono," snorted Sadie's father, and he turned to her mother and laughed. "I rather suspect no no mbwele. And did it like the taste, then, your leopard, Monday?" "Leopards like turkey, Bwana Monash," replied Monday flatly. "And what did it do with the feathers, I wonder," pursued Mr Monash, "will it keep them to stuff its mattress?" "Come and see, Bwana," said Monday, taking him to the hen-run, showing him the clots of sand and blood, the white fluff, the unfinished meal. "Yes, yes," said Mr Monash briefly. But he added the leopard to his repertoire of after-dinner stories about thieving servants. Sadie's mother would wince and explain that there really had been a leopard, and her husband would chime in with a sarcastic falsetto, "Really there had."

' "But what did you feel about it?" asked Kim. "I mean, just that word 'Bwana', it goes right through me. Imagine someone calling my Dad 'Bwana Ultimo'."

' "Feel?" repeated Sadie. "Feel? Colossally guilty, that's how I felt. I was four years old when I went there and I still think it's all my fault. What use is that to anyone? You only get resentful towards the people who make you feel guilty. A resentful tyrant! Jesus. And I can't go back there. Ever. Because it would mean walking right back into a system where Black people would wait on me, serve me in a hundred different ways even if I didn't actually hire servants. That's not true of other women remembering their childhoods. I used to wish Monday had

*Sadie had never seen it written down and was unsure of the spelling.

eaten the bloody turkeys. And burnt the house down while he was at it."

' "Delusions of grandeur," Kim replied, meaning to be understanding.

' "Well I imagine your Dad's employees have to call him 'Boss', Kim," Polly snapped in Sadie's defence.

' "It's different," said Sadie.

' "Yes," agreed Kim.

'And then she explained how she failed her maths A Level when she never thought she could. How a few weeks before the exam her mother set to worrying what would happen to Kim if she failed when all that school had taught her was that she must succeed. Kim's father managed a shoe shop in Streatham, her mother worked there sometimes, only she said he was so flipping fussy she'd rather cook his dinner any day. She wrote out slips of paper: Kim Ultimo, A Level Mathematics, Fail; gave them to her daughter to put in her sock drawer, her school books, her dressing-gown pocket, so it would not be a shock when the time came.

'Kim failed of course, and went to live with Riza in a hard-to-let. Decided to brighten the place up by painting a mural on an archway. Riza lifted the paint from college. They weren't exactly gifted but Riza reckoned if they kept it simple it would pass for naive art. Kim pencilled in a jungle with enormous ferocious-looking leopards. Mostly people liked it though they had a bit of trouble with the water-lily. Kept asking was it a monkey.

'The Estate was being upgraded, had its own community worker, let out flats to young professionals, started a Tenants' Association where they could meet up.'

'Oh, I like that bit,' said Hakea, turning aside briefly from what was really happening on the other side of the window. 'Kim and Riza go to one of the meetings to ask for more paint, don't they?'

'The room was full when they arrived, they'd been down the pub, so they sat at the back and listened. "Someone's half-baked idea about what people want." "I mean, who's ever actually seen a leopard." "Ludicrous." "Better to paint something that represents the reality of ordinary people's lives." "Much better." "Picasso had a good grasp of that." "Indeed yes! Take *Guernica* for example. I mean there you have it. The suffering on those faces. Haunting." "*Guernica*!" "Of course, of course. Perhaps we could ask Max, he knows about these things."

'Riza and Kim looked at each other. Perhaps leopards were a bit escapist for Brixton but they're easier to draw than the Spanish Civil War. Bright yellows and orange and as far as Riza could remember, *Guernica*'s all black and white. Besides, who wants to walk past smashed faces and broken horses every dreary day of their lives?

'For a short while the three women in the living-room are silent. Polly is remembering *Guernica*, was it in the Prado that time she went there with Margot? Sadie is still thinking about her leopard; if she told the story again, would they get the point this time? And Kim is thinking of Vivienne, the conductor at Tottenham garage, for no particular reason except that she likes to think of her.

'Now it is Polly's turn and she remembers her family; this seems to be the thing to do. "I became a Socialist," she says, "because it wasn't the Protestant Ascendancy." And she thinks of her father's prize hedges and his crescent lawn, the gold Buddha in the drawing-room brought back from Burma, and the tiger rug. And she realises that what she has been brought up to admire it is best to keep quiet about. But Kim recognises her silence and blurts out, "One thing I can't stand is women with money behind them making out they're hard up." And Polly thinks, that garden, Jimmy landscaped it; that Buddha, who made it? What tale of torment and humiliation accompanied its passage? And she says: "We had a tiger rug, it was my playmate. It had yellow marbles for eyes and I would jump on its back and play 'Guess who?' "

'That's what her Grandpa said you did when you were in India and a tiger was after you. "Jump on its back, dig your thumbs in its eyes and shout 'Guess who?' loud as you can. Then if it eats you it's a sore loser. Ha, ha." She played that game for hours.

'She taught English to some Indian children over the long vac. It was her first year at Trinity. She compiled worksheets and they went to Dublin zoo because it was hot and summer and no one wanted to be indoors. There were seven of them, Embassy mostly. They spent ages watching a rat being swallowed and passed down the body of a snake; looked on

173

admiringly as a camel had its toes painted yellow. Polly remembered the children's parties of her girlhood when the whole zoo would be hired and there were free rides on all the animals.

'Her pupils were very well behaved, all but the youngest girl, who was tired and wanted to eat her sandwiches. But Polly said they must first finish the worksheets. "Can't we buy sweets now?" asked the little girl. "Not yet," came the firm reply from one of the older children. 'We've still got number thirty-five to fifty." "We can tear them off!" said the little one brightly, beginning to fold her paper. "Now you stop that," said Polly, as crossly as she could. "You're going to hand in one fully completed worksheet on Monday morning, young lady, or else." "Or else what, Miss?" enquired the others, curious as to the horrific fate about to befall their classmate. "Or else," Polly floundered, but one of them interrupted, "Why don't you feed her to the tiger?" All eyes turned to the cage, full of respect. Just behind the little girl was a long, strong, golden Bengal tiger. For a moment it simply returned their stare. Its eyes were yellow marble like Polly's rug at home. Then it threw back its head, opened its mouth on white, flashing teeth and roared a loud, rounded belly roar and leapt off, front legs skimming back legs, nought to sixty in ten seconds.

' "Oh, Miss," said the little girl. "It's very, very . . . very, very . . . very, very tiger."

'And so it was.

' "My grandfather used to say that when a tiger is after you," Polly began, but she couldn't do it. Had no idea what tigers meant to them but suddenly her old nursery rug came to symbolise everything tyrannical and brutal about the white regime.'

'Everything?' questioned Melaleuca sarcastically.

'Delusions of grandeur,' Quercus agreed.

'If they can't have absolute good they settle for absolute evil,' said Melaleuca.

'Just as long as they can settle,' said Quercus. 'None of that awkward thinking.'

'So,' said Melaleuca, 'three leopards . . .'

'One of which is a tiger,' Quercus pointed out.

'Is that the only connection?' asked Melaleuca.

'Who knows?' said Quercus. 'You think they stop to listen?

174

Sadie's father counts Monday's wages into his hand, making him stand with upturned palm like a beggar. Polly's father leaves Jimmy's envelope in a saucer, as if he were leaving a tip. Kim's father gives her mother loose change from the till, but it goes straight back into the housekeeping. There's a pattern to this, but you think they even hear each other speak?'

'And if you listened, Quercus,' said Hakea, 'instead of assuming you know it all already, you'd hear something a lot more interesting than the half-remembered anecdotes you misquote.'

'I still don't want it rammed down my throat all the time,' Kim was saying.

'I'm not ramming it,' said Sadie, 'you asked me, though I don't suppose you want to know.'

'But it's all you ever talk about. Africa.'

'Bullshit. If I mention it once, that's once too often for you. You two aren't the least reticent to talk about your childhoods.'

'We've been too busy looking after you the last few months to talk about anything at all,' Kim snapped.

'Come on,' said Polly, 'that's past history now. It's getting very late and we've all had a bit to drink. I think we should go to bed and talk about it in the morning.'

Polly gathered up the glasses and the vodka and put them on a little tray as if to emphasise that the evening was over. 'You can borrow some of my sheets, Sadie,' she said. 'We had to throw the sleeping-bag away.' And she took the tray through to the kitchen.

'Oh,' said Sadie dully, remembering all that she owed them. As they had saved her life, did it mean she could never be angry with them? But she was. Angry. With someone.

'Why?' she asked. 'Why did you throw my sleeping-bag away?' Suddenly her sleeping-bag was very important, like her rucksack, it had seen her all round France, was some connection with the past. Something important had been forcibly removed.

'Because it was soaked with blood,' said Kim cruelly. 'We also scrubbed the lino, turned the mattress, and swept up the glass. Did you want us to keep the pieces?'

'That much blood?' said Sadie dazed.

'What makes you think you can do these things neatly?'

175

yelled Kim. 'Someone always has to clear up afterwards.'

'I didn't think . . .' Sadie started.

'You thought "poor little Sadie, everyone's cruel to her".'

'Well, thanks for doing what any caring human being would have done for their pet bush-baby.'

'You think because you grew up in Africa with servants that you had a deprived childhood?'

'No,' said Sadie more steadily, recovering herself. 'I was very privileged. In London we lived in a two-room basement, shared a bathroom with the family upstairs.'

'Come off it,' said Kim, 'your father was a farmer.'

'He was a cameraman,' Sadie corrected her. 'The farm was worked, as it always had been, by Monday and his family.'

'Till your father sacked him.'

'Yes,' said Sadie, 'till my father sacked him. But don't you see? His wages with Anglo were so high he could chase Africans off their own land.'

'That's disgusting! It's disgraceful! It's the most racist thing I ever heard.'

'To say it is racist? You think it's better to believe only the top drawer can buy up land in Africa? Make it seem less widespread, more exceptional.'

'It's horrible to think about.'

'You surprise me. Most white English people like to hear racist horror stories. As long as they're set in Africa. Make them feel nothing like that happens over here.'

'Not like that, no. So blatant!'

'You can get away with not noticing, that's the difference. "My brother Sylvest, killed a thousand Zulus in the West." One of your popular music hall songs; I heard it on TV last night in hospital. When my friend Beverly had to have her appendix out they asked her for her passport. Pretty subtle stuff, hey?'

'Shit, Sadie, I don't choose the telly programmes. And why are you so cross with me? You're not Black.'

'Because I am sick to death with this being the only conversation I can have with people about the place where I grew up. When I talk to Lorraine or Beverly it's different. Lorraine was born in Nigeria, well it's a long way north of Zambia, but when we talk it's a conversation, not a hysterical battle.'

'Yeah? Don't see much of her now, though, do you?'

'She's not a dyke, though I had hopes.'

'You two still up?' said Polly, padding into the living-room with her dressing-gown on. Sadie and Kim were standing by the mantelpiece glaring at each other. Or rather, because of the difference in heights, Sadie was glowering down, arms akimbo, hands in the pockets of her shorts; Kim was staring belligerently up, one hand on the mantelpiece as if to assure her of her position.

'Sadie thinks we're hysterical because we're not totally obsessed with the life and hard times of Cassandra Monash,' sneered Kim, not taking her eyes off Sadie.

'Oh give it a break,' said Polly, 'for Godsake, she's only just out of hospital.'

'Don't baby me,' said Sadie, 'I'm sick of it.'

'What a time to duel till dawn,' said Polly, sinking on to the sofa, dissociating herself from either party.

'Planning to referee?' Kim jeered. 'Ensure fair play? That'd fit. That's the liberal position. You can just sit there on your comfy sofa with your toes curled under you and tell these brawling louts you picked up off the streets how to behave in your house.'

'Let's discuss that later, Kim,' said Polly, 'I think you've had a bit too much to drink.' She looked at Sadie wondering was the row with Kim a way of putting off speaking to her.

'Don't you like people to raise their voices?' Kim raged. 'Afraid the decibels'll crack the china?'

'Oh sit down before you fall down,' said Polly solidly from the sofa. 'You'll have a rotten head tomorrow.' What was this anyway? Rivalry for her favours?

Kim could feel herself swaying despite her hand on the mantelpiece but to sit down now would mean complete humiliation. She propped one thigh against the chimney stack and endeavoured to remain upright. It was really no more difficult than collecting fares on a moving bus.

'I used to have a Saturday job,' she told Sadie, once assured of her balance, 'in a cut-price shop. Sold all sorts of odd bits, from remaindered china to cheap washing powder. The manageress told me to sell Ariel for fifteen pence to whites, and eighteen pence to coloureds. I said it was against the law. She said it was all right because eighteen was the retail price so the Blacks just missed out on a bargain. I said I wouldn't do it. So she told the owner's wife I was messing about with the boss. Got me sacked that did. Do you call that subtle?'

'What do you want?' snarled Sadie. 'Congratulations for not pushing a blind woman under a bus?'

'Trying to decide who gets more Brownie points for common decency?' asked Polly dryly from referee's corner. 'Ten to one it was the boss suggested the price difference in the first place.'

'So what do you know about cut-price shops, Polly?' Kim rounded on her again.

'They sell cracked mugs,' said Polly. 'I prefer teacups.'

'Some of us don't have any choice.'

'No, but if it has a saucer under it you two are less likely to spill it down the hallway,' Polly replied sharply. 'Anyway, you know, they disinherited Dorica Maud once she started living with the Lady Cicely . . .'

'Yeah, great, Polly, must be wonderful to have a thesis to fall back on. Sound so bloody knowledgeable. But as for your rich, bitch, last ditch twenties dykes, I'd've been honoured if they'd let me polish their jodhpurs.'

'You don't polish jodhpurs,' said Polly factually.

'No? And I probably don't pronounce the effing word right and what's more I don't give a monkey's.'

Finally Kim gave in to the demands of gravity and wobbly knees and slumped down into the carpet. She looked vaguely surprised to find herself now with her back against the chimney stack. Everything in the room seemed to have grown much taller. Sadie paced the room with an awkward and nervous energy. It was a small room and did not take many paces. Polly was relieved that so far no one seemed to have hit anyone else. She felt she ought to take responsibility for getting everyone safely into the right beds, but it irritated her intensely that she must be the one to do it. Perhaps a milky drink? Oh to hell with it. Let them heat their own cocoa.

Sadie stood for a while at the window, holding the curtain aside, but there was nothing to watch in the street save the curtains of the house opposite, which didn't move. In the left-hand corner of her eye she thought she glimpsed three figures, but when she turned to look all she saw were the shadows of three new shrubs Polly must have planted out front. She swung round and set off again across the room from the corner cabinet to the sofa but the swing veered her course slightly and she blundered across Kim's feet.

'Ouch! Watch what you're fuckin' doing,' snarled Kim.

'Your legs were in the way,' retorted Sadie.

It occurred to Polly briefly, as she looked at the two women, that she would not like to lay bets on which could do more damage to the other. Sadie was bigger and stronger, but Kim was at least three hours drunker. As they arched their backs and spat at each other, there came a loud crash and a groan from the back garden.

'Probably the cat,' said Polly, knowing Augusta was asleep on Sadie's bed, but she was only too glad to get out of the living-room. It is difficult to extricate yourself from someone else's row even when you know you're not wanted.

She switched on the light in the kitchen and was relieved to see it was only a gust of wind which had blown open the window. In the sink lay a broken glass jar, the one Kim used to take her washing powder to the launderette. Why Kim had to lug two bags of dirty clothes to Brixton High Road every week and sit in laundry fumes for half an hour, Polly never could fathom. There was a perfectly good front loader in the bathroom. Well, Kim preferred not to discuss the matter and Polly was pleased to discover she had quirks.

'But who groaned?' Polly wondered out loud, 'Only my imagination and the wind through the leaves.'

'It was me, dear,' said Buddleia, poking a branch through the open window. 'It was meant to be a cough, actually, a discreet little ahem, but what with the sawing and sighing . . .'

'Soughing, you mean,' Polly corrected her, 'or is that the wind?'

'No,' said Buddleia firmly, 'winds wuther.'

'Ts,' said Polly, 'so they do.'

'Well, I've been trying to have a little chat with you for quite a time, my dear, but you're a difficult lady to get hold of.'

'I know,' sighed Polly, 'all this carry on.'

'Been doing a fair bit of carrying on yourself,' commented Buddleia, 'what with the going out with and the staying in with, the getting on with and the getting off with . . .'

'The looking forward to and the looking after . . .'

'The having it off with and the having it out with . . .'

'The putting up with and the playing down . . .'

'The putting off, putting down and pushing over, the pushing up the daisies . . .'

'Steady on!' Polly protested, 'Don't get carried away.'

'So sorry,' said Buddleia, 'I'm just practising.'

'For what? Are you thinking of staying with us permanently?'

'Well, it's very different from what I'm used to of course; seems to rain almost uncontrollably here.'

'Yes,' said Polly gloomily.

'But then,' suggested Buddleia, 'maybe you don't mind that?'

'Well,' Polly considered practically, 'you can always bring an umbrella, or put on last year's gumboots.'

'So that's how it works,' said Buddleia, 'you adapt yourselves to the weather?'

'Have to,' said Polly, 'it's a rare fool doesn't know to come in when it rains.'

'Ah,' said Buddleia, 'we didn't think of that.'

'Well, when they beam you up, you can tell them all about it.' said Polly.

'Oh no dear,' said Buddleia, 'we don't beam.'

'What then?'

'We just sort of . . . grow.'

'What, backwards and forwards?'

'More or less. You see, Polly, I'm not really your mother-in-law.'

'I knew you weren't Mrs Murphy.'

'How could you tell?'

'It's the way you spend all your time in the garden. Bernie was always afraid she'd meet a slug if she so much as opened the window too wide. And anyway I couldn't stand the woman. Sort to hold strong convictions, if only she knew what they were.'

'Ah!' said Buddleia. 'An aggressive wimp. "Full of passionate intensity." '

'I knew you weren't her the moment you laughed but I thought you'd just done your research badly. I didn't hold it against you.'

'Oh dear, we don't seem to know much about you. We live in circles, you see, we don't actually die whereas you seem more urgent. Everything seems a question of priority not absolutes. I mean, how has it been?'

'Since you interrupted my despair?'

'Assuaged. Cured.'

180

'I don't think despair is like that.'

'Looked pretty awful from where I sat. Quercus couldn't hack it.'

'Yes. But things change. You come out of it again.'

'Sounds like a measured number of tears to cry and then it's over.'

'It seemed disrespectful to Margot not to hold on to her for as long as possible.'

'And are you pleased it was Sadie and Kim moved in?'

'How can one tell? If you did one thing, it means you didn't do another.'

'What a typical bloody lukewarm fencesitting liberal thing to say,' gushed Kim, bursting into the kitchen with no idea what they were talking about. 'I got no idea what you're on about,' she continued, 'but I can tell you this, you do something and you're fucking responsible for it and you better have a bloody good reason for doing it.'

'All right,' said Polly, warming to what seemed like a new side to Kim, 'I'm pleased.'

Buddleia wagged her branches.

'Sadie still in the sitting-room?' Polly asked Kim.

'Yes,' said Kim. 'What's the matter? Afraid I've floored your girlfriend? Listen, Polly, Sadie's nearly twice my size. She could flatten me any day of the week. You should know that about her.' Kim heaved herself up on to the kitchen cabinet still staggering slightly.

'Well?' said Hakea. 'Are we going to stay out here all night?'

'What do you suggest?' asked Melaleuca loftily.

'Only one thing for it,' said Quercus. 'We'll have to knock.'

'So what is this place you come from?' Kim asked Buddleia. 'I keep bumping into you, don't I, but you're not from round here.'

'Oh, it's really not very exciting,' said Buddleia. 'A cross between County Hall and an arboretum.'

'A fern bar?' suggested Polly.

'Who is it?' called Sadie from the hallway, wary of opening the door so late at night.

'We are Liberty Boddesses,' announced Quercus, 'from the

181

far-off land of Hortus whither we are anxious to return.'

'Quercus, what are you saying?' protested Melaleuca.

'Stranded for all eternity,' moaned Hakea, 'the beached whale of the . . .'

'I only wish you could,' said Sadie pacifically, from behind the closed door. Usually if you were pleasant to them they staggered off home quite affably.

The rest of Hakea's words were lost for at that moment she turned back into her prickly, cabbage-like self. She looked around as Melaleuca metamorphosed to a great, dangling, grey paper bark and their old friend Quercus became her usual crusty, crabbed old oak.

'Who was it?' called Polly.

'Goddesses, I think,' said Sadie, 'but I've no idea what they wanted.'

The sky turned briefly violet. Sadie glanced through the chink in the curtains and as she gazed she saw, she could have sworn she saw, three gleaming, glittering lustrous shooting stars, real bobby-dazzlers and so bright she would have sworn she saw them, had they not been shooting in the wrong direction, for whoever heard of a star which shot from Earth to Hortus? Sadie shrugged. Then she walked down the corridor towards the others, and as she walked she smiled. She smiled so that the corridor, the kitchen, the garden, then the whole of Stockwell were lit up and shining like dusk in the Dordogne. She smiled so that magnolia petals and cherry blossom floated through the window in a pink and white cloud, so that camellias, rhododendrons and azaleas dropped their flowers thoughtfully over the kitchen table, gardenias, hibiscus and oleander settled in the sink. And Polly was no longer tired, Kim no longer drunk and Sadie no longer ill. And it was possible for Polly to finish her thesis, for Sadie to paint her bedroom and for Kim to decide what feminism meant now that men were the enemy. And it was possible for women to think in public, on park benches and crowded buses, out loud and in front of others. And it was possible to rinse the washing-up so nothing need taste of detergent ever again, not even at breakfast. And it was possible to speak now of terrible things that had been done to you, and to cry and to go on speaking.

182